Who Can You Trust, Colby?

Hollis Kennedy Martin

Keys & Tale Publications, llc

Things whispered in vain are perhaps better kept hushed, for to say
them aloud is to define insanity.

Joey,

I don't know when you will get these books, but I can't imagine a scenario in which you get them before I die. The doctors say I have little time left. I am writing to you my story, but I so wish to know your story more than anything else.

At this point in my life, I learned to trust your father with everything, and I want you to know how he earned that trust. You're lucky to have your father. Of the two of us, he is the one you should have. I didn't always know this, so I want to make sure that you do. You can always trust your father. For everything that we were and everything we weren't, the one thing he was good for, is good for, is his word. In this world, who you can trust can change on a dime. And looking back, anytime I didn't trust your father, that was more me than him. I tell you this because someone, something, is going to break your trust in life, but your father can be the one who you can always trust. He loves you, oh, how he loves you, Joey.

Trust is fickle, Joey. It is never permanent.

I love you, my little Joey, your mom,

Colby

Part I: Unrequited (adj.)

/un-ree-'kwi-ted/

a) unrewarded feeling; not reciprocated,

b) another person not feeling the same way, particularly felt emotion

(esp. love)

Similar: unrecompensed, unanswered

1

THE BULLET CRACKED THE TV screen with a special crick that splintered across the screen. The sound traveled down my spine and instinctively caused me to contract and slam my body to the floor. The sound stuck to me. I had never heard a bullet like that before, not loud compared to others, but it stuck to my soul.

I no longer had the option to run. So, I slid my way through the doorway that adjoined the two motel rooms and pulled the door shut behind me. Maybe they wouldn't notice I'd escaped to the connected room. I left the room as bullets filled it. Some even entered my new room. I focused on the task at hand, locked the doors between the rooms, and high-crawled to the bathroom; I used my arms to pull my body along the ground. I wouldn't normally even touch a motel floor, but I think I could make an exception just this time.

I heard yelling outside; it didn't slow the bullets that much. Now I knew I had good reason for my suspicion of the man in the parking lot. He wasn't alone; he probably had connections to the drug cartel. This also confirmed that they were angry with me. I reached the bathroom and climbed into the tub and curled up and listened.

How the fuck did I get into this position? I never thought I would beg the FBI to show up, but everyone has a breaking point.

I should go back farther, to how I even ended up in that little motel room. It was a long road from there to here.

I wiped the mirror clear of the fog and looked at myself. I found my broken body in the mirror again. Although I had looked worse in the mirror before, I felt more destroyed than ever. Mentally, my brain felt disjointed. It took about a day to reach the safe house after my team rescued me from the prison. I took a shower as soon as we arrived. The pain of movement reminded me I did not die. I stood there and stared at it all, trying to understand the difference between reality and fiction. The last few weeks between my gunshot and interrogation felt like dreams, altogether too real and too much to actually be real at the same time. I felt the shock and burn of the cattle prod on too many parts of my body to count. My swollen face did well to hide the cuts, but not the bruises. Black, purple, red, green, and yellow covered my tortured body, but nothing felt as bad as my right side. There, my body had broken ribs, more bruises than I could count, and the surgery from the gunshot wound sewn shut just prior to the torture. I couldn't find reality in any of it. Too much happened for me to process it all, and the pain remained the only thing real to me. I now questioned my memory, especially since my interrogator broke my ability to grasp reality. *How did I fall for all of it? What else wasn't real?*

I tried to connect with the eyes in the mirror. I didn't recognize myself. My eyes welled up. I reached out to touch me, to touch the girl on the other side of the mirror, *it's okay*, but I couldn't reach her, *it's not okay*. I looked down at the sink, and the tears poured out. My breath went shaky. I couldn't face the trauma. I couldn't feel it, not now, maybe never. I myself took a deep breath and blew it out. I looked back at myself. We, I, would need to get it together. I just escaped a secret Defense Intelligence Agency (DIA) prison with the help of an elite team led by my agency, the Drug Enforcement Agency (DEA).

I pulled some clothes from a bag Asher had for me in the rescue. It felt good to be clean and have that place washed off me. I took the splint Doc gave me and put it on my mangled finger, compliments of Larry, my former training liaison. Larry proved essential in my escape.

He gained access to the facility and broke my finger to give me a shot of adrenaline to power through the pain of my injuries during the escape. Doc gave me a sling to minimize the movement of my ribs. I didn't want it and shoved it back in the bag Asher gave me. I left the bathroom and went toward the stairs of the log cabin safe house. I saw almost the whole first floor from the top of the stairs as it overlooked the great room and kitchen. The place looked empty. I made it down the stairs and opened the fridge. Now that I had access to food again, I wanted to eat healthy.

The front door opened, and Asher walked inside with a pile of wood. "Hey, Jack, how are you?" he asked, then dumped the wood by the roaring fire in the fireplace. It felt safe and warm in the cabin. The DEA partnered Asher and me. We spent the last year doing everything together to prepare for and go on missions. We got really close to each other. In this situation, he remained the only one I could tolerate.

I let the fridge door shut and turned to him. I shook my head from side to side and shrugged. I didn't have an answer to that question. I finally said, "Hungry," as I tried to smile at him as he came up to me. I could see the concern on his face. He opened his arms and stepped in to hug me, but I stepped back away from him. I didn't want to feel touch from anyone. I didn't know whose side anyone was on anymore, mine or the prison's. A different agency in my country captured me, tortured and interrogated me, and used someone close to me to do it. I didn't know where the betrayal started and ended. This felt like limbo. We both stopped. He reached out and touched my left shoulder. We stood there for a moment. He didn't do anything, but it felt like a dream to me. Yes, my team came to get me, but it was too easy. Maybe the DIA planned this so I would tell my team everything and they would report it back to the DIA. I couldn't discern reality, and I couldn't even trust Asher, my partner and best friend–or maybe I made that up in my head. It made me want to cry. It washed over my face, but I held back the tears. I turned slightly and pulled my shoulder from him and looked down. I had to regain my composure. I didn't know the location of this safe house, and that meant I would have to stay put for now. No matter what their plan, I would take the time here to recover from the prison before I figured out my next move.

"I'll fix you something," he said, breaking our silence and reaching out for my face.

I stepped backward, with my eyes on the ground and nodded in agreement. I headed to the table on the edge of the kitchen that separated the grand room from the living room. The wood table matched everything else in the cabin made of wood, and I needed it. I couldn't take cement walls or metal tables that made up the prison. The wood felt safer. I rubbed my fingers along the table and took in the new surroundings.

"Where is everyone?" I asked him as he dug through the fridge.

"Taking care of things, making sure we are safe here." He stayed focused on his task.

"Are they coming back soon?"

"I don't know," he said. "Guess it depends on what is going on."

I nodded to myself. "Is CJ coming? I haven't seen him on all of this." CJ led our team of six. I didn't see or hear about him in my rescue operation or anything that had happened since then. I saw him in the prison, and he took the prison's side in the interrogation. He told me I had to talk and tell them everything.

"No, I don't think so," he said as he chopped onions.

I thought about this place, and the journey of how I got there blurred together. Larry got me into the yard of the prison and broke my finger. My team pulled me via rope over the prison wall, and I ran to a nearby car. When the adrenaline from the rescue wore off, I felt exhausted and needed sleep. It made the journey blips on a radar from the prison to here. We traded cars and I think we ate. I had an IV of fluids, maybe more than one. I remember I fought Doc's touch too, and he had to convince me to let him do his work. Doc is a medical specialist on our team, which meant he was pretty close to being a doctor and could handle just about any injury thrown at him. I could still see Doc's face when he pulled up my shirt to check my surgery incision from my gunshot and found burns and bruises that covered me. I remember that.

I pulled myself out of my daydream. "Was I right to think we crossed a border at some point?" I questioned my memory, my fucked up, cracked reality of a memory.

"Um... Yeah," he said, now doing something on the stove.

"Where are we?"

"America," he said with a slight chuckle. Maybe he did not believe I didn't know where they detained me. "They had you up in Canada, if that's what you're asking."

"I didn't know I had left the country," I mumbled. The thought strangely disoriented me. I didn't know I had left the country and had to re-enter. I thought that prison was somewhere near Boston, not outside the country. It made me nauseous. It only added to the distortion in my mind about what to believe and what to trust.

That reminded me, the team had planned to head to Venezuela while I recovered from my gunshot. "Did you guys find out what the radiation sensor picked up?" I asked about the sensor we put in during a mission last year at a suspected drug transfer point ran by a cartel in Venezuela. Just before my imprisonment, the radiation sensor picked up a reading. They planned to go back down and investigate.

"We didn't go," Asher said and shot me a puzzled look.

"What? They could move the dirty bomb materials to the US at any minute. That place is the last stop before they move drugs into the country. It's logical to think the materials follow the same trajectory," I said, genuinely shocked the team didn't chase the lead.

Asher stopped and turned around to look at me. "Jackie, you disappeared. When CJ looked into it, the hospital said some people, possibly government, came and took you by helicopter and left no paper trail. What was he going to do, just say 'okay?'"

"I don't know. I thought getting a hit on radiation when we have been chasing a credible threat of an Iranian militia group trying to smuggle dirty bombs into the U.S. would be more important than me." I felt so guilty that I took the place of such an important mission. I now felt responsible if that material made it into the U.S. I knew now I didn't have time to recover. I needed to chase it. I tried to think of what we could do as a next step. We would need to think ahead and get ahead of the materials or the bomb-makers. There had to be a way we could still stop the bombings. I hoped the materials remained in Venezuela.

"Jack," he said while he stirred the food in the skillet. I snapped out of my other world.

"Yeah?"

"Why did they have you in that place?"

"Um..." I didn't have words, and I dreaded what would happen once he knew. I dreaded more once they all knew. "Asher... I want... I mean... CJ didn't tell you?" I really hoped he did. Then I wouldn't have to go through this. CJ came to the prison and even questioned me about my involvement in the bombing. He told me then he found out moments before coming into my interrogation room. At the time CJ said I broke trust with him by lying about my involvement in the Boston bombing. After they rescued me, I hoped differently.

"No," he glanced back at me, "he just told us to go get you and bring you here." I pulled that thought through my mind. CJ sent them after me. I hoped that meant he believed in me and he understood. In the prison, I hinted that perhaps some part of the government sanctioned what I did. Then again, based on him telling me I broke the trust, I had a nagging feeling this might be an elaborate ruse. Perhaps CJ arranged with the prison to pull me into a space with the team where I felt safe, and the team could get me to talk.

Fuck. I pulled myself back into the moment and out of the mind-game thought process the prison gave me. If I took the situation at face value, if the team already knew I took part in a bombing before I joined the team and they rescued me anyway, it would make the conversation easier. My mind guarded me. In this moment, with my partner and best friend, I could tell he, at the very least, didn't know who I was, and I owed him that much. "I guess I was hoping to tell you all at once," I said and looked around the empty room. I bit my lip. My heart climbed the ledge to break again, a possibility I had not considered. It put a lump in my throat, and I closed my eyes. I pulled my right arm in, to hold me together, to remember the pain, and to make it real.

"They might not come back for days," Asher said as he pulled out a dish for me.

He is going to hate me, I told myself. Even if they planned this interaction as part of one ruse to get me to talk, I had to do it. They won. I couldn't lie to Asher, my closest companion on this earth. When I joined the DEA, they stipulated I cut off myself from my old life, especially those I worked with to orchestrate the bombing. Then I got partnered with Asher and we planned, trained, and went on missions together, and it made us very close. "Okay," I said, "I owe you at least that, if not way more," I said. I sat there for a second. "I don't know where to start," I racked my brain.

He slid a bowl in front of me. "Simple, veggies, scrambled eggs," he said. "Is this good enough for you?"

I smiled at him and looked down at my bowl, and my breath left me. I shook. The bowl he slid in front of me mirrored that of the same blue bowl Ross used for cigarette ashes. Ross was the one who turned on me in the prison. I loved him and he told me he loved me. He worked for the DIA. I knew that, but he gained my trust in time. In the prison, they made it look like they tortured him to get me to talk, but it was a trick. I saw him during my rescue, and he was fine—not dead, like my interrogator made me think. I didn't realize until that moment that he always worked for them, and anything I thought I had with him, he fabricated. When I saw a bowl that matched a bowl he used for cigarette ashes, my stomach turned over. I had not processed the complicated things that happened with Ross in and out of the prison. Now in a safe house hidden from those who captured me, I felt like Ross and the people he worked for at the DIA invaded the space. It felt like anything but safe. "Where are the bowls?" I asked as I stood and stumbled backward.

He pointed at a cupboard. I went to it and opened it. There I found more similar blue bowls and some white ones. I grabbed one white bowl and all the blue bowls. I took the white one to the table and dumped my food into it. Then took the blue one with the other ones and threw them all in the trash can. Then I sat back down.

Asher's eyes were wide. "Got a problem with the bowls?"

"It's a long story, and not the one you want to hear right now."

He nodded from his seat across from me.

I took a few bites of food for courage. "Here goes," I said out loud to myself. "I'm... I'm Colby James." I lifted my eyes to meet Asher's. The leadership in the DEA knew I committed a bombing. They also helped me cover it up, changed my name, and invited me to join this tactical covert unit. They required me to disconnect from my past and assume a new identity. No one on my DEA team knew what I did or anything about my past. They called me Jackie Ericcson.

He looked confused, "Like the Colby James?" the question slowly slipped his lips. "As in the Boston Bomber, Colby James?" They caught me quickly after the bombing. For the last two years, I was the only one charged with crimes around the bombing. Which gave my old name, Colby James, infamy.

"You're the hacker who facilitated those two bombings that killed 39 people? Using car bombs in Boston?"

I stared back at him, chewed the inside of my bottom lip.

"What the FUCK..." he got up from the table and let his chair fall to the floor. He stared down at me and shook his head. I kept my eyes on him. "How are you in the DEA? How does that even happen? The DEA knows this about you, Ericcson, that you aren't Jackie Ericcson, and your real name is Colby James?" His questions were faster than I could answer.

I gave a slight nod.

"That's a mind fuck!" he shook his head. I could see the sentences form and leave his mind. "How did I miss... you..." Suddenly, he bent over and swiped the candle off the table and smashed it into the cabinets.

"Who had a hold of you in that prison?" he pointed over his shoulder.

"The DIA, Defense Intelligence Agency, they have not left me off their radar since the bombing."

"Somehow you get a government job after that?"

"I... uh..." I started, and he cut me off by raising his hand in my face and he shook his head from side to side. He didn't want my words, and he went outside and slammed the door behind him.

The only picture of me released to the public contained the bruises and stitches of a beating I got right after my arrest for the bombing. Honestly, I looked nothing like that. Other than that photo, they buried me, hid me from the public. Asher probably saw that picture and even if he saw a resemblance. He never imagined that someone like that could work for his agency.

I sat there for a while with my eyes closed. I had to face it; tell Asher whatever he wanted to know, no matter the consequences. I had to suck the poison out of this, if it broke me, if it killed me, and maybe it would put me back together.

I finished my meal and headed toward my room upstairs. The railing for the stairs sat to the right. I couldn't climb the stairs without the railing, but I needed my right arm to hold me together from my broken ribs. My screwed up lower back shot pain down my legs whenever I strained. I went slowly and reached across with my left hand to the rail and held my body together with my right and took it one stair at a time. I had to take a break every couple of stairs. The exercise left me in a light coat of sweat. Once I got to the top, I looked behind me for signs of Asher. I didn't see any.

2

It went from hard telling Asher I was Colby to harder when the rest of the team came back to the cabin.

I heard some people walk into the cabin downstairs. I closed a book I'd found on the bookshelf in the room and tried to listen in. I couldn't hear what they said. I strained my ears and closed my eyes to concentrate. Then all the sudden I could hear, "Are you fucking kidding me?" Mac's voice wafted through my door; his deep voice bellowed. My eyes went wide. I knew then the rest of the team took the news of my involvement in the bombing much worse than Asher did. Mac drew hard lines, and it took more time to gain his trust in the beginning. "We risked our fucking lives, put our lives on the line for that bitch?" The conversation continued, louder than before, but not as clear as Mac's words.

I took what little I had and shoved it in the backpack Asher had brought me. I included the book in my hand. I slid on socks and boots. I hit the end of the line and had to go. I knew the feeling. I welcomed the darkness like an old friend. I had hoped for more time to recover before I left, but I knew I would have to leave, eventually.

I took a slow breath as I put a hand on the bedroom doorknob. *God, I need you,* I said to myself as I twisted the doorknob. I got to the top of the stairs, and they went silent, and their eyes trained on me. As I made my way down the stairs, I looked at each of the members of my

DEA Team, Doc, Lee, Asher, and Mac. I tried to imprint them into my brain as my last memory.

I broke the silence at the bottom of the stairs. "I'll go," I said. They froze with their eyes fixed on me as I headed for the door.

Suddenly, Mac stepped between me and the door. "No," he said, "you're not fucking going anywhere until you explain this shit to us. We just fucked over our lives, our careers to get you. We helped a known bomber escape an American prison. You don't get to leave. Since we're going to prison for you, you are going to tell me why. You're sure as hell not going to go free." He pushed me back. Until this moment, he thought he rescued a DEA agent from illegal confinement in a secret U.S. prison in another country. He could stand behind something like that. He now knew, in his eyes, I am the terrorist known as Colby James. He felt like he rescued a terrorist. Which meant that made him one, too. The rescue not only put his career in jeopardy, but put him at risk of going to jail. He had a family and kids, like everyone else.

"Mac," I dropped my bag to the floor as I stumbled backward, "I just lived through hell for the second time. I'm not afraid of you." Mac liked to use loud blustery statements and violence to get people to comply with him. After surviving torture, I hardly put stock in his presentation of bravado, like I would before.

"I don't care if you are afraid of me," Mac said. "You at least owe us a good reason we shouldn't turn around and take you back right now."

I turned and looked around the room at all their faces. I loved these people and trusted them with every ounce of me. Asher was my partner. Doc and Lee were my fellow teammates who I felt really close to after the last year and on several overseas missions. Even Mac–our second in command on the team–we had grown close, I thought. They were all I had for the last year. I lost everything when I left Colby James behind. I buried myself in work and they were the only actual relationships I gained in that time frame. It wasn't the same for them, not anymore. I knew each one of them, their families, their hearts, and at the core of each of them were good people who all valued the same thing as me. "I broke our trust," I said. I echoed what CJ told me in the prison. "I know it's sacred. I'll leave. You will never see me again."

Doc stepped forward. "Ericcson," he stopped after he said my new identity last name. Then he shook his head, "whatever your name is..." He stepped between Mac and me. He knew Mac, I knew Mac, Mac wanted to deck me. He wanted to prevent it.

"Fucking Colby James," Asher chimed in with clarification that Jackie was not my real name.

"Colby," Doc looked at Asher and used a calm tone to acknowledge what he said, but still reduce the tension in the room. "Colby, CJ said to go up there and get you, bring you here, and figure out the next steps with you. He didn't say why or how you ended up in that prison. Although, he said he would respect the decision we made, which now makes sense. I thought at the time he meant getting back at those people. Now I see it's something entirely different. What do we do with this bomber who ended up on our team?" Doc swept his hand around the room at each person and urged them to nod at CJ's words to them. "I assume he does, but I need to know. Does CJ know you are Colby, and you did that bombing in Boston?"

I nodded yes. The anxiety from needing to know what they would do to me filled me with dread. It also gave me powerful visions of wanting to run out the door. "He found out when he found me there, not before." He and they didn't know the details of the bombing or why the DEA would cover for me. I understood on the surface it made little sense.

Doc shook his head. "CJ wouldn't put us in this position unless he knew something we didn't. You are going to have to explain this to us and we will go from there. You owe us at least that much," he said with his hand out and waited for me to agree with his statement like everyone else.

I nodded.

He turned to Mac, who shrugged his shoulders and rolled his eyes in agreement.

They all stared at me, and tears filled my eyes. I reached up and wiped them away and pushed the next set down. I did not let them reach my eyes. They were right; they had a very real probability of going to jail for helping me escape, and therefore ensnaring them to cover up my involvement in the bombing. When the DEA stepped in after I got arrested, I only got sentenced to the lesser crime of hacking, which came with probation. After the public interest died down, I moved away. This allowed me to change my name and fall off the face of the earth. The DEA couldn't openly clear me of my crimes without admitting that the government sanctioned the bombing of American people for a real purpose. The person, me, had slipped away. The DEA warned me if my true self resurfaced, they could not help me. In that thought, I had hope. Maybe if I told them what the leaders of the DEA already knew, they would accept it and help me like they did.

"Okay," I turned from Doc to look at each of their faces, "I trust all of you with my life. I will tell you everything." I stopped. The thought crept back through my mind. This could be another approach, just a way for those people from the prison to get me to tell everything about my bombing. The memory of Ross's fake torture and betrayal felt like a punch to the stomach and reminded me that my interrogator effectively altered my perception of reality. I didn't have a fight left in me for this stuff anymore, though. Even if the DIA conspired with the team to get me to talk, I didn't stand a chance of resistance any longer. "I will respect whatever decision you make." I looked up to God. "I hope when we're done you send me to the FBI instead and not to that place you got me from. Whatever you want, though, I'm at your mercy. I know you share a heart for our core purpose, but I don't expect you to understand." I lied. I wanted to be back on the team and nothing else. Everything I was and wanted to be intertwined with this team. I would give anything to get that back.

I closed my eyes for a moment. When I opened them, I went to the table and pulled out a chair. I pulled it out just wrong and my ribs reminded me that all of this was real, and I was here and alive. "I ask that you let me tell you all of it. I got away with it because the government approved the bombing, but there is so much to tell, so please let me tell the story." They looked at each other as they came and sat in their own chairs. I had a fleeting thought. Maybe they would understand, and everything could go back to normal.

"I was working as a contractor, a hacker, for the government, and then... I was approached by..." I stopped for a second and closed my eyes. I blew out a breath as I got ready to tell them what I had held so close for so long. The one thing Chin and the DIA wanted to know. Chin was the nickname I gave for the nameless interrogator who tortured me in the prison. They completely broke my body and my will to get the information. I had to trust my team or just accept that if the DIA concocted this elaborate ruse, I had no choice but to give in.

"Working up some lies?" Asher shot at me.

I looked him in the eyes. I knew my body could tell a better story than my mouth. I reached back and pulled off my shirt, and stood up in my sports bra. I showed off every inch of my bruised torso. They mangled my body. I had healed, but I broke first. I had burns, cuts, and still had stitches from my surgery to remove the bullet. "I just spent the last, I don't even know how many days, being tortured: broken, burned, electrocuted," I said and felt some strength grow in me. "I didn't eat or sleep or any fucking thing to protect this information, Asher." I took a second to look down at the black and purple that adorned my right side. I brushed up against a burn from the cattle prod. I turned my body, showing off the scars, the pink and mangled parts of my left side from the car bomb from so long ago. Probably none of them had seen that part of me before. It's not like I tried to hide it–but how often do you take off your shirt around your coworkers?

Someone said something, but I missed it. I had let too much of my feelings out and I had to rein it in. I went to the sink and got a glass of water and drank it down.

"Jackie," Doc came up behind me. "You don't have to do this right now."

"Yes, she does," Mac called over.

Doc put his hand on my right shoulder, and I jumped. "Ignore him." He waited for our eyes to meet. Doc's greatest downfall rested in his kindness until you crossed him.

"It's okay," I said. "I just needed a second."

He nodded and went back to the table.

I followed behind him. "Here's the bottom line: the Iranian militia that we have been chasing had a much wider grasp on our government. I planned the bombing to set in motion a series of events that removed that grasp. Prior to the bombing, blackmailers compromised several members of the President's cabinet. They convinced them to do all kinds of things to stop all investigations that would lead to related activities." I leaned forward and put my arms on the table and focused on each person.

I had a team for the operation that culminated in the bombing. We called the operation Fortitude. I decided the best place to start was to tell them about how I recruited my lieutenant into Operation Fortitude. It was a formula that worked for him and those that followed. Four years ago, I had to convince him too. I worked for the good guys. This came after I already had one partner, Crystal.

"Well, are you two going to tell me what that was all about?" Jason asked after we got into the back of the blue Ford rental car. We parked on a residential street a few blocks away from the restaurant. In the car, with Jason in the back seat with me, I flipped on my laptop and opened the program that monitored the Secretary of Defense's email traffic. I installed it a couple of weeks ago. I found out about a meeting by his blackmailer. Crystal and I brought Jason along as we tried to listen and track who he met with, but we didn't have enough people or the right equipment. We stayed cut off from the rest of the government until we rooted out the corruption. It meant we had to figure out everything on our own.

"What if we told you that meeting you just saw may have compromised our country's safety?" I said and looked up from the laptop and at Jason next to me.

"Right," Jason said and shook his head in disbelief.

Crystal started the car and pulled out of the parking spot. "We aren't joking."

"That was the Secretary of Defense. He isn't compromised," Jason scoffed.

"Show him." Crystal made eye contact with me through the rearview mirror.

I turned the laptop to Jason, "This is his email, and…"

"Stop right there," Jason said and reeled backward into the door. "Are you serious? You hacked into his email?"

"It's my job," I said. "I work for the government. I hack into their systems to find vulnerabilities and report it back to them. My job is to make their systems stronger."

"You've gone outside the bounds of that job," Jason said. He turned and looked outside to the streets of downtown Alexandria, Virginia. "Crystal, stop the car. Let me out." He pulled on the handle, but Crystal locked the door.

"Calm down," Crystal said.

"I also have the job of tracking down who in our government has been assisting an Iranian militia group. It's sanctioned work, Jason."

"Oh, yeah, then why are you telling me?" Jason adjusted how he sat to pull a phone from his pocket. "Pretty sure that sounds highly classified, or at least sensitive enough not to tell someone who is not working on your mission."

"Because we can't hope to do this alone," I said. "And before we can bring in an agency, we must be sure there aren't foreign actors acting upon them. So far, seven of the agencies we investigated have had major issues."

Jason shook his head in disbelief and fumbled to turn his phone on.

My computer dinged; the Secretary of Defense, Roger Bismark, emailed. I opened it.

Admiral,
Send USS Bolivar to assist with Operation Kentucky Coffee.
/R

"Look," I said to Jason and turned the computer screen.

"You are showing me you have access to classified information. It is not helping your cause," Jason said with his phone fully on. He tried to make a phone call, but as planned, Crystal activated a signal blocker.

"Jason, trust me." Crystal zoomed us onto I-95 southbound away from Old Town Alexandria, Virginia.

"I thought I could trust you," Jason said, now exasperated with his lack of a phone signal.

"We can pull over and kick you out, or I will show you everything, and then you do whatever you want with the information. Turn me in, whatever you want." I placed the laptop in his lap.

He looked down at the email and looked up at Crystal. "At least listen," Crystal said.

He took a moment and read the email again. "Why does this matter?" he said.

I reached over to the track pad and opened an email I had saved. "This email is from a weird email address. I opened the extension; it doesn't have a proper path. Someone with a depth in skill or inside knowledge got this injected into this classified network requesting a meet with Bismark."

"And?" Jason said and rubbed his forehead.

"We see this every time, a request to meet from a deep coded email, the meeting occurs, then an order comes out of the blue. If we looked hard enough, the USS Bolivar was probably in some area that disadvantaged this Iranian militia. It's hard, though, because we don't know what the militia is doing to figure out what happened here. We know that after one of these meetings with a high-ranking member of the staff for Secretary of State, Jill Peterson halted a few investigations in Venezuela. We can show you all the details."

Crystal pulled off on the side of the interstate. The cars zoomed by fast, the shoulder barely fit the car. "Stay and listen, or get out," Crystal said.

"Seven agencies?" he asked.

I nodded.

"I can't help you," his eyes bounced from mine down to the laptop.

"You can help, just until we find a place to turn this information in to someone who can handle it."

Jason shook his head, put the laptop back in my lap and pushed the door open, and it slammed against the guardrail.

I reached out and touched his hand. "Please, listen and then all of this is yours, the computer and anything else you want." I closed the laptop and held it out to him. A semi-truck zoomed by and shook the car, barely missed our side. Jason stood up; I held the laptop out still. He stood for a moment longer and then pulled the laptop from my hands. He stepped backward, away from the door, then came back and sat back down in the car. "I want your bag too and that other laptop I always see you with, the red one."

"Anything you want," I said.

He shut the door to the car.

I didn't know it at the time. Now, with retrospect last year with my DEA team, we went down to a small town near the shore of Venezuela to see if the militia used it to transfer radioactive material. Sitting here now after I just told my team, that conversation with Jason became more poignant.

"So, you're telling me our top government officials were assisting Iran in potentially attacking our country?" Mac asked with an array of disbelief.

"I don't think they knew the culmination of their actions, just little things here and there," I said. "Stopping an investigation, changing resource priorities, and things like that. I doubt they had any idea what all of it amounted to."

3

My DEA team listened but didn't seem to like my answers. "Who were you working for?" Mac said and pounded on the table.

"I had high-level government officials bring me in," I said. I really didn't want to reveal the only card I had left.

"No, you fucking tell us," Doc said, now standing and leaned against the cabinets.

In reality, it was Senator Brickman, the head of the intelligence committee out of Florida, but I couldn't give his name. "Our director of the DEA Admiral Holmes .... he was involved." I didn't know how the Admiral was involved, but I used his name and it would probably give me clearance to not give up Brickman's name.

"Why not just turn them in?" Doc asked. He kept coming back to the bombing. His anger level about the bombing portion of what I did foamed at the top of his mind and questions.

"I tried," I said. "When we finished our investigation, I turned it over to the only officials I could trust."

I told my DEA team about trying to turn over the investigation to the authorities. Although, I didn't tell them who the person I met with. Senator Brickman recruited me and set my mission. I had to protect him. I told my team I turned it in to Admiral Holmes, but in reality, it was Brickman.

"Ms. James, your work is exemplary," Senator Brickman looked up from the summary file I prepared for him. I dropped the files with his team yesterday. He made time for me between the events and dinner in the middle of the Southeast Peace Brokerage Conference. He flipped back through the pages. I peered across his desk and out the windows with the tree leaves that softly waved on the other side of the window. You wouldn't know that you were in a hotel room unless you walked up to the window and looked down over the sprawling conference center. "You really captured the breadth and some of the depth of the problem," he said from behind one page. I had laid out which agencies had corruption and the highest levels of it. I included examples of what they have done and how entrenched I thought they were or the level of knowledge of what their actions did for the Iranian militia. Many of them didn't know who they worked for or didn't understand the subtle influence that was exerted upon them. Nonetheless, if the militia compromised an agency, I at least grabbed the highest levels of who and what was involved.

"It should be enough evidence, on all of them," I said, confident we reached the edges of what we could without giving away our investigation.

"Do you know how long an investigation like this by a Senate Committee, the FBI, U.S. District Attorney or some sort of Special Prosecutor will take?" Brickman let the papers flap down and pointed at the file and looked at me over the rims of his reading glasses.

"We did most of the legwork. So, what's left ... six months, a year?" I asked.

"Years and years," he said and took off his reading glasses, throwing them on his larger-than-life dark cherry desk in his hotel suite.

"I spent years. I did that leg work," I said defensively. I knew our work and that it provided details of the corrupted officials in the agencies and that could get rid of the problems.

"You are not a special prosecutor; you are a Joe-shmoe regular old civilian, with no authority, who used some unsavory and illegal hacking and bugging tactics to piece together a very complex case. They can't use that information legally."

"You are the one who told me to do that." I scooted to the edge of my fancy armchair and leaned forward to his giant desk. This is as close to a regular meeting I would have about the case. I stayed away from all his other offices in DC, in the Senate building, or at his rented house, or at his offices back in Florida.

"I'm not saying the work you did wasn't good."

"Then what are you saying?" I did not expect this conversation to go this way.

"I applaud your reporting and the depth of information here, but this will not work," Brickman said. "Paperwork can be buried, investigators can be bought, things and people can be shuffled, and nothing will be stopped, at least not on time."

"So, what do we do?"

"You figure it out. That's what I hired you for. Stop them, all of them. Now that you know how big the problem is, you know how much work you have to do," he said and stood up. "These leaders need to be stopped, remove their blackmailers, their influences, or figure out a way to remove them. Whatever it takes to stop this." He stacked my folder onto the box of documents. "Now, I have dinner to go to with these defense firms."

"Defense firms? Isn't this a Peace Conference?" I questioned his comment.

He let out a chuckle and pulled his suit jacket off the hook and slipped over his shoulders. "You should remember, the best of our defense contractors are always involved in the..." he paused for a second and smirked, "...the bringing about of peace, or the need to bring about peace."

"I never thought of it that way."

"They don't choose a side if they are any good. They survive no matter what is going on." He went to the mirror and adjusted his tie and buttoned his suit jacket. "Now you need to make sure this Iranian militia group doesn't use our own people to bring us out of peace."

I stood up and soaked in his instructions. I did as he said and found the lengths of corruption and used whatever tactic I found necessary. It wasn't enough, though; any legal or official channels would not work in rooting out the corruption. I had to still stop it, and I didn't have an agency to back me up. It was still just me and the team I created, all off the books. I bit my lip and watched him shuffle the papers on his desk. I am not a prosecutor; he hired me to suck out the poison, something to stop it all at once.

A man walked into the room, and Brickman nodded at the box. The man went and picked it up.

"Ms. James," he snapped out of my deep thoughts on what to do next. "You did a great job, but it's not enough, not even close." He nodded the top of his head toward the door. He warned me when he hired me. I had to suck out the poison, even if it meant injecting radiation to get the cancer.

"Understood," I said and turned for the door.

When I reached the threshold of the room, he called out, "Ms. James, do me a favor and go out the back." I figured as much. Our relationship could never become public at all costs.

"Your bomb didn't kill them, your bomb killed innocent people," Doc said.

I shook my head and held in my sharp retorts. I would need to be calm and understanding to get through this. "I'm getting there."

"I don't know how you might get there," Doc said. At that moment, the way he looked at me had changed. In this moment, I was not his patient, but under his keen investigative eye.

"We spent years figuring out who the Iranian militia had a grasp on, who knew about it, and ways to break it free," I said, moving us forward.

"Sum it up already," Mac said.

My Fortitude team, Jason really, had pieced it together. I told my new DEA team the story of when we figured it out. Dan, one of the original members of my Fortitude team, dropped a box of donuts in the middle of the table. He had one in his mouth. He kept us fed most of the time. "Fuel as promised. I have a bunch of coffee in the car too," he said and turned, heading toward the door.

Furi, our security for the team, was the first one into the box while Crystal moved the documents under the box. Over the last two days, we compiled all the information and drew it on the board to make sure we didn't miss anything. Jason insisted he drew the connections with markers and he spent most of the time configuring and reconfiguring what he drew on the board. He kept at it while we all waited for the coffee to come back in with Dan.

I found the information fit methodically in my head, but I could see the need to draw it out to find the gaps. "There, other than the agencies that are everywhere, I separated out Boston, Detroit, and Atlanta from each other, and now it all logically fits," Jason said.

"You think that clears things up?" Crystal said rhetorically.

"What about an expose article in the newspaper?" Furi asked.

"Did you not see the sad drawing Jason has up there? We can't even draw it on the board. How are we going to tell the story?" Crystal asked.

"What if we kill them?" Dan asked.

Everyone stopped and looked at him.

"Not a bad idea, but probably difficult to execute. Especially since you kill one and even if you get past that and kill two, the FBI will have us pegged in no time," Jason said.

I walked up to the board and reviewed what Jason drew. He had coupled everyone based on where they were located and not based on their agency. Then I saw his name, Ashenhurst; I knew the name, but I didn't think he worked for anyone. I went to the table where the mess from the donuts covered the top layers of paper. An argument broke out between Jason and Crystal over executing some of the cabinet members. I pulled out Ashenhurst information. He knew about three of the corrupted cabinet members. That is all we had on him. He knew and did nothing. Brickman knew and tried. Maybe we could find something with Ashenhurst. Brickman made it clear we had to solve this, and because we weren't on the books, our tactics didn't have to be either.

I summed it up to my DEA team. "We found out Ashenhurst, the old mayor in Boston, was aware of the corruption and was not making a move. He had floated the idea with his advisors of pushing all of those people out using his special connection with the President but was waiting for the right moment. We made him think one of them was turning on him, that was the bombings. Within weeks, all the corrupted cabinet members were out of power and now all are under investigation. Our push on Ashenhurst worked. I got it cleared before I did it."

"Who would clear that? Killing Americans?" Doc said and looked over at his partner, Lee, who had his arms crossed and had gone silent, much like Asher. Lee didn't connect back with him. He had lost himself listening to everything.

I moved past his comment. "Look, the reason we know about the Iranian militia trying to bring in materials for a dirty bomb is because we removed the blockers of the investigation."

"This is insane," Asher said and shook his head. Silence fell upon the room as I could feel the word clouds from over us, everyone lost in their own thoughts.

"If this was all sanctioned, why were you in a prison? Right or wrong, why would they be torturing you for this information?" Doc asked.

"Larry told me he thinks we missed the DIA director," I realized now how insane it all sounded. "That's who runs the prison, the DIA."

4

AFTER HOURS OF TALKING, Doc cut into the middle of a different story. "There had to be a better way to get rid of corrupt leaders than a bombing. You're not telling us everything."

I looked over at him exasperated but tried to not show it. "Jason and I on the Fortitude team decided on the bombing as the best course of action." I thought of the decision we made, the one that set me on this trajectory.

"A bomb is a little extreme," I said to Jason as we sat out on the beach late in the evening. I lit a cigarette and stared at the streaks of light as the moon bounced off the water.

Jason leaned over on to his elbow, his head toward me. "We have to make Ashenhurst make a move. We know he has the power, and it's the only thing that will sway him into action. He is not afraid of publicity, congressmen, and we do not know where the President lands on this."

"Can't we threaten him?" I asked, almost rhetorically.

"He doesn't respond to threats." Jason took a long drag. He knew I knew that information.

"Maybe if we can get to the President, we can..."

"We can ask if he knows almost all his cabinet members are on a blackmail list?" Jason said and finished my sentence. "And somehow, he didn't know? Or that maybe he knows, but we are the people who figured it out. Also, please don't kill us." Jason clasped his hands together and mimicked a beggar.

I pushed his shoulder, and he rocked onto his back and sat up. We talked about these things and only sometimes with Crystal. We tried to come to the team with action, not questions.

Jason continued, "Ashenhurst knows, and he isn't doing anything. He is waiting for the right moment to make his move. He wants to capitalize on the moment. We have to force his hand and make him remove these people. At least two of the corrupted cabinet members, maybe three of them, know Ashenhurst knows and has done nothing to them. If we can convince Ashenhurst the corrupted members are after him, he will get them removed. That will be his moment and he can't wait any longer. He knows everyone who is dirty, and he has enough pull with the President to kick them out. With them out of the way of blocking legitimate investigations, we can find the depths of the Iranian militia group's plan."

I continued to stare into the ocean. "I have spent days trying to find a better way."

"He is terrified of bombings; a bombing killed his father and brother in Beirut, and he is almost paranoid about it."

"I know. A bomb is perfect. He will immediately think some of them are after him, most likely more than one; that will force him to make a move. Something we can move around easily," I said, finally agreeing with Jason. I knew I would have to, eventually.

"We need to disguise its purpose from the public for his sake and ours. It makes him feel safe to enact his plan. A sniper or something like that wouldn't do that. We will look like terrorists; it will be perfect," Jason said. He had thought about this longer than I had, and I knew we would make it work.

"We will need clearance for collateral damage," I said and felt the plan form in my mind. I pulled my knees up and wrapped my arms around them. I turned my head to Jason.

He nodded at me.

I smiled.

"How am I supposed to believe this? You can be making this all up. Where is your proof?"

"Doc, you're asking me to download years of my life into a few hours of conversation. I'm exhausted, I need rest. Can we pick this up tomorrow?" I said. He would barely let me talk. He tore me apart whenever I talked about anything that led up to the bombing. Lee had moved to the living room and sat in a chair. He listened but didn't take part. Asher had left the cabin several times and would make quiet comments to Lee. Mac and Doc grilled me.

The room went silent as everyone bounced looks off each other. "Let her go," Asher said. Lee and Asher in the very least wanted to talk to everyone and not to me, that seemed obvious.

"I will be right upstairs if you need me," I said. I pushed myself up, stopped for a moment to take a deep breath and remembered how much it hurt to just breathe.

I headed back to my room and decided I needed to sleep. We made a decision to turn our will and our lives over to the care of God as we understand him. Step 3 for Narcotics Anonymous. I spun the Bible from the side table in my hands and felt the beautiful leather worked binding under my palms. I sat it down on my pillow. I had found it in the room earlier in the day after I told Asher I was Colby. I got into bed. I moved the Bible to the pillow next to mine and moved wrong and felt my ribs scream at me. I was afraid to crack the Bible open, what would fall out of it, out of me? After all this time since the bombing I still did not feel worthy for God. I believed my bombing was for good, but the one place I could not reach for was God. If I opened the Bible, I would have to face that part of me and with everything that happened, I couldn't do it.

My life was completely unmanageable, and it had nothing to do with opioids. I was a recovering addict, and I could find a way through this mess using the tools given to me in recovery. Maybe I could make it through the safe house. I also placed my trust in a team that might put me right back in that prison. I placed my hand on its cover and closed my eyes. I felt exhausted yet relieved from finally letting go of my secret, that the government hired me and the government sanctioned my bombing. The torture that broke my body and mind to protect it somehow didn't hurt as much now that I shared that secret with my team. The government formed my team to continue to track militia activity after my bombing. It felt better to tell my team, but it left me vulnerable and afraid for the future. They could send me right back to that prison, or back to the FBI or Justice Department. If the DIA planned this, then it worked, and I was okay with it, for now. I fell asleep quickly.

Laura flooded in, the child I lost, her little body so small wrapped in that white hospital blanket with the two blue lines. She had never known the world, never tasted its air. I worried about her little neck, but what was there to worry about? My baby left the world before she entered it. I kissed her forehead and ran my fingers across her face. I let the tears stream before I left her in that room.

She grew in my dream, my hand in my former lover Lars's as we watched her grow. She ran and laughed. Her blonde hair wispy in the wind. My heart was so happy. I looked back at Lars, and his smile warmed my heart. Our fingers intertwined. I looked again at our daughter and her beautiful blonde hair turned red and curly. I loved her so, and she giggled and ran through the grass.

I looked back at Lars, and he was gone, and it was Ross there instead. His hand in mine. I looked back at our daughter, and there was the girl with the Kool-Aid smile who died in my bombing. I saw her right before the bomb went off, and she haunted my dreams ever since. I chased her, she cried and so afraid of me, afraid of what would happen to her, what did happen to her.

I couldn't run. I fell to my knees. "I'm sorry," I said. "I'm so sorry. Please forgive me." I cried as she slipped out of sight. I looked at the grass and my hands covered in blood. I felt it again, not right, not knowing why I couldn't get my body to respond after I got shot, "Damn, blood."

I looked back up to see her one last time. There was Ross, laying there in his own blood. He turned his head to me, "Are you not sorry for me, Colby..." In the prison they made me watch what I thought was torture of Ross and his death. Until I saw him alive, I thought he died because he loved me.

"I didn't want them to hurt you," I said desperately.

I was back in the room, my tears streamed as the snot dripped from my nose. "Please, please stop hurting him!" I screamed at Chin, my interrogator.

"You know how to stop it, Colby," he said.

"He's dead!" I screamed. "STOP, STOP THE WATER!" He wasn't moving. I had to get to him. In the prison they made it seem like he died by waterboarding.

I got to him in a hospital bed, and I had his hand. "You're mine, Colby," he gave my hand a squeeze. I smiled as he got out of bed, and I thought he would kiss me. He put his hands on my throat and squeezed. It wasn't gentle. His face turned angry, dangerous, angry. I tried to kick him. I grabbed his arms. I wanted to scream. I kicked hard.

I woke to find Lee who tried to stop me. "Whoa, Jack, it's okay."

I breathed heavily as sweat dripped down my face. I grabbed the covers and threw them off the bed. Lee sat on the edge of the bed and looked at me. I felt like I was still ready to fight for my life. I scooted past him and went to the window; I needed air. I went to open it.

"Jack, we don't open the windows at safe houses." Lee put his hand on mine and looked down at me.

"Fine," I left the room headed for the bathroom. I splashed the cool sink water on my face. I took a towel and wet it and placed it on my neck. I wasn't sure what was worse, that dream or living in this moment, waiting to know what they would do to me. Were they going to send me back to the prison or turn me over to the FBI, or maybe just maybe let me continue our mission? I took a few sips of the water from the sink with my hands. I went back to the room. Lee was still in there; he looked out the window.

"Are you okay?" he asked.

"I don't have an answer for that question," I said and sat in the chair, the towel still draped around my neck.

"What was that dream about?" Lee said.

I leaned back and shook my head.

"I will not accept that this time; you said you would tell us every-thing."

Almost every Monday since I met Lee, he spent the first 30 minutes of the day telling me about his weekend. I think the last time was not too long before Nicaragua. That was our last mission where we went to track the cartels actions. I got shot on that mission. That was right before the DIA got me back in their prison.

"So, did you do anything interesting over the weekend?" Lee asked me when he walked into our team room. He rolled up a chair and had a large coffee in his hands.

I smiled awkwardly, "No," I said. Ross flashed through my mind; he had been here all weekend, but we ended up on a bad note. We got in a big fight and he left after it. All too much to tell Lee.

"There is so much story there you are not telling me," Lee said and shook his head. I never told him anything, mostly because I had nothing to tell. This time, Ross would be way too much to unpack. Ross worked for the DIA and led an investigation into me after the bombing, I never told him much. Through time though we became really close and intimate. It was better the less who knew about that complicated part of my history.

I changed the subject, "Did you guys end up having that party?" I asked Lee. Dale, his partner, invited me, but when Ross showed up, I forgot all about it.

"Thanks for coming," Lee said sarcastically.

"Sorry, I got distracted," I said, and for a moment a flutter went through my stomach because I really enjoyed being with Ross. He was incredibly sexy. He was tall and strong. He had red hair and had various states of a beard every time I saw him. The thought of him stirred me up inside. Probably because I shouldn't be with him, which made it so much hotter.

"You have to tell me his or her name," Lee said.

I smiled and blushed a little. "Did Dale survive the party?" I ignored his question and asked the one thing that would fire up Lee to tell me all about the events of the weekend. Dale packed every event with drama. I knew asking that question would spark a story about some minor thing like shortage of food turning into a major drama to address it.

In the cabin I stared back at Lee and decided it was time.

"That was not my first time in that prison," I said and sat up and rested my forearms on my legs trying to find any position that didn't feel so horrible. "There was a guy, Ross, who was my interrogator the first time I was there. After that and since I got out of that prison the first time, he has been a constant in my life, there every step of my life. I dreamed of him hurting me."

"He did all of that to your body?"

I shook my head 'no.' I felt the tears well up in my eyes. "That was a different guy. Ross, he umm... he spent years gaining my trust. For the last two years he inserted himself into my life, my training, and came to see me in DC. He made me think he cared about me, and I guess I cared about him too." I felt so stupid saying the words. The emotional pain drew up the pain in my ribs.

"Jackie, that is fucked up."

"I know," I said. "The prison this last time they tortured him in front of me, and killed him. Or at least I thought they did." I stood up and blew out my emotions trying to find a new position that didn't hurt. "But it wasn't real, and I fell for it. He is alive, I saw him on the way out of the prison." I motioned for Lee to get off my bed.

I laid down on the bed and took in the ceiling. "He was all I had for the last two years and it messed with my mind. I lost my family and everything I was before the bombing. Ross was the only person on earth who knew everything about me, and in that kind of isolation you don't think right. I couldn't tell anyone either, because the agency warned me about anything from my life coming back. It would be the end of my career."

"Reset," CJ called out, and a bell rang through our radios.

"What the fuck was that?" I said aloud to everyone and stood up. I needed more blanks to run that again. I crossed the yard to the shipping container used for ammo supply. I filled up my spent magazines. Jackie Ericcson, our newest teammate, walked up next to me and did the same.

"Hey, Mac."

"What branch did you say you were in?" I asked her. I knew nothing about her.

"I didn't," she said, as she slid rounds through the fast loader into her magazine.

"You didn't say?" I stopped and looked at her face.

"I didn't say, and I didn't serve," she said.

"Now I know why you keep fucking us up. I didn't know you could get into this unit without military training. In our team, Doc and I served in Army Special Forces. We knew each other before this task force. I had even met Asher a couple times, when Asher was an Army Ranger, although just casually. Asher was DEA now. Lee spent time in the Navy too, but now he was ATF. CJ spent almost his whole career in the DEA, but he had a short stint in the Army. Then there is you, with no military training."

She cut back at me, "I had a lot of military training."

"But no real-life experience," I said and threw the box on the table. Pulling in an unexperienced operator would challenge us. I couldn't believe that CJ put us in that position. "You're going to get us killed," I said and walked away. No need to sugar coat it, better she knew where she stood.

I went straight to CJ who sorted through a stack of papers on the hood of his truck, "She's fucked this practice run twice. How many times are we going to run through this before we kick her off the team? She doesn't have it." It made sense now, why CJ had us out here running drills on clearing buildings and pre-running operations when we had done them 100 times already. He didn't think she could either.

"Give her a break, Mac. You will not come across a techie hacker that's tactical like her easily. She's been on the team for not even two weeks. We got to bring her up. We need her on this team," CJ said and didn't even look back at me from the papers on the hood of the truck in front of him. He looked at our first mission on paper and adjusted different scenarios for us to be ready for anything.

"Asher can do it," I said. I liked Asher, and I didn't know what she could do that he couldn't.

"Not like her," CJ said and glanced over his shoulder at me. Our eyes locked and his face said this conversation had ended and he didn't want to hear it again. Doc and Lee hadn't expressed their frustration yet, but I could see the annoyance on their faces. Asher liked her though; he made that clear. He liked all women.

5

I DIDN'T SLEEP LONG; My body needed motion. I got up and put on the only clothes I had. Boots weren't ideal for running but I didn't care. I headed down the stairs. They were already all awake, or they never slept. They watched me move slowly down the stairs in awkward silence.

"I need to go for a run or a walk, whatever my body will let me do," I said on my way to the door. I reached out and grabbed the handle.

"Jackie, wait," Doc said. I did like that he called me Jackie and not Colby.

I turned around, the thought of being told I couldn't leave made me combative. I turned with a scowl on my face, "I'll be right back."

He came toward me, "It's freezing out," he said and took off his black thermal, long sleeve shirt with DEA sprawled across the front.

"Thanks." I put it on and turned back for the door.

I pulled the door open and let the fresh air fill my lungs and heal my broken soul. I walked out past the shrubs that buried the door into a hidden cove. We were up in the mountains; I could tell by the crispness. The trees were tall and blue green. I could see the hills behind us and in front of us. There was a Toyota 4Runner in the driveway, and as I got into the driveway, I saw a Chevy pickup out back. As I got further from the cabin, I turned around. It was a log cabin. There was a big, detached garage out back, probably fuel inside, 4 Wheelers, maybe snowmobiles. A large wood pile sat by the garage. The back of the cabin was up against a hill. The gravel driveway was long, twisted down a hill through some trees from the cabin to the road. I took it all in.

I needed to know where I was. I had to feel in control of something and at least know where I was, unlike wherever I was in the prison. I started down the driveway. First, I walked, and started walking faster. Then I jogged. I landed with my right leg and my body jostled, and a sharp pain shot up my right side, my ribs, the pain under my ribs, bringing me to my knees. "FUCK!" I screamed.

I got up, angry. I couldn't have my body fail me. My mind already failed me, and I didn't need it to be a part of the problem. I started with a walk again and went quickly down the driveway and out to the road. The road was dirt mixed with gravel. All the traffic seemed to come in and out of this driveway from the left. Few turned right. I needed to check both ways. I turned left down the tree-lined, one-lane road. I ran again; the pain screamed back at me. I pulled my arm in and held it. I let the pain wash over me. I had to run. I didn't care about the pain; it made me feel alive. This was something I could fight. I kept running, but I was slow.

I heard footsteps behind me. I checked over my shoulder, Mac was running up. It made me run faster, but I was still slow. He screamed up to me, running without a problem. He slowed his jog to my speed as he came alongside me. "Are you sure you should be running?" he asked me.

I was in pain, and I'm sure it registered on my face. I glanced over at him but tried to run as fast as my body would let me.

"You gotta let your body heal."

I let go of the run and went for a walk. "This is how I heal," I said. I breathed heavily and held my side.

"I've been shot before, it needs time to heal," he said with genuine concern on his face.

"My gunshot…" I laughed at him, "I don't even notice it. That has nothing to do with what I'm dealing with." I took a couple breaths, felt the crisp air agree with the part of me that wished to escape my life right now. "Look, you can see I can barely move. I don't need a babysitter, let me move. I need to get my heart rate up for something good, and I'll be right back."

He stopped moving and let me walk past him.

"If I'm not back soon, don't worry. I will have only made it a mile or so, just come and find me, shouldn't take you long." Mac gave me a hard time through our initial training, then more so in everything I did. I was never good enough.

I don't know if I would call what I did a run. I tried to move through the pain and sometimes that meant walking, sometimes it meant I cried. Cried from the pain, cried from not being able to be myself, or cried from being so overwhelmed. I wanted my body to be fixed. Mac was right, my body needed more time to heal, but my mind couldn't wait for that. I needed on this first day free of that hell to move my body the way I wanted. I needed the sweat, and I needed my heart to pump not out of fear, pain, anxiety nor adrenaline.

I had Doc's black thermal DEA shirt tied around my waist by the time I got back. When I walked in, they were at the table still deliberating what I had said to them the night before.

"You are really too tough for your own good," Doc said when I walked in, as sweat dripped down my face and soaked through my clothes. "You might have done some damage doing that, I'm going to look later." Doc put me as a patient clearly above the hostile feelings he had toward me for being in the bombing.

I nodded.

Someone made breakfast. "Want some?" Lee said. I went and washed my hands and sat back down at the table.

"How are you feeling?" Mac asked. "You look like you were in a lot of pain out there."

"I feel better, thank you."

Asher squirmed in the chair and was noticeably uncomfortable with me sitting there. It made sense; since I revealed I had lied about Colby James, it basically invalidated any feelings he had about me for the last year.

I wolfed down the food, and gratefulness suddenly overcame me. I didn't know what would come next, but I wasn't in the prison being tortured. I stopped and looked up, "Thank you for coming to get me. I know you might regret it now. I don't think I would have made it a few more days in that place, hell one more day might have been the end of me." I looked around the table at them. "Seriously," I knew they might send me back, but I hoped they wouldn't. "Thank you."

Mac nodded. "I think I get you now," Mac said. "I also get why CJ sent us after you. He saw what you went through and on some level believed you. He also knew our team broke. It would break us, and how can we trust each other anymore, certainly not you," he pointed to me. "CJ sent us here to find out what we thought and to see if we could fix it. We can't go out on our mission until we have decided what to do with you. We have to be good before he even floats anything with leadership."

The weight of his words fell heavy on me; I broke my team. They have a chance to catch the materials, and they came after me instead, a choice I wish they didn't make. What if the new team didn't get down there on time to find it? Would it come to the U.S.? This would be my fault. The weight of the situation landed on me and squeezed the air from my lungs. "I will do whatever it takes to fix this." I knew not being there would be the easiest way to fix it.

"It will take all of us, Jackie, not just you," Mac said. I nodded.

I picked up the dishes and took them to the sink.

"Colby," Doc said. I shuddered. Colby still belonged to Ross. He ruined the name when he was my interrogator, and he was the only person who called me that for years. That name was inextricably linked to torture. After I talked to Lee last night, it wasn't lost on me how screwed up my feelings were for him. I decided the best medicine was to tell the truth, no matter how screwed up it was.

"What was that?" Asher asked.

"The only person who called her that name in years is her first interrogator, Ross," Lee said to me. We talked for hours last night after he woke me up from my nightmare. I was honest with Lee for the first time about everything, about Ross, and who I was.

I continued to clear the table; I was the last one to eat.

"Isn't his name actually Aaron?" Mac asked.

Everyone looked at me. "Is that a question to me?"

"You're the one that has spent years with him," Lee said.

"Yeah, as Ross."

"Is that all you know?" Doc asked.

"Umm, his real name is Jack, but he doesn't go by that," I stopped for a second. He told me that, and I assumed he went by his last name. It didn't occur to me he went by another name entirely.

"His last name is Ericcson," Mac said. I turned around to the sink. Just like that, they all knew I took his name—a fact I never thought another soul would know. I took his name when I thought he was out of my life, a decision I would not have made had I known he would come into my life and stay.

"That's fucked up," Asher said. "Jackie, you're gone. He really fucked your head up." There are some truths about yourself you wish wouldn't come out. I, Colby James, took Jack Ericcson, my interrogator's name. According to Mac, though, he went by Aaron.

"How do you know him, Mac?" I changed the subject away from the fact that I took his name. I never thought I would see him again when I took his name.

"I've been in training with him. Never really talked to him. When I saw him in the hospital and you called him Ross, I wasn't sure what was going on, so I let it lie."

Lee leaned forward, "You knew he was running game on Jackie, and you said nothing? He lied about his name, even without knowing why he lied about his name, he was up to something and you didn't protect her."

Mac shrugged his shoulders, "He seemed genuinely cut up about seeing Jackie in the hospital. I didn't give it more thought than that."

"Where is he stationed?" Lee asked.

"I think Ft. Bragg, last I knew," Mac said.

Lee said, "It has to be. He was at Jackie's house all the time when she was there. No way they gave him reign on her like that or sent him to do that."

"Did they ask about us in that prison?" Asher asked.

I looked over at Asher who wouldn't look at me, he avoided eye contact all morning. "He asked one time, but not in there. All I told him was DEA, and he accepted that. He knew my current job was legit. He just didn't understand how I got it after what I did. He knew I did the bombing, and that is why he stayed in my life. I see now they put him in my life to get intel, it wasn't that clear but hindsight is 20/20."

"I don't get how you can join our team," Asher said.

"Me too," Lee piled on top.

"Maybe they saw passed the emotional reaction and saw the big picture," Mac said, a surprise ally in this situation. The room fell silent. They had argued about this all night, I could feel it. "She stopped major espionage and corruption of our government by the Iranian militia. Maybe she is unorthodox, but she did something no one else could." Everyone was silent again. You could feel the tension between everyone.

"Does he have a family?" I asked Mac.

"Aaron?" he looked up for a moment, "I don't know, I really didn't talk to him."

"Why do you care?" Asher asked.

"He was around all the time, I didn't get it."

The room went silent again and everyone looked down. I was sure I was the source of their lack of words and the argument that had gone on for hours.

Joey, I couldn't imagine letting you read these books before your mom passes. I found them before you could read them, or at least I hope you didn't. If you are reading this now, I am guessing she has passed. For that I am truly sorry. We all wished you had more time with her, even me, and I know you don't believe me, you never have. I held these back because it will ruin what little time you have left with her. I can, though, help you understand all the things she talked about. I added these amendments to help you understand her story.

After Colby's escape, we were in a tailspin in the jail. "We know from the video that McNally is on the team that came to get her. We know him. We can connect those dots and find her," he walked me outside the door from the operations room. McNally went by Mac, but I didn't know him, not really, just knew of him. He was Special Forces, and I had trained with him a time or two, nothing serious. I had never worked with him though.

"Me finding her sounds like someone else's problem, she thinks I'm dead, she was devastated by it. We were going to use it to break her down, we were using it. It worked; we just needed more time." Colby called me by my cover name, Ross. Before she escaped, we faked my torture and death to break up her grasp on reality. She had grown attached to me over the last couple of years while I made sure to always be present in her life. It was the best way to figure out what she was up to. When I found her in the hospital after her surgery from her gunshot and I knew the DIA would come for her and return her to prison, once I reported it, and I felt bad. I knew I had to do it, and I knew they would torture her. She was already hurt. In the hospital I could tell whatever had happened between us, she did not hide her feelings for me. I used it against her. The first time I heard her cry for me in the prison, it hurt; the pain ate at my stomach. I hid it, but I hated doing that to her. This was easier when I didn't get involved the way I had with her. I didn't like that I had crossed that line with her. We knew Colby would need a mental breakdown to get into her head. I have had almost all men in that same seat as her and they broke a lot easier. Her strength made her stick to my mind. She intrigued me. A puzzle I couldn't solve and therefore was always on my mind. I came back to the moment, "I can't track her down if I'm dead."

"Her team lead, CJ, saw you alive, as did that son of a bitch, Larry." Larry helped her escape. Larry told us he is the one person in the world she couldn't say no to. After she escaped, he knew, and we knew there wasn't anything we could do to him. "You're the only one that can gain her trust, Ericcson." Chief Steiner said as he gave me the nod to walk with him. Most people called me Ericcson, but I also went by Aaron, my middle name. I didn't like my first name, Jack. "We better get you to a place where you can find Mac."

"That sounds suicidal without a full team." I wasn't about to go poke around looking for Colby's team which would expose my location and they come and get the person who put her through a hellish interrogation for the second time. I know if the roles were reversed, I would pay that person a visit and they would leave in an ambulance. "Why do I want to find them?" There must have been something at play that I was missing.

"Find out more. We are missing something big. The DIA Director Young came to this facility over one detainee. He just left, tore us to shreds. Yes, we were bested and lost a detainee, but for him to come here over this, that seems over the top."

"He was here?" I asked Steiner.

Fahrenbacher, her interrogator walked up to us, "I don't understand how it's my fault some two-bit DEA agents got the better of our security. I was her interrogator, not in charge of security for the prison," his face was red. He looked pretty pissed, he obviously talked about the director who ripped him apart.

"At least one was Special Forces," I referred to Mac. "Maybe they all were, and if that's the case, we should not be surprised they bested our contractor-led security company."

"You know all he asked about was shit related to investigations into former presidential cabinet members. He didn't ask about the bombing or who she worked for, not that we had answers," Fahrenbacher said as he paced back and forth in the hallway.

"I told you, she told me she worked for the government for the bombing," I said back to him.

"Yeah, fucking right," Fahrenbacher said.

"Why else would Special Forces come break her out?" I asked. "Why not just work channels to get her officially?"

Steiner piped in, "She wasn't officially here; there are no channels to work. We let her team lead and Larry in; that was a mistake. I've been thinking, you know, FBI let her go after a bombing, then let her fall off the radar. Why isn't the director okay with what the FBI seems comfortable with? Then for the DEA to hire her. This has to be so much bigger for that to happen. Then they send Special Forces after her? Something big is happening. She knows what it is. Why else would she put you through that? It's big enough for her to take that punishment and not say a word. You got to get back in her proximity. Use Mac to find her. We have to figure out why the director is so riled up over one detainee and why, as you claim, the government sanctioned a bomb in the U.S."

"You think even if I find him, he will take me to her?" He wanted me to offer myself up as bait.

"If you do your job right, which I'm sure you will figure it out. Get her alone and bring her back. Save our asses and find out what else is going on. This is big, I know you feel it. She knows what it is. In the very least, get Mac on your side. They will fight back if we send a team."

"Why not Fahrenbacher?" I had played my last card on her. I did not know how to bring her around to that. She loved me though, that much was clear. That's the only thing I had to start with. It would be a lie to say I didn't care for her.

"Me? She is in love with you, you are the only one that stands a chance," Fahrenbacher scoffed.

I nodded. "Send me home. I will make sure people know I'm home. I will ask around about him, news will travel fast." I would figure it out. Maybe I could talk to her too. I usually could get her to feel the way I wanted, even if I couldn't get the information I wanted. Maybe Mac was the key.

6

ASHER WAS THE ONE person out of all of them I was dying to fix things with. I came out of my room in the safe house later in the afternoon, the day after I told the team everything. I got to the top of the stairs and looked down at the great room of the cabin. I slowly went down the stairs and over to the door. "Hey, you guys know where my bag went?" I said to whoever was around.

Asher was sitting in an armchair in the living room. He pointed to the couch by the windows, and I saw my bag dumped out and gone through. Ironic, Asher was the one who originally packed it. I grabbed what was on the couch.

Asher and I always topped the day working out together. He trusted me with everything, good and bad. One of the last times we went to the gym was right before we went on our last mission.

"Asher, I need a spot, put your fucking phone down," I yelled at Asher before pulling the bar off the rack. He had a smile about him, as he set his phone down and came to spot me. When it was his turn, his phone went off, and I grabbed it as soon as he pulled the bar off the rack.

Tinder notification. I knew it. I unlocked his phone and clicked on the notification. This girl was all over him, she was basically begging him to come over to her place. "You're ridiculous."

I typed a message back to her, "This is a first for me."

"What's that?" I could hear her giggle in the subtext.

"I think you are so hot, just rarely think thick girls are that hot." She wasn't, but I enjoyed messing with Asher's toys. After I hit send, Asher snatched the phone out of my hands.

"Damnit, Jackie, why do you do this to me?" he read what I sent to her.

"Because it's funny, plus you find the most desperate girls, and WHEN you go to her house later you will know for sure how desperate she is."

"I thought my phone locked."

"I'm with you twenty-four/seven. I know the code."

"She will not talk to me anymore," Asher said as he scrolled through her photos.

"Watch... do me a favor do NOT use me as an excuse for why you're not home. Your wife hates me enough."

His phone buzzed, "She doesn't... hate..." He got a big grin on his face. She was still in.

"I shouldn't have helped you with that app."

"It's fun."

I snatched the phone out of his hand, "Let me find a girl out of your league, then we will know if you really have it." I turned my back to him and swiped through girls.

"She was hot, why did you swipe her away?" he said, looking over my shoulder.

"Let's find you a less desperate heap. See what you are really made of."

He wrapped his arms around me, and I stretched my arms away from him. He pulled me to his side and pulled the phone out of my hand. "You're a piece of work, Jack."

"Let's work out; play with your girls later." I headed back to what we were doing before his phone interrupted us.

"Fine," he said, putting the phone down.

Here in the cabin, I peered at the back of his head while he read in the living room chair. I wanted that relationship back. "Are there any more clothes around here or a washer and dryer?" I asked him and looked around the first floor of the cabin.

He pointed at a door by the kitchen.

I opened the door, and it was full of supplies, clothes, food, gear—and the washer and dryer too. I was relieved. I grabbed a few sets and stocked up my bag. If I needed to get out, I would need these things. Gloves, hat, sweaters, and just the basic clothes. Everything was too big, meant for the stereotypical DEA agents they were expecting, but it was better than too small. I grabbed food and water too. I didn't know what they would say or decide, but it would have to be unanimous to get me back on the team. I packed it all up, zipped it and dropped it by the stairs.

"Where did everyone go?" I asked Asher.

"They ran out to get resources for our next steps. Also, to check in with CJ too."

"What's our next step? What are you guys going to do with me?" I asked.

Asher turned himself around in his chair and shook his head. He didn't want me to know. "Me and you for a while," Asher said.

"Come on, Asher, do I at least get to know if it's my last day of freedom?" Asher and I prepped for missions together. We did the studying, the dry runs, quizzed each other, challenged each other. He would come to CrossFit with me, and I would try to keep up with him on runs. He didn't say it, but his wife hated me. I would hate me too, but not for the reasons he hated me right now. We were close, really close. He probably felt stupid; he thought I was someone he could trust with my life and then found out I'm not who I said I was at all.

He stared back at me. Whatever they had planned I didn't get to know the information, and it filled me with dread. If they wanted to keep me on the team, they would just tell me. If they needed me to stay put before they turned me over to the authorities, they would probably leave me in the dark about the next steps.

"Wanna work out?" I asked him, trying to put an ounce of what was once us back into the situation.

He cut his eyes at me, "No, Jack, not with you."

"Ash, I'm sorry, I should've told you."

He stood up, "I dunno, Jack," he came over to me. "I maybe could've understood, but I dunno..." he looked down at me, "I don't know you at all."

I looked up at him, "Still me."

"You know my wife, my kids, shit ... you know about my affairs, my past, my time as a Ranger, Iraq, all of it. I trusted you with every piece, and I don't even know your name."

"I know."

"You have this fucker messing with you and you don't even mention that?" I think Asher wishes he could have removed Ross from my life sooner. "And Colby? Boston? Fuck. I think I could've maybe understood it up front, but fuck, Jack, you... I don't know."

"Okay, what do you want to know, it's all fair game."

"How can we trust what she says?" Lee asked CJ. We met CJ at a smaller office branch office for the DEA out in Winchester, Virginia.

"We can't take her on face value, we need some evidence. How do we know the government sanctioned that? She could have made up that entire story," Doc said and leaned against the door with his arms folded. We had crowded into an office that belonged to someone else who actually worked here. It was in a little strip mall that seemed all but abandoned.

CJ rubbed his chin. "I talked to the leadership; they don't think Jackie's original mission was done. There are still remnants of the Iranian group having influence on our government. We need to fix that. We also have to stop the bomb. Because of the interrelated nature of the missions, they have expanded the scope of our special team to cover both items with Iranian militia dirty bomb plot and the corruption in our government."

"Does that mean we get a bigger team?" Lee asked.

CJ shook his head 'no.' "Only augment if we get a solid lead. They are pulling a team to send to Venezuela for us though, since we can't go soon."

"So a couple Special Forces guys, a couple DEA agents, an ATF agent, are supposed to be enough to chase this threat?" Doc asked.

"We can use Jackie," I said. I understood now what CJ meant when he said to go get her and he would respect the decision we made. He meant we could keep her on the team and mission or not. He could not decide and put it on us.

"That can't be our best choice," Doc said.

"Unfortunately for us, Jackie did this off the books and there are very little records. She is the best shot we have at doing this," CJ said and shook his head, pausing when his phone rang.

"Did they know she was Colby James?" I asked knowing Doc was thinking it.

"Mac," he said and looked at me, "give me a minute." He swiped to answer the phone. "Yea?" he said to the other person on the line.

He sat in the desk chair; Lee and I were across from him. We watched CJ intently listen to other end of the line for a couple minutes.

"No, not yet," he said and paused a moment. "We will maintain control of her, and I will advise." CJ hung up the phone.

He pointed at his phone and looked over at me, "The Admiral wants us to make sure whatever happens Jackie stays in DEA custody, so we don't leave her alone anymore." He paused and slid his phone into his pocket.

"As I was saying," he looked up at me, then around the room. "I talked to leadership and at first, they floated around not answering my questions. So, I called Larry; he seemed to know about all her work as Colby." CJ used to work with Larry when CJ was a rookie. Larry was in charge of Jackie's training. "It took time for him to come along, but ultimately agreed she would be a great asset for the DEA." CJ took a minute and looked over at Doc, who seemed increasingly agitated with the thought of Jackie returning to work with us. "While we were talking about it, Larry and I discussed what happens in those secret prisons, and it just didn't sit right with us. I couldn't leave her there."

"That's a government facility; you don't get to make that decision," Doc said.

"You didn't see her there. She deserved a fair shot, a trial, not that place," CJ said and stared off for a second. He didn't say it, but I knew him better than everyone else. He thought he was in for much worse torture or death when they captured him in Venezuela. Jackie went above and beyond to set him free.

"Doc, you saw the way she was when we got her; hell, she probably has injuries only you know about."

"Look, we got her out of the prison, and we can't change it. What does leadership want us to do with her?" Lee asked. One argument we had was that they should not have sanctioned a rescue mission without all the information. Lee, on the other hand, liked to deal with absolutes. We can't undo that decision we have to concentrate on what will happen next.

"The leadership was clear. It's up to you all. We keep her and chase this Iranian militia down, or do it without her. No matter what happens, we never lose control over her, and they will deal with her when are done," CJ said. "Some of the top brass implicitly trust her. Others are more middle of the road."

"Do they have any evidence to back it up? How do they know she isn't involved in something worse?" Doc reiterated our earlier question.

"Her mission to root out government infiltration by the Iranian militia, which culminated in the bombing, was sanctioned but off the books. So, there is almost no paperwork. But her mission is linked to our mission. She knows it better than anyone else."

"I don't think that works for me." Doc folded his arms. "How could you send us to get her out if you didn't know what to do? She might know about these Iranians because she is involved with them."

CJ sat up in his chair and made eye contact with each of us, "Judgment call. Plus, someone slid an envelope under my hotel room door with all the intel we needed to get into and out of that place. Someone else wanted her out, so I went with it. There is not an ounce of evidence to suggest she is involved with the Iranians."

"Who wanted her out and gave you that info?" Doc asked.

"I don't know, but the person was on the inside," CJ replied.

"I thought we agreed to follow this?" I said back to Doc.

"We did," Lee said.

Doc nodded, "We did, but I mean, we can't just let her run free."

"We won't let her free; we treat her like an asset," I said, and then an idea popped in my head. "What if we pull in people that know this whole situation better than us?" I said to the room. I believed Jackie;

she was braver than I realized, and I was impressed by her. I couldn't have done what she did on her own. I gravely underestimated her. I also knew a person in the DIA who could give us some information from the other side.

7

"Colby," his voice danced in my ears. "Colby, wake up, we need to talk." I hated how much he still occupied my thoughts and my nightmares. "Colby?" I felt a presence near me, and my half-asleep state became fully awake. I sat up all the way and climbed backward to the pillows.

"Colby, it's me, we need to talk before..."

OH, FUCK. "Ross!" I said out loud while my adrenaline shot through the roof. My team wanted to send me back to the prison. My go bag sat between Ross and the door. FUCK. I couldn't go back, I wouldn't. Mac was next to him; he was talking, but I couldn't hear him. At the door, Lee stood with Doc. In one fell swoop I ran, opened a window, and jumped out taking the screen with me. We hit the ground together, the screen and me. It knocked the wind out of me. I struggled to suck air in as the pain in my ribs reignited their feud with my body. The alarm on the house went off, and it jolted me back into action. I glanced back at the window. Ross's face peered down.

I got up and ran. I didn't have shoes, just shorts and a T-shirt in the frozen evening. It didn't matter, I had to go. I couldn't go back to that torture chamber. I guess I really didn't think my team would do that to me. I guess the only thing I thought they would do was let me back on the team. *FUCK.* Something stabbed my foot. My side burned, but my fear rose above it all. I had slept a lot to recover and even though the sun had gone down, I don't think it was that late in the evening.

When I was out earlier, I saw a house a couple kilometers away; it was where I was going. It had good signs for me, well kept, Marine Corps flag, and a rainbow flag. I knew when I was falling from the window that is where I should go; it just popped into my mind. There was a strong chance they would help me, fight for me, or shoot me on sight. They were all good options given the alternative of going back with Ross, back to the prison with Chin.

I cut into the tree line and my feet screamed at me as they landed on twigs. I kept moving away from the house through the trees. I pulled myself between a tree and a bunch of bushes, and the brush cut my legs. The moonlight helped me as I continued to run. The fear and the pain kept me warm; my foot found a sharp rock then a stick stabbed my foot just wrong, and I had to slow down. I was definitely running faster than I was earlier, but I was still slow. I knew if I kept the sound of the river within ear shot, the road that ran along it was close, and I headed the right direction. As I continued, I collected cuts on my arms, legs, and feet. I finally got near the house, and I slowed down. I was behind the house; I went toward their first outbuilding, some sort of barn. I got to it and took a minute to catch my breath.

Sneaking up to this house wouldn't be a good option. I would have to make myself known. It seemed there was someone in the kitchen that had a window to the back of the house. I went around the barn and into the middle of the yard. I put my hands up as I got closer. I wanted them to see me. As I got close, a small motion light clicked on and blinded me. I kept my hands up and kept facing the house. I stopped for a second and headed for the stairs on the back porch.

As I got to the second stair, I heard a shotgun cock. I stopped. "Please, help me," I said to the stranger I couldn't see. "These men are after me," I continued. "Please, I have nothing." I waited a bit, and they were not responding. "I just need shoes or something and I will be gone." I stopped there; it was best not to talk too much when someone has a gun to you.

"Where are your clothes?" a woman said to me.

"I had an opportunity to run; I didn't have a chance to get clothes."

"Where are you coming from?"

"I ran from a house, I don't know, I was out in the woods and lost; it's been a while. I saw this place." I didn't want them to get into more trouble by knowing where I was coming from.

"Did he do that to your face?"

I nodded yes.

The silence came again. I tried to find the face of the voice. It was somewhere in the dark to my right.

"Come in. We can protect you," a voice said from in front of me.

"No, I can't do that to you. There is a lot of them, and they are dangerous. Please, shoes, maybe pants. I have to keep running. If I'm here, they will find me and hurt you to get me."

"Are you running from the cops?" she asked.

"No, I wish, but no." I wish it was the cops. It was the problem that Ross didn't seem to have any rules.

The light that blinded me turned off.

"Here," the woman said as she leaned the shotgun against the banister and sat on the stair next to me, taking off her shoes.

"Oh, my God, thank you," I couldn't believe it worked.

Then the other woman brought me pants. I slid on the pants and then the warm socks and shoes. I hugged the shotgun lady, "Thank you!" I turned and went down the stairs to run back behind the barn.

"Wait," she said. "You are going to want to go out front, cross the street, cross the river, there's a place downstream to cross the river and stay dry. Then go up and over the ridge. The ridge is steep, but you can make it up. They won't think you went that way."

"Okay," I took a few steps backward now in my new direction.

"One more thing," the other woman called out, "Here." She walked out with a coat and a bag. "This is one of our hiking bags."

"I swear you are saving my life. If I survive this, I will come back and thank you, somehow." I slid on the jacket and put on the backpack as I went quickly toward the road. I was about halfway there when I heard someone running up behind me.

"Here, take this gun," she said, holding out a pistol.

"If they catch me, they will trace it to you," I warned her.

"They won't," she replied.

I could see something in her face, her concern and maybe some level of knowingness. My heart hurt for her; she shouldn't know what I was going through at this moment. I put my hand on her shoulder and turned back for the road.

I really wasn't that far from the cabin and crucially on the same road. The guys could move faster than me; they weren't slowed by injuries and not having shoes and what just happened. All of this made crossing the road a tricky proposition. I got up close to it and got real quiet. I had to listen for them looking for me. *Were they coming? Did they pass?* After a minute or two I decided I had no choice. I had to keep moving.

I ran across the road and quickly descended to the river. It gushed past me but wasn't wide. She said I could find a dry spot to cross. I moved along following downstream—looking for my opportunity. There was enough moonlight that it felt almost like daytime. I saw a combo of a fallen tree and rocks. I ran to it; it seemed steady. I climbed up onto the log and walked as far as I could across the tree then jumped out to a rock, then another.

Once on the other side I saw the steep climb in front of me. I checked the safety on the gun and slid it into the back of my pants. "You are going to fight the pain," I whispered to myself. If the stairs hurt, this would be way worse.

Where I started there were plenty of saplings and roots that promised to hold me as I made my way up. I grabbed the first tree with my left hand then lifted my foot to find a footing. I pulled and reached out with my right hand, placed my left foot. I pulled and winced from the sharp intense pain that shot through my side. I asked too much with running and now this. I laid my head on my right hand. "Little victories." That's what I needed. Not the whole ridge, one step at a time. I slowly focused on each task. One pull, I found I had to mostly climb with my left side, and the right was just for stabilizing. Reaching far and pulling with the right hand was not an option.

I had made it quite a way up the side of the steep hill, almost a cliff. The sting of my broken ribs and broken body begged for the finish line. Then I heard a noise on the road below. I stopped moving and laid against the hill. Dread filled me up, and I struggled to control my breath. I told my team I would respect their decision and go back to the prison if they wanted to send me there, but how could I? I could not fathom the thought of subjecting myself to torture. I had not healed yet, and mentally I don't know if I could from what happened. Something told me to run, and I knew I had to, to survive. I listened to them move along the road and river below me. I couldn't even process how Ross ended up with them. I hoped they didn't have that much gear up here in these mountains. All it would take was one of them using a thermal sight or night vision goggles, and they could see my warm body pressed against this cold hill, a bright shiny hot body on the cliff above them. My body needed the break from the climb, and the damp cool ground felt good against the pain. My left foot that held me up slipped and a rock let loose. I grabbed a tree with my right hand, my body dropped all the weight onto the right arm, and I wanted to scream with the strain as it shot through my body. Instead, I held my breath as my foot dangled, tears filled my eyes, and I waited for the rock to hit the ground below. The river sloshed and covered the faint taps as it found its way to the bottom of the cliff. I let out a breath of relief. Even after they passed, I waited longer to make sure I didn't knock down something else.

Instead of chasing the dirty bomb now enroute to the U.S., my team chased me. They thought I was involved or worse planned it all. They wasted resources on me; now it would be up to me to stop it. First, I had to get free of them. I pressed my body against the cold hill, and the chill on my body reminded me of the cement in the prison. It reminded me of why I had to push through all the pain, especially these broken ribs.

I finally climbed again. The grade decreased, and the climbing got easier. Slowly I got upright. My right side burned and poked at me. The need to survive was stronger than any ounce of pain. It finally flattened, out and as I got farther along, I saw a clearing.

There was a town down below, I could see the lights. I could get there by morning, or the old me could. I would shoot for lunch time. *Would they be looking for me there?* I would have to get there and find a way to another place as fast as possible.

8

The library sat on the main road in front of a school in Clarksburg, the town I saw from up on the ridge during my escape. I would have to move fast; they would probably think I was after Internet. I walked across the street and into the library and past the distracted librarian. I found a computer, but it needed a card to turn it on. I looked around. There was only one lady in the library with her kids. It would be difficult to lift her card off her.

I went to the lady at the desk. "Excuse me. Can you tell me how I can use the computer?" She was still distracted. "Use your library card."

I pulled my hood off and crouched down. "Please, help me," I showed her my broken face.

She looked up, "Oh, honey," she said with concern, "I can call the police," she said, reaching for the phone.

"Please, no, please." I held my hand over hers on the phone. "I just need to look up something on the computer."

"Are you sure, I can't do anything else?"

"No, I have to figure this out without him knowing," I implied I was on the run from an abusive boyfriend or husband. She caught the subtext.

She got up and came with me. "Thank you," I said as she logged in for me. She walked away.

I searched for battered women's shelters. My mom taught me how to use this system in high school, well, showed me anyhow. They could get me out without public transportation or stealing a car. I found nothing local, but I found one in nearby Morgantown. I wrote down the number.

I headed to the Dairy Queen; it was around lunchtime, and it was pretty crowded. I went in through the crowd and lifted a cell phone off a young kid. I needed to spread my forensic evidence around. I couldn't use everything in one place; it made it too easy for them. I went outside and behind the dumpsters. I called the number.

"I need help," I said to the lady. "I ran, he's after me, but I have nothing."

"Can you go to the police?" she said.

"No, he knows them and will look for me there. Or on a bus. Please," I pleaded. I was desperate, but the situation was not quite what she was used to.

"Where are you?" she said to me.

"Clarksburg."

"Can you get here?"

"No, I don't have a way. I don't even know if I should go to Morgantown, it's too close. He is going to find me." I felt guilty exploiting this system, but I needed an out and if I went to that prison, they would torture me.

There was a pause before she spoke, "Can you lie low for a few hours?"

"Yeah, I can do that."

"We will call you back…"

I cut her off, "This isn't my phone."

"Hold on." I could hear her talking to someone in the background. After a few minutes she came back to me. "Okay, there is a tattoo shop on Twentieth, Red Swing Tattoo, close to the nursing home, do you know the one?"

"I will find it."

"Go there and wait. Someone will come and get you."

"Thank you!" I said. It gave me hope that I might actually get away. My coverage on the bombing would be gone. My team turned on me and thought I should go to prison; it would mean the DEA would stop covering for me on probation, and they could get all the agencies including the Marshall services to come after me. It wouldn't take much digging to figure out that Colby James dropped off the face of the earth not long after going on probation.

"Honey, I will pray for you," she said. I took the phone and ripped it apart, the sim card and the battery. I smashed all the parts, threw some in the dumpster and tossed the rest into the drive through to be run over by the lunch rush over and over.

When I arrived at the tattoo shop on the main road through town, I first tried to open the door and found it locked. I felt panic creep into my body. It would be so easy to find me right on the only main thorough-fare through town close to the cabin, and I did not like being on it. I knocked and tried to resist the urge to look over my shoulder at the road. If they were in town looking for me, I was incredibly exposed in this moment. I saw Ross in my room, in a safe house. A place he shouldn't be. "They went to get resources for our next steps..." That's what Asher said. In reality, they went to get Ross and probably Chin. I knocked again, and I couldn't help it, I had to look up and down the road. I was so afraid I would be captured at any moment.

Someone came out of the back, and I pulled my hood down. The man opened the door. "Come on, they called me, told me you were coming. You can hang out in the back. I have a client so you can wait in my office."

"Thank you," I said.

He showed me to the office. I needed to refill the water bottles I had found in my pack from the ladies who gave me a go-bag. I pulled them out and poked my head out and crossed the hall into the bathroom. I looked in the mirror. I really looked like shit. Should I thank Chin for the way may face looked? He was making my escape possible because I looked the part of a battered woman. I checked the back door—I needed a quick escape, just in case. If they tracked me here, I was trapped, I knew it.

After a few hours, a knock came at the back door. The tattoo artist came out of his room where he tattooed. I pulled the gun out and leaned up against the wall.

"Hey." The tattoo guy knew him. I slid the gun back into my pants and left the office.

It was a man in a big Dodge Ram. "You called us?

I nodded.

"Let's go," he said.

I ran out and opened the back door to find a car seat.

"You are going to sit up front." I shut the door and ran around. You don't realize the innocence in a child until you see them, two of them in the back seat smiling at you. Both of them unaware and unable to comprehend how I ended up in that truck. My heart dropped; I didn't want to put them in danger. I slouched way down in the truck.

He jumped in the driver's seat, "You're okay now," he said, nodding at me. I looked over at him, I was at his mercy. "West?" he said.

"Please."

"I can take you to Jackson, Ohio. Someone else will take you from there." He left town onto U.S. 50. The kids in the back reminded me of something kinder in the world. I was exhausted. I let my eyes close and fell asleep.

9

I WOKE UP AS we pulled into a rest stop. "How long was I out?"

"Not long," my getaway driver replied. "We are past Parkersburg, just crossed into Ohio."

I got out of the truck, and I felt free.

"My kids need to run around. We started driving a couple hours before we got to you," he said as he pulled one out of the car seat and sat him on the ground. I smiled at the kid. I figured the less we knew about each other, the better it would be for both of us.

He set up their food at a picnic table behind the restrooms. I sat at the far end of the table and pulled food out of my bag. There were four or five-days' worth of rations in my bag, I took inventory at the tattoo shop. I watched his kids play as I ate. I was lost in their screaming when I saw a pickup truck pull into the rest stop. It was the truck from the cabin. I dropped my food and put on my pack.

"Fuck, they're here."

"What? Where?" the guy said, looking up from his kids.

"You need to run, they are after me, not you."

"I'm not afraid of this guy," he said.

"He isn't alone, and they will stop at nothing to get me," I pulled at my gun and moved behind the restroom. My driver's eyes got big when he saw the gun.

He ran and scooped up his kids as he ran for his truck. I owed him a clean getaway. I stepped out from behind the restroom to let them see me. I saw the 4Runner from the cabin stop on the side of the road off to my left.

Lee got out of the truck with Doc. "Jackie, come on," Doc said.

I pulled my pistol out front to the low ready. "I'm not going back." I realized the DIA would stop at nothing to find out who I worked for, and my team got pulled into that. I would never reveal that without him this country would have nothing as a last line of defense; they would torture me to near death over and over.

"You aren't going to shoot us," Doc said.

I saw my getaway truck drive off. I hoped they'd leave him alone; it wasn't his fault that I got him wrapped into this. "I think you underestimate me. I'm not going back to that place to be tortured."

"We aren't taking you there," Lee said.

"The fuck you aren't."

Doc and Lee came near me with their hands out to their sides and their palms facing me. "We promise," Doc said.

I didn't believe them; Ross was in my room. I saw Ross in the safe house in the place I should be free from the DIA. He was there, so how could I believe what they told me? My thoughts jumbled, maybe I imagined it all. My head was so fucked. I shook. He was right, I couldn't shoot them. I could run though. I let go of the pistol with my left hand and took stock of my options.

Wham. Someone tackled me from behind. I hit the pavement hard. My broken body was brought to the forefront, my crack in reality was pushed back. I forgot the other car was behind me. I wasn't on all the way. It felt like they all piled on me. Someone took my gun and my pack.

In the end, only Asher was left on my back. "You're safe, Jackie, come with us."

I closed my eyes and nodded.

"I'm going to let you up, just come with me to the 4Runner," he said.

"Okay."

"Don't run, Jackie," he warned. He slowly let me up and kept ahold of my arm. We walked across the grass to the 4Runner, which was on the side of the road. I was sure then my mind had broken from reality. I couldn't trust anything, but I had to trust at least Asher, couldn't I? Ross wasn't in the cabin; it was in my head. A bad dream. I had a lot of bad dreams. Asher got into the back seat with me. Mac got in the driver's seat. He took off back toward Clarksburg and the cabin. Lee and Doc came behind us.

"I'm pretty impressed," started Mac, "Less than twenty-four hours, and you are over one hundred miles away with a gun and a go-bag. You left in shorts and a T-shirt without shoes."

"It wasn't enough," I said.

"Why are you running?" Asher asked.

"I don't want to go back to that prison. I wouldn't survive it. I would rather die than go through one more ounce of that place." I said, looking out the window.

"We aren't sending you back," Asher reassured me.

I still didn't believe him. I felt crazy. I had to trust them, but I didn't believe them. I trusted them over my own senses. "How did you find me?" I looked at Asher and then at Mac. Mac and Asher were exchanging looks in the mirror. They were weighing something out. I kept glancing between them. "Ash, how did you find me?" Asher didn't answer me. "Mac, come on, I have to know, how did you find me?"

"Well..." Mac started and shifted himself in his seat. "You know, your guy, Aaron, or Ross as you call him... he knew exactly what you would do. Then Asher used that info to find you." The words settled on my ears and slowly worked their way into my brain.

"Ross?" I said, making sure I wasn't breaking from reality again. He called him Aaron because it was his real name, but I called him Ross. I looked over at Asher and he nodded.

I lost my shit; I wasn't breaking with reality. "I fucking knew it; you are sending me back!" I decked Asher in the face and opened the door. We were going fast, but I had to jump. Asher grabbed me and pulled me back in. Mac swerved and pulled over. Perfect. I ripped Asher's arms off me. The door was still ajar, and Doc was behind it. I kicked it hard, slamming it into Doc, and then jumped out. Fuck, nothing around. I ran to the edge of the road and peered over the guard rail, there was a drop—we were up on a bridge, but not over the water yet.

Lee wrapped his arms around me. I threw my head back into his face, and it caused him to tumble backward. I took off running in the opposite direction of traffic. My body reminded me it was not in shape to run and move the way I just did. Mac came around the back side of the truck and got between me and my getaway route. Mac's hands were up. "I'm not going with him," I said, terrified they were sending me with Ross to see Chin. Chin electrocuted me, broke my ribs, and caused me to break my grasp on reality, all in a short window of time. It would be much worse with more time.

"We don't want you to," Mac said. I was surrounded now. Asher and Mac were in front of me, Doc and Lee were behind me.

"Why is he at the cabin? Why is he telling you where I am?" I asked, facing the truck and trying to watch both of them at the same time. I was a few seconds away from a full-on panic attack.

"He's going to help us," Mac said about Ross.

"With WHAT?" I asked, losing my mind. "Why am I forced into situations with this son of a bitch?"

"To get the last cabinet member, DIA director. We have to stop him and the Iranian militia from getting the dirty bombs into the country. All the things you told us. We believe you and we are chasing them down," Mac said.

"This makes little sense," I said as they stepped closer and drove me into a higher sense of agitation.

Asher chimed in, "Jackie, come on, we will explain it all, but not on the side of the road."

"We aren't sending you back," Lee said. "You're on our team, we wouldn't do that." His nose bled.

Asher walked toward me, "Come on, we promise, we aren't sending you back, never." I stood up all the way as he got near me, his arm out as if to put it around me. I stopped for a second and took a deep breath. Nothing seemed real, *was I using again?*

"Don't touch me," I said to Asher, shoving his arm down as I walked past him and back to the 4Runner. I got back in; I had to trust them. What choice did I have?

Asher turned on the child lock for my door. Mac slid in next to me this time, and Asher took the wheel. My mind felt fractured; it was a fog. I really didn't know what was real. I stared out the window all the way back, chewing my lip. Ross's presence at the safe house made me sick. I didn't know what to do with the information. How could I believe him after he faked his death to break me? Now I'm supposed to just accept and trust him like my team is doing. The anxiety pulled into my veins and made my heart race and skip beats. I concentrated on my breath to calm down, to no avail. I needed to see what would happen next. It made every mile of the drive feel longer. They wouldn't talk to me in the car, I guess they didn't want me jumping out at 60 miles per hour. It's a trick, when Aaron, or Ross, whatever he is called, is involved; it is a trick, isn't it? Would they do this to me? They rescued me from him. My stomach tied up in knots from the anxiety; it made me physically nauseous.

10

<hr>

We pulled into the driveway of the cabin. CJ and Ross came out to greet us. I followed Mac out his door because of the child lock on my door. The fear had turned to anger and pulsed through me. I didn't want to be caught, and the thought of having Ross involved made me want to kill someone. I saw CJ, and I felt the urge to kill come down to a simmer.

"I don't know how many times I will send this team after you," CJ said.

I cocked my head to the side, "Tell this fucker that..." I pointed at my Ross but didn't look at him. "You wouldn't have to come and get me if this asshole was out of my life." Ross seemed to be present at every screwed-up portion of my life for the last couple of years. In my mind, if he wasn't around I would have avoided quite a bit, including the prison and running away.

I paused and turned around to look down the drive to the main road and calm down. CJ walked up to stand next to me.

"Why did you have to find me? I don't need to be around him." I motioned my head in Ross's direction. "The team does not want me around either. You should have let me go." If I would not be on the team, I wanted as far away from the chance of going back to that prison as possible. Ross here, that was too close.

I turned to face CJ; he kept his eyes on me and kept mine on him. It helped; it calmed me just to be near CJ. A few breaths passed, and Lee and Doc pulled up. I turned my head, bit my lip, and watched them get out of their truck. Doc exited the truck and pulled out the bag and gun that they had taken from me. Lee had blood on his shirt, probably from when I hit him. Seeing my gear, I felt indignant. I was so close to gone, and here I was again and so close to the grasp of Ross.

"What happened to you?" CJ asked Lee as he came near us.

"She didn't want to come back here, because of Aaron," he pointed at Ross. It would be difficult for me to transition to a new name for him; he still was Ross in my head. Ross took that as his signal to go inside behind Lee. I still had not looked at him.

I turned back to CJ, who stood there. He examined me. I imagined I looked at least as shitty as I felt. I owed him; he saved me from that place. He saved me from the torture, like I saved him in Venezuela.

"I wish I could say you look better today than last time I saw you, but it looks like things got a lot worse for you there before we got to you," CJ said. I could feel the guilt push out through his face. He reached out and touched my swollen, cut, and bruised face. I pulled my head away.

"I am a lot better though, my body just hasn't caught up," I replied.

CJ nodded and put his hands on his hips. We were alone now as the sun glared at us right before it set. He was taller than me, so I had to look up at him. He seemed to search for words; so did I. I let my eyes drift to the surroundings. I still felt like running.

"I talked to our leaders and to Larry. We decided your mission isn't done; the Iranians still have influence on our government. We all agreed we need to fix that. The truth is, Jackie, no one knows this case better than you. We could never catch up on that information you collected and the work you did. It was off the books, and while that made it successful it meant we had nowhere to start from. We would be at a disadvantage trying to stop them without you. Our agency is backing finishing this mission, and now it's this teams' mission. That being said, your tactics are unacceptable to all of us. We will not bomb Americans to achieve our ends."

He moved his head into my eyeline. I nodded to show I understood what he just said.

"My rules now, Jackie. Honestly, if things go south, we plan to give you back to them," CJ said matter-of-fact like. "You want your life back; help us. It's a win-win situation. You don't get to run off. If you don't want to help us, then we give you to the people who will make you pay for the bombing to the full extent of the law. Those are the only options."

"Okay," I nodded. It was harsh and churned my stomach. I wanted my life back and I would do anything not to go back to that prison, or any prison. It took me away from my anger and into myself.

He reached out and grabbed my shoulder and gave it a squeeze. I guess that was as close to a hug as he would dole out right then. "I wasn't sure what to do with you, Jackie, but I would not let them do what they were going to do to you. It seems though, we were a little late." He shook his head and looked off for a second and came back to me. "Especially after you told me Aaron was dead, and I had just talked to him. I knew they broke something in you, and it would only get worse." Even if he didn't understand the bombing, he didn't believe I should be tortured over it.

I nodded; I was embarrassed that I was duped by Ross. I hated that my mind fractured, and I didn't know what was real anymore. I hated it more that CJ knew they distorted my reality.

"So, we got you out, the team did. Now that they know everything, they still stand by you."

"Thank you for sending them," I said and felt the anger leave me, grateful to be out of prison.

I didn't have words for what he did for me. I bit my lip, looked at the ground and back up at him. I wanted to hug him but also knew I was just the means to their ends and some part of him wanted me back in the prison. Maybe he still would after this ended. After a few moments I walked past him into the cabin.

"Jackie," he said and waited for me to turn around. I paused on the concrete slab that led to the front door. "They chose you, the team, every single one of them, don't forget that."

"I won't," I said, half-smiling at him. It knew it was a big deal that after all I did, all I had said, and the trust I broke, the team chose me, to believe me, to bring me back into the team and to even finish my mission. They chose me. Words to live by.

11

I WALKED INTO THE cabin, passed Ross, Aaron at the kitchen table, who talked intently to Lee and Asher. I sat down on the couch next to Mac and turned my attention to him. Still with the man who put me through hell sat across the room and talking to my team, I was in complete shock. I turned my attention to Mac, who was going through my go-bag. "Where'd you get all of this?" He held up the maps and money.

"Some things have to remain a secret," I said back to him. "I know it was you."

"What was?" He pulled one of my meals out of my bag.

"Aaron," I said, referring to him getting pulled into the fold.

"We didn't set out to bring him back, it just happened."

I looked over at Ross, Aaron at the table with Doc and CJ. "He's not on our side." I leaned toward Mac with my voice low.

"He's a good dude. I know he fucked with you, but he is on our side."

"Come on, Mac, how the fuck did he convince you of that?" I wanted to catch Mac's eye, but he studied the map.

"We um... went to talk to him." He looked up, "Come on." He stood up and put down the stuff in his hands.

We walked out the front door of the cabin and toward the garage out back. "Well at first, I had one friend said he was looking for me. I told Lee, and Lee had this idea that we were going to kill him, but you know..."

I shook my head, I didn't know.

"Just fuck him up a little... or a lot," Mac said, "for what he did to you."

I grabbed him to stop him walking and look at me. I liked that idea. Them going to fuck him up for me. "How did you find him?"

"I called around, found out where he was. When I did that, I found out he was actively looking for me. From there I found out he was at home. He wasn't surprised when we showed, he knew I would come." I wanted the words to fall out of his mouth faster and into my ears for processing.

"He said the DIA director lost his mind when we got you out. Came down on top of them, even came to the prison. The director wasn't focused on who in the government worked for the bombing. What he was upset about didn't really align with anything, and it was clear he was more concerned with the large-scale investigation into the former cabinet members, maybe himself. He wasn't concerned about you doing the bombing. Aaron knew something bigger and fishier was in play and wanted to figure it out. He knew the DIA director seemed off."

"Do you believe him, Mac?" I knew I couldn't trust my instincts with Ross, Aaron.

"Look, I know he fucked with your head for a long time. He checks out, he is good. I know his team, the guys he works with. I've trained with him. He only has the interests of our country at the heart of what he does."

"Just like that you bring him here?" I frustratingly said, pointing back at the cabin, the supposed safe house, that felt anything but safe to me at the moment.

"Not just like that. He helped us get you out."

I shook my head; there was no way that was true. I bit my lip. If it was true, then it would only confirm I was still in their control somehow. That is why they chased me down; they were using this whole experience to keep getting intel from me. "No, I don't believe that."

"I wouldn't have either, but CJ only spent a few hours there, and when he sent us on the mission, he had all the security protocols, where the cameras were, when shift change was, the works. That would have taken us weeks to figure out. He had to have an inside man. Plus, Larry does not have enough pull to have them let you go outside; Aaron convinced them to let him talk to you privately outside. Only Aaron could do that for us. They were messing with your reality; they needed to keep you in the only few rooms you saw. If you didn't go outside, we could not get you out."

My heart raced; this was all bullshit. I gave up all that intel to who I thought was my team, but they were just furthering this ruse. Aaron was involved, maybe it was a fake escape like I originally suspected, to get me to talk. "CJ knows many people." I thought maybe CJ could do these things without Ross's, Aaron's help.

"Jackie, he helped us. Aaron told me he couldn't stand to watch what they were doing to you."

"He FUCKING put me in that place. He KNEW what they would do. He..." I felt so stupid for falling for him. He did those things to me; he knew what would happen. I stopped, "All he had to do is not put me in that place."

"Look, admit, with the amount of information he was working with, you were a threat. You committed a bombing that killed many people and got away with it. Then you worked for a government agency. To me, to all of us, you seem like you should be in jail. Without the full story, I would've thought the same thing. I certainly did. It changes a lot knowing everything. It changed my opinion of you. I would have done the same thing he did and followed orders and got you detained to figure out what is going on. I see his side, Jackie. I see yours too. You were both operating on what you actually knew."

On some level, it made sense. I just couldn't trust anything Aaron said.

"Once they figure out what he did to help you escape, he will be in deep shit. He has to lie low anyway, so he came with us. He is going to help us with the DIA, get us insights and allies on the inside," Mac said. "I trust him. He is the only lead we have inside the DIA and he wants to help us. He believes the director is compromised. He wants us to help him prove or whatever we need to do. We could not do that without him."

I trusted nothing from Aaron; I trusted Mac. The two worlds collided in my head. The ache that fractured my reality hurt. I needed Mac more than I needed Aaron gone.

"You better have Colby James in that trunk," Chief Steiner said as I walked up to his front porch.

Asher held back and talked on his phone, and I got ahead of the conversation with Chief Steiner. "I need you to play along, this guy is on her team, he knows what we want to know," I whispered as I reached out to shake Chief Steiner's hand.

"Ericcson, I told you to get her, not bring some member of her team here," he said in a low tone.

Asher walked up behind me, "Chief Steiner, this is Special Agent Asher Findlay from the DEA, Colby's team," I said and stepped to the side.

"Pleasure to meet you. Come on inside," he said and let us into his home. He held it open, and we both walked into the small foyer of his home, and he shut the door.

"You were right about the director; Colby knew something we didn't," I said to get ahead of the Chief blowing up my entire pitch to get Colby's team to cooperate and that Chief would come along too.

"Sounds like we need a beer, do you guys want one?" He pointed at the kitchen.

"Sure," Asher said.

I followed both of them into the kitchen and picked up the conversation before Chief Steiner could hand me a beer. "The Iranian militia is connected to this case." I threw out more information he didn't know or expect. He had worked human intelligence long enough; he should grab it and move forward.

"Shit, what did we stumble into?" he said.

I tried not to smile; he played along.

"Looks like there are several high-ranking government officials involved," I said.

"There were several high-ranking government officials involved, many have been taken down. We believe there is one left, as far as we know," Asher said.

"Care to enlighten me?" Chief Steiner said and pulled out a chair at the kitchen table and sat down.

"Your director," Asher said. Asher had not touched his beer. He took this seriously.

"My director..." Chief Steiner paused for a moment. "Are you talking about Andre Young?"

"Yes, him," Asher said. "He is entwined somehow in this Iranian militia plot, infiltration into the government and smuggling materials for a dirty bomb into the country. Most of these people are being blackmailed or bribed on some level—we don't know what is going on with Director Young. We know, based on what is going on, that somehow, he is involved," Asher said.

Chief Steiner sat his beer down on the table and leaned forward. I took a seat to his left. He looked at Asher and then back at me.

"You're convinced of this too?" he said to me.

I nodded.

"Well, that explains why Ericcson here is AWOL, and he is a person of interest in assisting a prisoner escape."

I didn't like the sound of that, but I didn't know if the Chief was playing something up like I asked or not. It may be possible he told the truth, but I didn't like it. I didn't like my character and my service besmirched. I would have to ride this line, and maybe I could ask before we left if that were true, if I got away from Asher.

Since Asher was off with Aaron, and the rest of the team was at the cabin, Lee and I headed down to train the team going in our stead to Venezuela. Sensors that Jackie put in place during our mission had picked up radiation, and we needed to find out what exactly emanated that radiation. The DEA asked Special Forces to take on the mission, since our team was not at operating capacity.

"This point is the real pinch," Lee said and pointed to the map. "It's the only way you can get in and out of that valley. They secured the other paths. It took us awhile to get in there. Its highly guarded." Lee provided the lay down of the geography of the Venezuelan small town where our sensor had picked up radiation.

"How armed are they?" asked Siobhan, their team lead.

"We got pinned down by them; they captured one of our guys, and we had to extract him before it got worse," I said, referring to the close call that CJ and I had with them.

Lee pulled out his marker and wrote on the map. "I will give you the positions we held and the positions they held."

Siobhan pulled me aside. "Mac, you guys want to come with us?" he asked with a grin.

"Of course, I do," I didn't like that Jackie sidelined our team; we were, for the time being, not quite ready for operations.

"Do we know where the material is headed?" Siobhan asked.

"The U.S.," I said. "There is a lot of talk of a multi-city attack, coordinated, and super deadly with the material they could get a handle on."

"How did this end up in the DEA's hands? Usually this is always Special Ops?" he asked.

"Drug cartel is the main mode of transportation. Besides, they got Doc and myself." Doc and I both were assigned to this task force from Special Forces. I missed my old Special Forces team sometimes, but I did like this task force. It made it a little more predictable for my family. I was still gone a lot, but it was different.

"Apparently not," Siobhan said as an offhand jerk remark.

"Alright, come and check this out," Lee said. He had covered the map with red and blue x's which covered what we did and encountered. This team would have leave the next day.

12

My team had mostly let me recover at the cabin for the last week while they ran off to DC and other places to prepare for the next steps in our mission to track down the incoming dirty bomb and the surrounding conspiracy to facilitate it. Today, though, it was different. They left Aaron and me alone. Aaron couldn't show his face anywhere they were going because he was warned he would be arrested there. For me, in the end they probably didn't trust me. They told me it was because I wasn't up to it physically. CJ had to get back to headquarters, and that left Aaron and me.

I got up early to run or walk or whatever I could do to get my cardio going. I also wanted to stash a go-bag outside but didn't want to be caught doing it. No way I could convince my neighbors to give me another one. I also considered taking this opportunity to run. I knew I had about three seconds before the alarms rang out on the window being open. I used the same window I jumped out because the screen was out and still laying on the ground where we landed together. I opened the window, tossed the bag, and shut it. I waited for the alarm; it didn't go off. Good.

I headed out of the room and down the stairs. It was silent, no Ross. I headed out the front door. It was still dark out, but the horizon threatened to lighten up as the sunrise approached by hinting the mountain ridge. The plan was to run out and circle back, get the bag, stash it, and come back. I walked down the driveway mentally prepared to move through the pain on the run. As I got to the end of the driveway, I heard the front door shut. *FUCK.*

I took a right out of the driveway and picked up a slow jog hoping it was a coincidence. I heard rocks as they shifted in the gravel; the sound came my way. I didn't look back; I wanted him to go away. His footsteps were quick though, and he rapidly closed the gap between us.

"Hey, Colby, I will go with you," he said to me. He used my old name; he was the only one who had called me that in years.

I stopped running and turned to look him in the face as he caught up to me.

"It will be just like old times," he said.

"This isn't your fucking game anymore," I yelled, "Back OFF!" I shook my head as he slowed to a walk. He began to talk, "NO..." I said, cutting him off. "This is my time, my healing and you are counterproductive to any of it." Aaron found out where I was training for the DEA, and he spent that entire year interjecting himself in my life. He was kind, thoughtful, and helpful. He was the only person I had for over a year after I joined the DEA with my new identity. I left my whole life behind and he was the only person I had. He was a partner in crime to everything I had to do and wanted to do. He didn't ask me about what I did with the bombing. In time I grew feelings for him. Retrospectively though, I understood he did it all to get information from me. I thought he cared about me, but I was wrong.

He stood right in front of me, so close. The swirl of all the emotions swelled in me. I was happy he was alive but profoundly hated him. The DIA found out I had feelings for him, maybe loved him. They used it against me, faked his torture and death, and I believed that too. So seeing him alive was a good feeling but also represented a profound betrayal that spoke to my foolhardy ignorance. I hated the part of me that fell for it all. He hurt me in a way that I didn't know was possible, and he would do it again. I wanted to hug him and punch him at the same time. It was all too much. I turned my head away looking at the rocks at the side of the road, "Please." I didn't know what else to do at that moment.

We stood there for a while, for me an eternity. I wanted him to turn around. He waited for me to say something else. I slowly turned and jogged again. He didn't follow.

I actually had a good run, not fast, but steady. I guess having Ross on the mind, so present, dulled the physical pain. I slowed to a walk as I got to the driveway. I don't think I could stomach however many days with him. I was at the mercy and grace of my team. If this is what they were giving me, I would take it. I didn't think they would get this far with me, and I didn't think they would leave us alone.

I opened the door, and he stood at the stove cooking, his hair slicked back, and his shirt stuck to his sweaty skin. He glanced back at me and smiled. I looked away as I went to the sink to get water. I smelled him as I passed him, his sweat, his deodorant, his smell, and my stomach flipped over. I wasn't sad or happy or angry, I felt overwhelmed. As I downed a glass of water, some tears escaped my eyes. I turned my body to be sure he didn't see. Then I headed for the stairs.

"Alright if I make you breakfast?" he asked.

I nodded, not looking at him. I was hungry, and I would not turn down food. The stairs had been getting easier as I gained my strength. I was still slow though.

I headed back down after my shower, driven largely by hunger because the rest of me didn't want to put myself near him. There was a plate on the table, and he had slid a cup of coffee into place as I made it to the table. I hated to admit he knew what I liked, it would be easier if he fucked it all up. "Thanks," I said and sat down.

He had already eaten, I thanked God for that. I hoped that meant he would leave me alone at the table. He filled up his coffee cup and sat down to the left of me. I concentrated on my food and tried to my best to pretend I didn't notice him.

"How long do you think they'll be gone?" he broke the silence.

"Interesting," I said back.

"What?" he said.

"They didn't tell you. Hmm… I thought you were in with them."

"Wow," he said to me.

I took a few more bites, I finally looked over at him, "What?"

"You're jealous."

"Excuse me?" I said, aghast at his comment.

"You don't like me being with your team."

"Oh, you must be confused, you can end that sentence with, 'I don't like you'," I snapped back.

"That isn't true, Colby," he said.

I shook my head in exasperation and dropped my fork. "What did you think would happen, Ross? You would just come up here and I would be so happy to see you." I said, clasping my hands mimicking a giddy girl, batting my eyelashes.

"No," he said, raising his eyebrows, "but it doesn't mean you don't like me."

"You're right, I fucking hate you." I kept the rest in, my mind was so fucked because of him. I bit my lip and stared down at my coffee cup. "I don't even know what is real anymore," I whispered to my cup. I stood up; I couldn't have this conversation with him.

"Colby, wait," he said, putting his hand on my hand.

I pulled it away hard and fast. "You have lost all right to touch me. You are ONLY here because my team wants you here because I sure as fuck don't. You are here to help us crack the corruption in the DIA, be our inside man, other than that you serve no other purpose." I stared down at him. I boiled over with different competing emotions, I hated myself for falling for his tricks, I wanted to hug him, and I wanted to hurt him. Each one overtook the other in a turbulent fight for my attention and response. I went over to the living room and sat down on the couch. I twisted to look out the window behind it.

He came to me after a few minutes and handed me my coffee. He sat on the far end of the couch facing me.

"We weren't nothing. We can figure this out, at least how to work together."

"The last time anything made sense to me was when you were dead. I watched you die on that table. My heart broke for you, and I blamed myself. Then I had cut off the feelings toward my heart being ripped out at your death and prepared for what would happen to me. With you dead, they would torture me," I said while looking out the window then turned to him. "I remember thinking I wanted to take your place. I would have given almost anything to put the air back in your lungs because I was so devastated. I thought you died for me, to protect me, for something we believed in. You told me, that was what was happening. I saw that was happening. I cried and hurt over everything they did to you."

The tears streamed down my face now, and so too from my nose. I sat my coffee down on the windowsill and wiped the tears from my face while I looked out the window. I turned to look at him. "You said you loved me. You said you did it for us, for me. You said you took this torture for me and believed in me." His hair fell into his face, and his beard was only a day old. His eyes pierced me. "That wasn't real though, none of it was, nothing we ever were, was real. That was your goal, wasn't it?" If there was a reason to remove me from the DEA, it was for believing him, my greatest defeat, falling for a man I knew had only one motive to be present in my life. That motive was to get information from me.

"It's so much more than that," he said as his eyes welled up.

"This moment is worse than you being dead. I wish you were dead, then all of that would be true." I wanted out of this place; I couldn't be here with him anymore. I could not face the worst failure in my life, caring for him. I could feel the need to flee ring in my ears and course into my veins. I stood to leave, and he reached for me and almost touched my thigh. I came to a complete stop and stared down at his hand. I was going to lose it on him if he touched me, especially there. He stopped himself.

"I'm still your Ross," he said.

"Your name is Aaron," I said back, like it was a piece of reality I had to affirm to put myself back together. I stood up all the way and turned away from him to head back to my room.

"Colby," I hated to admit hearing him say my name was good, but not if anyone else said it. "Please, sit down. We can talk about this, please." His kindness, fake as it might be, felt like a knife in my heart. The mixture of paradoxical emotions only made them both more intense.

I turned around and his face met mine, he stood so close. The air between us grew thick, suffocating. I waited for his words, and he wanted to touch me. Like every moment between us, it was a battle of my will and my want. I let the moment sit and felt it all. I was, am genuinely happy he is alive. I am also completely and utterly betrayed by him, stupid, hurt, my heart was shattered. I now questioned everything from the moment I met him; I didn't know what was real. Each memory would flash, and I would ask, did that happen? Did I make that up? How stupid am I? The spiral would continue until it became as hazy as a dream. I wanted him and also therefore truly wished he was dead. If he was dead, everything would be real, and I wouldn't be like this. I wouldn't wonder if I was really here with a team or if it was all a trick. Was I actually crazy and so snapped from reality that I was still in the prison making this all up?

He broke the silence, "I'm still your ranga," he said. I called him ranga, after his red-hair. Ranga is short for Orangutan. Before I knew his name, I called him my ranga. I told him eventually that is what I called him in my head, my ranga. When he said 'I'm still your ranga' he wanted me to remember our close connection. I let his words sink in and wash over me, my skin covered in goosebumps. My eyes locked with his and my breath became heavy. My love for him pulled to the front. Being so close to him I couldn't fight the part of me that celebrated him being alive. Having his presence and his smell so close to me brought those feelings closest to the surface. I still fought it though. The chapters of us before stopped me. I closed my eyes to will it all away, I had to use my brain and tell myself this man did not care for me. That the emotions were actually a reaction to his manipulations. I had to resist any urge I had to fall into the arms of someone I loved, however wrong that love was.

He wiped his thumb across my cheek, softly with his rough callouses. I opened my eyes and let the tears fall down my cheeks. He knew everything I went through; I felt so uncontrolled and miserable, my emotions had taken over my body and I could not will myself out of them. Still, I leaned into him with my arms curled up, my head on his chest. He wrapped me in his arms and held me. I wept. I hadn't yet, not really, since I left that place. I was trying to be tough, and I didn't feel safe until this moment in his arms. I felt so confused. It wasn't lost on me that in this moment I was being held by the person who caused it all to happen. Somehow him knowing everything made it the only place to cry, and if anything, it made me cry harder.

He stood there holding me while I sobbed for everything that broke in my body and in my mind. The moment went against everything I wanted to be. I wanted to be strong and independent, but I hadn't been able to since I got shot. I needed my team, and I needed to heal from whatever Ross did to me, my Ross, my ranga, Aaron.

I woke in his arms on the couch and laid there long after I woke from crying. I didn't want the moment to pass, him holding me, knowing once I stood, we would be broken still. Were we ever really whole? The answer bored into my soul, and I didn't like it. It burned me somewhere deep inside.

I reached up and felt his beard under my hand. I loved the way his beard felt under my fingers. Before I touched him the first time, I dreamed of touching his beard and feeling it on my face. This time though, it would be the last.

His head turned down toward me, so we could look at each other. I looked up at his face. His eyes were red. He, maybe, had cried too. We could have been something, the two of us. I certainly loved him and maybe in his way he loved me. We both were bound by bigger things than us, those things that got in our way.

I ran my thumb up his beard to put my hand around the back of his head. He brushed the hair off my face. A part of me wanted him at that moment; I wanted to kiss him. I wished I could wash away all the pain and start fresh with him. My eyes went wet again, and so did his. Perhaps if we met in a gym somewhere, or in a training, we could work. I leaned up on my elbow. I kissed him on the forehead and let my lips linger there. This would be the last time I kissed him. I wanted to remember this moment. I knew it was wrong, but I needed him to know I loved him, even if it wasn't a real love. I felt his arms around me and it felt like he loved me too, like he said. My body tingled to his touch. I felt safe.

My heart broke anew; it wasn't real, none of it was real. This time the heart break was new, and it felt like the blood that contained our loved poured out of my heart and emptied into my body, and anger settled into its place. I knew then I would one day get him back for what he did to me, maybe even kill if I could. But for this moment, I let the tears fall as his fingers traced my neck and down my shoulder. We were at this moment in love with each other. In this moment, we let the other things fall away and I let them fall down my face. I still loved him. I moved my hand down to his chest and pulled back to see his eyes again. I ached for a time when this was real and wasn't shattered irrevocably.

A shell formed around my heart, and I knew the time would come when I would have to resolve this, just not right now. I don't think I could survive knowing what he did to me. He is the biggest threat to my survival and my success. My eyes danced between his and I slid my legs off the couch. I stood up, I kept my hand on his chest and my eyes on his. It was a goodbye from my heart to his, and when I let go, the break would be permanent.

"He is inbound," Doc said over our earpieces about DIA Director Young as he came into the building. I waited in the cafeteria with Asher.

"Freeing up a locker now," Lee said. We took the key to many lockers to ensure that when the director got there, he would have to use the one we left open for him. Everyone had to lock up their electronics before going into certain parts of the DIA building, we counted on him doing the same.

"Three-four-one-eight," Lee said, which meant the director took the locker next to that one. That was my cue. I got up and took the bag Asher prepared for me to the locker next to the one the director used and put it inside. The lockers sat in a large open room, near the first security desk. The cafeteria was just around the corner. I turned to go back to the cafeteria and saw Chief Steiner shaking the director's hand after he passed the turnstiles down one of the higher security hallways. Chief Steiner lured him into the office with a lead on finding Colby, and he took it because he showed special interest in the case, willingly clearing his calendar to get updates.

Asher had his laptop open, and it was his turn to do the magic. "Thanks, Mac," Asher said when I sat down next to him.

"There's two phones," Asher said.

I thought about it for a second, "One has to be a government phone."

Asher intently focused on his computer. "Okay, I've isolated the non-government phone, starting the process now." He was cloning the phone into the device we had in the locker. This would allow us to see everything that was on that phone.

I stood up and went to get us coffee. We had to act like we were supposed to be in this cafeteria, and not look too suspicious. Chief Steiner got us into this part of the building; it was as far as he could get us without sending out a flag.

I brought back the coffee and set them down next to us. "Thanks," he said.

"How long does this take?" I asked.

"I'm not sure. I hope we can get it done within the hour," he replied.

Asher stared at his computer while we waited for it to work. A janitor cleaned tables at the far end of the cafeteria. As he went along, he flipped chairs over. "I don't think we have an hour," I said, feeling a little on edge we would be kicked out.

"It's frozen," Asher said.

"What do we do?" I asked him. It was why we had Jackie on the team, she would know, I don't know.

"Uh, go restart the phone," he said to me.

On the scale of danger for missions, this sat on the low end, but still we didn't need to be identified by anyone in the building. I went to the locker and pulled out the phone and started the restart sequence. I sat there with the phone in my hand and wanted to make sure it came back on before I left it. It flashed back on, and it looked good, and I set it back in the locker and locked it.

Asher walked up to me, "Time to go," he said.

"Okay," I said, wondering where this sudden need to leave came from. I went to unlock the locker again.

"No, now," Asher said and nodded at the door. I followed suit. He must know something I don't.

"Why are you two coming out?" Lee said over the earpiece as we made it outside the doors.

"Yeah, Asher, what is going on?" I asked him as he smiled at me and slightly quickened his pace toward the parking lot.

"Chief Steiner and the director just walked into the cafeteria. We were running out of tables," Asher said. I must have let my guard down because of the building we were in, and I had no sense of need for security or danger, I didn't notice them. "I still need to back up from the carrier and restore the device. I think I can do it from the parking lot."

"Think, that's your plan, think?" I don't 'think' we put enough prep into this sad little mission of trying to steal the information from the director's personal cell phone to break into all his apps. Not to mention Asher was a novice at all of this. Jackie's skills made him look like a child.

I climbed into the front seat next to Doc in the pickup, and Asher went to the 4Runner with Lee. Asher got in the back seat, pulled out his laptop, and went to work again. "Okay, the restart worked," he said over the earpiece.

I looked out the front windshield and kept my eyes on the door.

"This is the long part, I'm running a restore from the carrier," Asher said.

"Little strange, isn't it," I said to Doc.

"What?" he said and looked over at me.

"Second time in a month we are messing with a DIA facility," I said with a shrug.

"Don't remind me," Doc said. "You know I don't like any of this, at all, Mac."

"Still?" I didn't understand everyone's problem. Maybe I did a little, but I trusted CJ implicitly, so I wanted to follow this trail to see where it went. I realized Jackie was a part of something bigger, proof or not.

"A bomb, in the U.S.," Doc shook his head then rubbed his face with his hands. He understandably was stuck on it. He argued over and over to that point but gave into the will of the team. We let the silence settle into the car.

"I need the phone restarted again," Asher broke the silence.

"And who do you suggest walks back in there?" I asked. We were just in there and it would look weird for us to go back into the building.

"Come on, Mac," Asher said.

"Who thinks this is a bad idea now?" Doc said softly, hitting me shoulder with the back of his right hand.

"Fuck," I said and pushed the door open and headed back in. "I'm not going back in after this, this is it." When I got inside, I showed my temporary badge and headed back to the locker area.

"Nevermind," Asher said.

I sighed. I opened the locker anyway. I couldn't turn around now.

"Pick it up, we are good now, we're done," Asher said. I grabbed the bag I put in there and threw it over my shoulder and headed for the door.

13

I SUCCESSFULLY AVOIDED AARON the rest of the day after crying into his arms. "Don't overdo it," Aaron said to me. "You've been out here going for hours, and your body isn't ready for it." He was right, but I hated him being right. I was out in the garage trying to find a place that was quiet to workout away from him.

"Don't you have something better to do than worry yourself with me?"

"Strange."

"What?" I snapped back.

"You are still asking me that question."

I rolled my eyes.

"I made you dinner. Come and eat," he said. I reluctantly followed him. I still didn't like his presence, and I didn't trust his intentions.

I sat down at the table, "How do you know what I like so well?" He was a skilled cook and made me meals often in the past.

"You're mine, Colby."

I smiled, "Not anymore." I reached out and touched his face, "And my name is Jackie." I turned my attention back to my food. The kindness of our moment earlier in the day lingered. Maybe he thought he got to me, but it was the opposite for me. Still, the barrier broke, and I knew I had to feign kindness for now, for the mission.

"Not anymore?" he questioned back, lifting my chin gently with his hand. My eyes met his, and I went flush. My lingering feelings were still there.

"I'm not your game anymore," I said. "Aaron." My eyes went wide when I said his real name. I wanted to emphasize that his name was new information to me. Hiding his name from me was part of his manipulation of me.

He used his fingers to push my crazy workout hair behind my ears and traced his fingers down my shoulder, arm, to my hand. "You aren't a game to me, Colby." I wanted to believe him, but I couldn't. Nothing was ever real if he was involved, even in my fractured state of mind I knew that. This morning taught me that.

He ran his fingers across the palm of my hand, and I watched him. Still though based on what happened, I let him touch me. My heart skipped a few beats. He got up, still held my hand and walked around to kneel next to me. He still played the game. "I promise, you weren't a game, this us, it wasn't a game. Why I showed up was one thing, but why I stayed was another. It wasn't because you were a game to me. I fell for you." I felt able to deal with these competing emotions now. I knew that if I held it together, I would get out of this. I could withstand my emotions and his manipulations. He was still in the game though.

I watched his face searching for clues of his intentions. He saw through me, why couldn't I see through him?

He kissed my hand then put my head in his hands and kissed my forehead, then on my cheek. I didn't want to give in. He wasn't doing enough to erase the hurt and pain, he never would be able to. He came down to have his eyes meet mine, inches from me. My head in his hands, my heartbeat to his touch, my breath matched his breath. I held back, I wanted to kiss him, but I knew better now. He held us there for a few breaths then leaned in and kissed me.

He kept kissing and moved one of his hands down and wrapped me into him and I finally gave in and kissed him back.

His food was bad for my will power, I would remember that for tomorrow.

I wrapped my arms around him, it felt so good. Then his touch, his kiss, it put me back in that room of our last kiss. The kiss before I thought he died. I stopped and stood up, pushed the chair backward. "I've always been a game to you," I looked at him still kneeling. He rose. "I have had no choice with you since the second we met and all of what you did was to mess with my reality." I felt stronger today; I could do this today.

"Not all of it," he stood in front of me.

"I didn't even know your name until Mac told me." I paused as my strength filled me up, as my will grew stronger. "I know nothing about you, nothing, except that we are exactly the same at our core. I don't know where you are from, if you're married. Guys like you are always married. I am only a means to an end. That's why you messed with me, why I was your game. That's why my team has you here now, you are a means to our end."

He stood close to me with his arms around me loosely. "That doesn't make our feelings less real. It only worked there because they were real."

A bomb went off inside me. I didn't know which part would come out first. "You think that was love? I would never do that to anyone I love, not for any price." I shirked his arms off me and pushed him back, so I had space to get around the chair. I reached a dangerous level of angry. My ears tickled by the rush of blood from the rage. I could feel it, and knew I had to get away. I could the feel the pain behind it, the hurt of him dying, and how mad it made me at myself for being so stupid for falling for him.

"It wasn't like that Colby..."

My voice pierced, "Explain it then, what was it like? To make me watch the man I..." I stopped—I couldn't say the word to him, that I loved him, my breath became shaky as the adrenaline and devastation piled into my veins at once. "To watch them torture him and die because of what I thought we believed in, torture and die for me, because of me, because of what I did." I was screaming now, "What do you call that, Ross? Aaron?"

"I screwed over my entire life for you," Aaron raised his voice. "I'm going to get court-martialed for this. I helped you escape from a government facility. Now I am absent without leave from the Army, not to mention a person of interest now in all the stuff you did. If they catch me, I will go to jail for you, for helping you escape, to stop them from torturing you," he pointed at me and stepped toward me.

I put my hand out. "I still feel that pain, the pain of you being hurt," I stopped for a second as I felt the twinge of heartache and the words became difficult. "The pain of losing you," tears burst through my eyes as anger rose right behind it until my vision became almost red. "It's as real as if had just happened. It wasn't erased when you showed up. It didn't disappear because you claimed you help me escape." I slammed the dining table chairs backward to the ground.

"I didn't have a choice, you know I didn't, it's duty. You of all people should get that," he said. I cut him off.

"You let that fucker break my ribs," I said and stepped over to him, "and look at my face!"

"It's not that simple; you know it's not."

"Yes, I know what you are going to say. You were just trying to get information from me. To serve your country and do what was necessary, I KNOW!" I turned and walked into the living room. I hated even more that I would have done the same thing if the roles were reversed. "I understand it, which fucks me up more." My back was to him, and I trembled now. "I'm happy your alive, I am truly, and I'm happy to see you, but I'm also completely and utterly betrayed by you using me the way you did." My mind was still fractured. I still felt unsure of whom to trust, which way was up, or more importantly, which way was out. Reality is still lost to me. I felt so stupid for every part of me that fell for every part of his act. It was too much. I sat down on the couch, and I put my head in my hands.

"You're surrounded by people who put their whole lives on the line for you." He was frustrated and trying to not be loud. "You have an entire agency backing you, again, for what you did. Do you know how dangerous that is? Your team is on the front line of it, and if anything goes wrong, they will lose everything, go to jail. What about their families? This is so much bigger than you and a few moments you had in the past. There is a serious threat to our country, and we are all putting it on the line for you," he shook his head and dropped his hands to his sides. "You don't even care about any of that. You are stuck on a few moments that are over."

I brought my pitch low and slow and tried to take in his words, "I know, the worst part is, my team chose me, and I don't believe it. All I can think is that it's another one of your tricks. I don't..." The knife from my go-bag was on the table next to the couch. I picked it up and played with it in its pouch. Something to fidget with. My thoughts clouded. I could only feel the pain and confusion. "You blew up my mind."

He came and sat on the couch near me, "let me help you put it back together."

"A month ago, I had everything, nothing was broken in my life. I had a great job with the DEA." I turned to him and blinked slowly. "We just completed a mission in Nicaragua, and even though I was shot laying at the edge of a jungle. I was completely peaceful, happy to die there. I was happy with what I had done in service to my country, what I had done for my team, and happy with whatever it was I had with you," I stopped. Aaron was my last thought when I thought I was dying. My uncontrolled last thought and memory was of him being there with me when he wasn't. "I have nothing now." I can't even accept my team's word that they have me. I don't believe them. Aaron made all the breaks happen. He stayed in my life and reported everything that happened back to the DIA. He turned me over and put me back in the DIA prison. He offered himself up as fodder to break my grip on reality. He was the only one that put all these wheels in motion. Without him in my life I would have recovered from my gunshot, rejoined my team and continued down that path with the DEA. Everything with him is and always has been a trick.

"I'm here, you have me," he said, maybe to be reassuringly, "I can help you, Colby." I couldn't tell his intent, like I couldn't tell what was real and what was a trick. I knew this much; with him it was a trick. "I know you; we can get through this part and focus on the mission."

"You broke me," I said calmly, as the tears on my face inexplicably dried.

"Colby, you need to get over yourself. Wake up! You're not in prison anymore. No one is hurting you. Why are you acting like they still are?"

I pulled the knife from its pouch. I had nothing left, and he took it all from me.

"What are you doing?" Aaron asked. "Give me the knife, Colby."

"Always afraid when I have a knife, Ross?" It was clear we defaulted to the original names we have for each other when our emotions got high.

He went for my wrist. I pushed him off me and sliced his arm at the same time. I stood up moving backward away from him, ready to keep fighting. I didn't mean to cut him, but I was okay with watching him bleed. It was nothing compared to what he did to me. "What are you going to do, Ross?"

"We should have left you there," he held his arm as the blood pulsed out of it.

If I was honest, I would say I didn't know what I was going to do. Aaron walked behind the armchair toward the rooms that lined the great room. I wanted him to hurt like me. He fucked up my mind, my body, my life.

In my periphery a truck pulled into the driveway, the light that bounced from the setting sun off the windshield temporarily blinded and captured my attention. I stood there a moment longer before throwing the knife into the ground, letting it stab into the rug and floor in front of the couch.

I went outside. He yelled after me, "I didn't sign up for this."

I sat on the curb of the concrete porch that touched the edge of the gravel driveway. It was Doc and Lee.

"You alright?" Doc asked.

"No," I said. "Why did you leave me here with him?" I asked them.

"Did he do something to you," Lee asked, and the few items he held dropped from his hands.

The last few minutes washed over me and pulled up in my face wanting to come out in tears, "No...but I cut him though. He is bleeding everywhere. Maybe would've killed him if you guys didn't pull up."

"What in the fuck is wrong with you," Doc barked as he opened the truck door again.

"You left me with the man responsible for my torture. You, of all people, saw what they did to me. What did you think would happen?" I screamed at him.

Doc pulled out his medic bag from the truck. "This is all so fucked," he said and kicked the door shut.

Doc ran inside to tend to Aaron.

Lee sat down next to me. "Jackie, you can't do stuff like that."

"I just...snapped, I can't believe he is here. How can I act like I'm okay with the man who helped them break me? I can't even explain what it was like in there, in that prison, that torture," I said while the last few moments twisted in my mind.

"Jackie, I don't know what you went through in that place, but..." he paused and looked around at the surroundings.

His eyes focused on the horizon. "Dale was so worried when he got to the hospital, and you weren't there. Over the next few days, I couldn't calm him down, he called hospitals all over Maryland and Virginia. I told him you were probably fine. You were always such a mystery that you probably went off the grid with your scheduled time off. I wasn't as worried as everyone else was about it. I didn't know how far from the truth that was."

I didn't know what to say to him at that moment.

He looked over at me and let his eyes settle on mine after he reviewed my face, "No matter what you did, for whatever reason you did it, you don't deserve that, no one does."

I broke eye contact to stop the tears from falling. I leaned my head on his shoulder, "Can I tell you a secret?"

"Hmm," he said.

"I think my mind is more broken than my body." I closed my eyes.

"I agree with that," he said. "I think you saying that means you're on the mend," Lee said. I could feel he was trying to look at me on his shoulder. "I shouldn't say it, but I don't know if I trust him either. Don't kill him though."

"Do we really need him?"

"Yeah, we do," he said, repositioning to put his arm around me. I sat there for a moment and let the anger subside. I let it all drain out, the shrapnel that attacked my emotions when the bomb went off inside me. I let it out one breath at a time. Lee was patient with me as I let it go with my head on his shoulder.

14

It was dark by the time CJ and Mac came into the cabin and I went out to meet Asher at the back of the Suburban. "I gotta know how you did it, how did you get the director's phone."

"I used this," Asher said, pulling out a modified phone. "He had two phones, a work one and personal one."

I sat down in the back of the Suburban to hear his story.

"I isolated on his personal cell, stole some basic information. It was enough for me to swap his number to a different sim, and we cloned his phone. We used the carrier back-up system to get everything and used texting one-time passcodes to get back into all his accounts. We put in a back door to everything, then loaded his phone back into his phone in the locker. We are in," Asher said with a smile and put the device back in his bag. He was so proud and full of himself.

"Okay, it didn't go as smooth as I just described and I might have had to call for help on some things, but it worked and that's what matters, right?" He was letting his guard down. I knew that would only happen with me. It made me smile.

"I thought you were literally going to steal it."

"People notice when their phones disappear. On the other hand, they expect when they lock them at the locker at work that they are completely safe."

"Has he noticed yet, like is everything reset?"

"Not that I'm aware of."

"Who's going through the phone?"

"CJ has some analysts on it. They are better at it than me, anyway."

"Man, I wish I was there."

"Next time," he said, smiling up at me as he finished shoving things into his bag.

"How was it here?" he said, sitting down next to me in the back of the Suburban.

My smile left, and I looked down.

"What did he do?" Asher said, barely hiding the anger rising in him.

"Nothing..." I shook my head, "He was fine, I guess." I paused for a second and met Asher's eyes. "I cut him though, pretty bad," I chuckled a little. I covered my mouth to stop the laughing from coming out. "I shouldn't laugh."

Asher stood up and looked back at me with his jaw dropped. "Jackie... are you serious?"

"I know, it's bad, I shouldn't have."

"I wouldn't want to be you when CJ finds out."

My face went straight, "I know."

"I'm glad you did though; he deserves it. He got off easy after what he did to you," Asher said, shoved my shoulder lightly, and picked up his bag.

"ERICCSON!" CJ yelled.

Asher looked at me knowingly. I wiped the smile off my face. CJ waited for me to walk back to the garage. He walked away before I got to him. I picked up a jog to come alongside him.

He shook his head and showed me his anger. "You did that to Aaron?" he asked, pointing at the house and put his face in mine as we came to a halt in our walking.

"Yes, I did," I said straight back to him.

"What in the FUCK is WRONG WITH YOU!" he yelled. "HAVE YOU LOST YOUR GOD DAMN MIND? Assaulting someone! What was your plan, Ericcson? Were you going to fucking kill him?"

He paused a moment, "Don't answer that, I do not want to know the fucking answer to that question." He stood up, took his face out of mine and put his hands on his hips and stared down his nose at me. "I do NOT give a FUCK what happened today or before, it doesn't fucking matter. You are dead wrong to do that. You know you are dead fucking wrong."

He bent down to my face again and put his hand up making the motion of a pinch with his right hand, with his thumb and finger close to each other. He yelled again, "My patience for your SHIT is BEYOND wearing thin. You are hanging by a GOD DAMN thread!" He stood back up and went back to staring down his nose at me. I didn't have a response. Everything he had to say was true and deserved. My words or objections would only make it worse; it didn't matter my justification.

"Ericcson," he said a little calmer, a little quieter but still at a high decibel. "I expect my team to do better than that," his taut jaw pushed out the words through his complete frustration with my actions. "Aaron insists he is fine and that while unprovoked it is understandable. He doesn't get to decide that. Aaron is on our team now, DO YOU UNDERSTAND?" he finished with a yell and got into my face.

"Yes, Sir."

"NO MORE SHIT FROM YOU!" He pushed his finger into my sternum, "YOU GOT IT?"

I nodded.

He went back to his clenched jaw, "We are in a God Damn SHIT STORM and trying to clean it up." His voice raised again; he couldn't pull back how pissed he was. "You are at the center of this fucking shit storm, and I don't need anyone ESPECIALLY YOU making it worse." He came within inches of my face.

"Got it."

"Why in the fuck...." He stopped and stood up. He put his hand over his mouth and looked up to the sky for a moment then dropped his hand. "Fuck that, I don't give a shit. You are going to go in there and get Aaron. Come out here and work it out. Don't fucking come back to that cabin until you are good! Then NO MORE SHIT between you two." His face tensed as he looked down at me.

"Yes, sir." I waited to make sure he finished before I went in. He stared at me. I took it as a sign to go.

When I opened the door open, I hoped to see Aaron at the table, no dice. "Doc, do you know where Aaron is?"

He pointed to his room. I walked back there and knocked on the door. He popped it open. He did not seem happy to see me, I could tell by his face. "Can I talk to you out in the garage?" I asked. His hand held the door up high, and he had his foot behind it to make sure I didn't open it further.

"Why would I do that?" he played with the dip in his lip.

"We got to work together, can't do that with shit between us."

"Something tells me this has more to do with CJ ripping you one than you actually wanting to squash things between us."

I shrugged my shoulders.

"Okay, give me a minute," he looked back into the room at something he was doing.

I leaned up against the 4-Wheeler when he finally came out. I didn't know what to say to him, or how to fix anything between us. I followed orders this far.

"So?" He stood far from me and close to the door. He had his hands in his pockets. His left arm was bandaged up.

"Sorry I cut you. I felt myself get out of control and I shouldn't have grabbed the knife," I said in his direction but not to his face. I did not feel sorry; I needed CJ to not send me back to jail.

"That's not our problem," Aaron said back, "but I appreciate it."

As soon as Lee and Doc showed up my thought pattern on my situation with Aaron changed from highly emotional to what we needed to finish the case. My team's presence, CJ, gave me a perspective I missed and couldn't form when they left us alone. It was easy to get mixed up when it was just the two of us. I bit my lip and stared off to the side of him.

"I'm not married, by the way," he pulled his hands out of his pockets, lifted his hat and pushed his hair back and put it back on.

I looked back at him confused.

"You said, 'Guys like me are always married.' I'm not." He stopped for a second to play with the dip in his lip, pushing it around with his tongue below his front bottom teeth. "I was once, but I was gone too much. Even when I was here, I wasn't here, it's been years."

I enjoyed hearing that, I wouldn't lie.

"No girlfriend either, no kids," he said.

It was like I just met him; it was the first time he let his guard down. The first words from him I found to be not contrived or meant to manipulate.

"Colby, you weren't a game."

"No," I shook my head, "We can't talk about that." I couldn't deal with my love of a man that was ... well, him. I couldn't talk about it.

He stared back at me for a moment then went to the pile of chairs on the side of the garage. He pulled two off and set them down sitting at a 90-degree angle to each other. I went and sat in one while he sat in the other.

He started first, "What do we... I mean, I don't know how to fix this."

"Me neither, but CJ doesn't want us back until we figure it out." We both sat there in our own worlds not looking at each other, no words for each other. My eyes were on the ground, and I saw his boots. I used it to break the silence, "What branch were you, or are you in?"

"Army, actually, still in," he said.

"Huh, I thought Marines for sure. Those boots are Marine Corps."

"Few people would catch that," he said.

"I spent a lot of time on the receiving end of those," I said with my eyes still trained on them. "I got a good look. Jason is a Marine too, well, was. I don't know now what is going on with him. Or with Crystal. How did you figure them out?" I mentioned my Fortitude Team's names, people I was asked about in the prison so I knew he knew about them, but I wasn't sure how they got that information.

"I didn't. By the time you started giving me anything to work with..." he stopped, "I didn't want it. Fahrenbacher had that intel from the FBI."

"Is that the big guy you left me with?" asking if that was Chin's name.

He nodded yes.

I remembered the times he held back questions. It reminded me of lying on his chest.

"I don't know what this is...or what it's not, but it feels like we have unfinished business. Our story isn't over; there is something big between us," he said.

"We have to be done. For our mission, for our team," I said. My words, my beliefs, my needs.

"I have to see where we go, together, Colby. I will walk away from this mission, any mission, if that is what it takes," he said.

I leaned forward in the chair. I ran my fingers through my hair and looked over at him. He messed with the brim of his hat in his hands. My stomach flipped. It all came back up, the good and the ugly. I stood up. "Ross," I walked forward. "FUCK!"

"You want it, admit it," he said.

"It's not that simple." I stared at the wall in front of me.

I heard him get out of his chair. "It is. I walk away, you guys finish this, and then it's me and you." He came up to the side of me. "I know you love me, and I love you."

"We can't finish this without you; we need you."

He was right about my love, but I would not admit it; I was also done with him. I still thought he was trying to run his game on me. I was made a fool enough to know better. There was so much there. I couldn't trust him; I couldn't believe him. I couldn't be with him. I wanted to hurt him way worse than I did today. I looked at him, and his hair fell down in his face. I pushed it out of his face and kissed him, and he kissed back. I gave in all the way and laid my body into him. I wrapped my arms around him, and he did the same to me. I wanted him. I stopped and smiled. I took his hand and took him to the ladder to the loft. I let go and climbed. He stopped me and kissed my neck, wrapped his arms around my stomach, picked me up and set me to the side of the ladder. Then raced up the ladder. It made me laugh. I chased after him.

We laid there afterward, my head on his arm. I looked up at the ceiling. "I don't think this is what CJ meant."

He leaned over and looked down at me, and traced my face with his fingers. His bandage was right in front of me.

"Did I cut you bad?" I tried to discern by the size of the bandage.

"No... well, maybe. Doc put a lot of stitches in me to put me back together." Aaron leaned over and kissed me again. "I'll leave; it will be fine." He got up and got dressed.

I got dressed too.

As he finished and reached for the ladder; I stopped him, "Ross, wait." I waited for him to stop and catch my eye. "We can't be us; it will not work. You know it too." I sat down on the edge of the loft and dangled my legs down and stared into the garage below.

He came back and sat next to me. "I don't know that."

"You do, I do. We just don't want it to be true."

He put his hand on my leg. "Colby, you flipped my world around. I put everything on the line for you, my life and career, and as much as I didn't want to admit it, I fell for you. I never in a million years would think I would be here ready to give it all up for you, and I am here willing to do that." I still didn't believe him; how could I believe him? He was great at manipulating me.

I put my hand on his. "There's too much damage," I blinked slowly, staring off into the garage, feeling the parts of me that felt so broken I didn't think they could mend. The parts he broke in me, from the time he was an interrogator and the betrayal of turning me back into that prison, helping them break my mind through his fake torture, and the torture I went through. "I didn't know a person could break like this."

I could feel his eyes on the side of my head. "I should probably leave anyway," he said.

"You can't; we need you," I said, somehow finding the perspective of my team and how valuable it is to have Aaron on our side given the situation. The DIA director was, at this time, the only target left, to our knowledge, influenced by the Iranian militia. Having an inside man would be way easier than us trying to deal with the situation without him. I moved my hand to his leg as he pulled it up so he could face me more directly.

"How do we do that?" he said skeptically. There was a lot between us. I knew I couldn't trust him, I wanted to hurt him, and I had to wait until this ended to do anything.

I looked down at my other hand and backed out into the garage. "We focus on what we share, not on what we don't, not again anyway." I couldn't look at him. That is how I would get through this.

He let out a frustrated sigh, "What's that, Colby?"

"You and I do, will give every part of us for this country, no matter the price." Those were words I knew were true. There was no fracture in that reality. We both will pay with our life and everything we cared about to achieve our missions. That much was clear in the prison, but for each of us on opposite sides of the fence. I will be hurt to hide my government secrets. Ross was willing to have me be hurt to get that information, assuming he did actually care about me like he said. He just said he gave up his marriage because of his work.

"What don't we have?" he said, slightly perturbed with my answer.

"Each other, not like this, not anymore. It's a price we pay for who we are and what we love first," I said, feeling strength grow in me. Feeling a small piece of me stop bleeding and move toward healing. We both loved our country, and the missions given to us. We wholeheartedly believed in that and followed that before everything else in our lives. We were the same in that way. Our country is our first love.

"I don't like it," he said. He wanted what he said to be true, not what I said.

I finally looked at him. "I didn't ask you to like it. It's necessary."

I could see he got it and was trying to come up with objections. He knew that our mission was important than us. He knew our mission was more important than anything we both wanted in our lives. I realized in that moment I knew what I looked like when I was full of it and why he could see through me. I could use this to put me back together.

"What's next?" he said, looking deep into my eyes.

"We agree to let this go, let the past go, focus on our mission stop the dirty bomb, root out the remnants of the Iranian militia influence on our government." I wanted to reach out to him. I wanted his touch to fix me. I wanted it all to be done. Maybe the one that broke me could put me back together.

He nodded and let a tear fall before he stopped others from falling.

"Don't bring it up; don't talk about the past. Focus on the mission. We are on the same team, that's it."

He gave me a puzzled look, "So does that mean you won't cut me anymore?"

I smiled, "No promises."

"Colby..." I stopped him.

"I'm Jackie now, you're Aaron. We have to stop with Colby and Ross."

"Well, we're both Ericcson," he said back. I wondered what he thought of me taking his name. It wasn't something I could ask about though, especially not now.

I shrugged my shoulders, "It is what it is." I couldn't help myself. I leaned over and kissed him one more time. When our lips touched, tears rolled down my face. I pulled away and wiped them.

"Okay," he said, holding back the emotions. He held out his hand, and I grabbed it to shake it. "Teammates." We shook on it.

"Well, teammate," he said, looking at me, "you are going to want to fix that hair before we go inside."

15

"Fuck!" I fell to my knees after Chin landed a blow right to my stitches. I was trying to regain my composure when I was backhanded across the face, over the cuts and bruises already there. I leaned onto my left hand, trying to hold myself up. I couldn't even hear him talking, I was so disoriented. He kicked out my arm, and I fell all the way to the ground. He landed with his knee to my side, and I heard the crack/pop explosion in my side. I screamed out then my air wouldn't go in or out. With my face firmly attached to the ground, I looked straight ahead at the legs of the metal table across the room. It's all I could do, soak in the pain. My eyes wide open, unable to blink. All I could see were the legs of that fucking table.

Finally, air, "Oh, shit," breathing hurt. I pulled my arms in and held my right side, to hold me together. My face was still on the floor. I pulled my knees in and whimpered. I had never felt something like that before.

He pulled on my right arm. "Get up, Colby," Chin commanded.

Jackie

"No," I whispered. He pulled harder. I screamed this time "NO! STOP, PLEASE STOP!"

He pulled anyway, I screamed again and cried. I didn't know what else to do. I shook from the pain and the fear. Shallow breaths. *Oh, the ribs!*

I couldn't stand; I fell to the ground back in my cement room. The sound they pumped into the room started, the noise of crashing metal and other loud noises. I hated that noise. I screamed loud and long over and over, and I couldn't drown out the noise. I wanted it to go away. I pushed my body into the wall and covered my eyes and ears. It hurt to move my body, my right arm, and my ribs. Tears poured out of my eyes. I couldn't take noise anymore. I screamed again to drown it out. Shallow breaths, little breaths. I felt the prod going to my back.

"Who are you working for?" Chin yelled in my ear.

Jackie

"Please, no, I don't know the answer. Please. No," the words barely shook out of my breath. Then he shocked me. It makes your ears tickle. It makes your teeth feel like they are breaking. It smells like dying. And you can't do anything but just feel it, no talking, no moving just feeling, seizing.

Ross put his thumb on my leg, "What's the next attack?"

Jackie

He shoved his thumb into my leg, I started to kick and grab at his arm. Throwing myself backward and away from him and falling back to the ground. I watched his feet; he liked to kick me when I was like this.

"Don't cross the line," the guard said. I slid backward away from it. It was so close, I didn't have room. I pressed myself against the wall. I felt pinned against it.

I felt pinned under the chair. He was dying. "I don't know how to find them, it's been too long," I screamed, "He's dying!" I flipped on my side; my forearm was pinched as it held my entire body weight strapped to that chair.

They pulled me from the room, I was screaming and kicking. "NO... NO... NO... ROSS!... ROSS!!!" I kicked them, fighting them. "Get off me."

"Jackie!" a voice was breaking in, but I couldn't place it. They were grabbing at my wrists. I kicked hard. "JACKIE!"

I woke up, and I was on the floor next to the bed. I jumped onto the bed and scrambled backward over it to the other side, away from whoever just touched me. I stood there and felt the remnants of hunger and dehydration, like I felt when I was there. I felt the devastation of the loss of Ross, just a remnant of how that felt. It diminished as I stared at CJ. Sweat poured down my face and my back. I held my hand up to keep him away.

"Jackie, it's okay," he said.

Fear and adrenaline poured through my veins; their effects shrunk though as I stared at CJ. I heaved air. My side hurt anew, and my burns all stung. My ears rang, and my jaw hurt.

They chose you. CJ's words were in my mind. They chose me. I closed my eyes and focused on the words, on the team. CJ walked around the bed and I heard him. I opened my eyes and backed up. I put both my hands up, trying to tell him not to come near. He stopped. I looked down and studied my hands. I lifted my shirt to check my stitches, no stitches, just a scar, new but healed.

I fell to my knees. "They chose me," I whispered to myself.

"It was just a dream," he kneeled in front of me.

"I know, I know," I said so quietly, I told myself more than him. "He's alive, he's fine. I'm safe." I closed my eyes and focused on my breathing.

"Jackie," CJ said, "come here."

"It's okay, I'm okay," I put my hands up again. I thought if I got touched again it would hurt.

He scooted toward me slowly and put his arms around me. "You're safe. You're here," he said. It didn't hurt. I breathed a little easier. I tried to let it go. I pulled my arms tight to my chest and protected my body. I laid my head on CJ. I shook as the adrenaline and fear tapered.

I felt the remnants of guilt and devastation related to Ross's death. I was so thirsty.

"He's alive, he's fine, I'm safe," I said again out loud to myself. I pulled back from CJ. I needed water. I used his shoulders to stand up. I still shook, but I needed water more. I looked over at the door. Mac and Doc stood just inside and watched the scene. I rubbed my forehead with my hands. I didn't want any of them around for any of this. I didn't want them to know that part of me. I got near the door and stopped.

"What happened to you?" Mac said.

"Are you okay?" Doc asked.

I stared at them and their shocked faces; I stepped toward them and waited for them to move. They finally moved a little, and I pushed past them and down the stairs.

I only had on a shirt and underwear, but I didn't care. I went to the kitchen and got a big glass. I went to the sink and sat the cup in the sink to fill it up. I closed my eyes; it felt so real. I could still feel it all. I hated it. I picked up the cup, and I shook too much. I set it down on the counter, spilling water everywhere. It made me angry for my body to betray me like that, which made the shakiness worse. I grabbed onto the sink with both hands, I needed it to stop.

CJ came up behind me and put his hand on my shoulder. "Sit down, Jackie," he said calmly.

I agreed. I nodded. I needed to sit. I put my head in my hands and walked over to the table and pushed out a chair with my foot and sat down.

"Can you put these on?" CJ said and handed me pants. I rubbed my face and grabbed them from him. I slipped them on as far as I could without standing up. It's all I had at the moment. It had to wait. He sat across from me. I stared at him. I hated this moment. I didn't want to be in it. I didn't want to be kicked off the team for it. I could feel it all draining off. I had to focus on my breathing, not anything else. I couldn't even look at CJ. His presence though, helped. I took my hand and covered my mouth. I needed the shaking to slow enough to drink the water and go back to the room away from everyone.

"Some dream," CJ said.

I blinked slowly as I looked at him; I had no words for what that was. It didn't feel like a dream; I thought I was there. I felt like I was just there. Like my room, that bed, was a portal to that place.

"It took me a long time to wake you. You were fighting me pretty good," he said, turning his hands, arms, and face to show some scratches and red spots.

"Sorry," I said. "Just a flashback; I'm okay." I stood to get away from this moment and pulled my pants the rest of the way up.

"I've been waking you up from these dreams quite a bit, although none as bad as that one. Little bird told me you think your mind is more broken than your body. Your body is pretty messed up, so we need to talk and figure this out."

"Sounds like a little bird wants me to break his beak," I said back as I sat back down. I looked around for Lee in the great room, but no one was down there with us.

"Jackie, what's going on up there?" he pointed to my head.

"It's better when you guys are around," I laid my head down on the table, onto the side, looking over at the sink.

"As opposed to?" CJ questioned back.

"You know, I thought..." I paused and bit my lip and let out a shaky breath, deliberately trying to calm my nerves, "I know it's not true, I just thought my actions killed Ross... I mean, Aaron." It was hard to find words with CJ right now. I lifted my head off the table and kept looking at the sink. "I know it's not real, but I feel it like it's real. Reality is so fractured for me. If that wasn't real, what else isn't real?" I couldn't tell him I questioned the realness of the team and what their intentions were for me. I brought my eyes back to CJ. "It's better with you guys around, really."

CJ looked at me concerned, puzzling out my words. I'm sure there isn't a response to, 'I think I lost my mind, but don't worry I know I did.' Maybe he understood why I wanted to kill Aaron yesterday, or was that still today? I didn't know.

"I'm getting better, I promise," I reached out and put my hand on his. Then stood. I still needed water. I wasn't shaking that bad anymore. I downed the whole glass and got another. I wanted this conversation and never-ending night to be over.

As I was drinking my second glass, I heard yelling outside. I turned quickly; CJ heard it too, and we ran outside. Lee, Doc, and Mac were watching Asher pummel Aaron. CJ headed straight for Asher and grabbed him, trying to pull him back.

"Stop!" CJ said in the struggle. Asher struggled to get out of CJ's arms. "Get off him." Doc and Mac jumped in and pulled Asher off Aaron now.

"Asher, stop," I could see the rage burning in his eyes. He wanted to kill Aaron.

He kept his attention on Aaron; who had made it back to his feet at this point. "This fucker did that to you?" he screamed at Aaron, loosely talking to me, pulling at CJ's arms and throwing Doc and Mac's hands.

"I'm okay; it's okay," I said, trying to pull his attention. I didn't want CJ to blame me for this.

"I can see why you cut him, but what I don't get is why you didn't kill him," Asher said, still focused in on Aaron. His fists were balled up and he was rocking from side to side, like he was ready to go back in.

"He didn't do all of that; it wasn't him. It's okay." I was desperate to stop him because CJ just told me he was inches from kicking me off the team. He had to cool down.

Asher finally glanced around at everyone, "Can someone explain to me why this asshole is here?" He finally landed his eyes on CJ. "We don't need him; we can do this without him."

"We need him to get into the DIA," I said calmly and quietly to him, "He's helping us." I got in front of Asher and put my hands up and slowly put them onto his shoulders. Trying to catch his eyes. "What you did yesterday, that wouldn't have happened without him. Asher look at me. I'm okay, Ash, I'm good. It was just a dream."

Asher's eyes finally came down to meet mine.

"I'm okay; he didn't do all of that. It was a different guy. It was just a dream, anyway."

Asher pushed me back away from him and walked away.

I turned my eyes over to Aaron; he was bleeding, and I liked it. I wanted him to hurt the way I hurt. I turned my eyes back to CJ who was clearly frustrated. The rest of the team was looking on at the chaos. I wanted out of all of this. I wanted to be a team member, not the reason our team broke.

"Asher," CJ called, "Jackie," I looked over at him. "Aaron." He waited for all of our attention to land on him. "Take a few then meet me out in the garage." I didn't like where this was heading. I went in and got more water, clothes, and boots before heading out to the garage.

When I opened the door, Aaron and CJ were talking. They stopped when I walked in. Aaron leaned up against the wall. He used his gray shirt to wipe most of the blood off his face. It had red/brown wet spots all along the bottom. CJ was in a chair. I sat down in the other one, the one Aaron was in earlier. I put my hands in the hoodie I was wearing. They weren't talking. I thought of the loft and Aaron. I couldn't look at Aaron.

Asher walked in; I opened my eyes. He closed the door behind him and didn't move much closer to us. I looked to CJ. I felt the tension ratchet up in the room. We all waited on CJ, who looked for words as he glanced around the room at each of us. He had a lot to deal with, and they didn't need me to move forward, I knew that. Dropping me from the equation was the easiest way to finish the mission. He studied each one of us with his eyes. He finally talked, "We are all on a team, all of us, seven of us now," CJ said matter-of-fact like, leaving no room for interpretation. CJ had an indescribable commanding presence.

He turned his attention to Aaron, "Our team works with partners: Me and Mac, Doc and Lee, Asher and Jackie," he said, pointing at us two. "You are the odd one out. I'm going to put you with these two."

Asher shook his head. I could hear what he would say if they weren't here. *Fuck that.*

"The three of you are going to go down to the analysts who have been going through the director's phone and figure out our next steps. Find out why he is cooperating with that militia and find out how we make our next move. All three of you are going to put together a plan and get us moving. While the other team is in Venezuela tracking down radiation source, we will focus on the director. Find out what you can from his phone and then let us know what we are doing next."

I nodded looking back at CJ. I wanted to go back in and was sick of being on the sideline.

"I need a verbal confirmation from all three of you."

"Got it," I said.

"I'm in," Aaron said.

Asher was still fuming but trying to pull it back, he nodded.

"I need words," CJ said.

"Roger, wilco," Asher said with flat effect.

Part II: Promnesia (n)

/pram nee za/

a) feeling of experiencing something twice

b) unpleasant familiarity

Similar: déjà vu

16

I WALKED OUT TO my car to grab a bag out of the trunk. Maybe I could wash some clothes I had. Lord knows I didn't have much, and I can't remember the last time I felt comfortable enough in one of these shitty motels to use their laundry. I pulled the bag out of my trunk and felt someone's presence. I shut the trunk. I could tell they were behind me, looking at me, but not close. I dropped the key to the car on purpose and used the opportunity to glance in that direction. A guy in a sedan behind me dropped his camera below the dashboard. *FUCK*. Surveillance. I had to get out of here. I knew something wasn't right then, I should have left right then. I never thought it would lead me to lying in a tub hiding from a barrage of bullets, asking God for the FBI to help me. I went back to the motel for the essentials and planned to leave out the back. I took too long.

Asher and I went from partners to a trio with Aaron when we had to find the source of a blackmailer. "Send the payment," Aaron said to me as he looked over my shoulder at the cloned device.

"Relax," I said, "we have to test the location intercept."

"I just did," Asher said. "It worked."

"I don't get it?" Aaron said.

Asher started, "The payment will only pass to the other account if the receiver of the other account is in a place expected by the device."

"Your cell carrier, they know where you will be normally, right? They take all the information about where you have been and have a pretty good idea of where you should be, like what is normal," I said on top of Asher's explanation.

Asher continued, "We are going to interrupt the location to cause the payment to fail. Instead of the payment failing altogether it will request location again. This will cause the app to actually request a tower ping and or Wi-Fi/Bluetooth, giving us a precise location."

"If they spoof the first location, this will get around it and make sure we are getting the actual location," I said to Aaron who picked it up quickly.

"So, what I need to know is that this will tell us where the person is who's receiving the payment, and we are just making sure they aren't giving a fake location," Aaron said.

"It's enough money that they will confirm the other phone location before giving them access when they get the notification of the payment," I said. We found out the director was being blackmailed and initiated payment to the last set of instructions he received and would trace that payment. We would then have it blocked by the bank and fail during the three-day processing period, but it would initially look like it went through. The tricky part though was figuring out where it was going because it could be anywhere digitally.

"All of this over a picture?" Asher questioned. "I don't get it; it's the director on a motorcycle."

"The picture has to have a deeper meaning," Aaron said.

"It doesn't matter why that picture bothers him; they obviously know and it's working so, let's use it to our advantage. Maybe when you talk to him later, ask him why it bothers him," I said. We found the source of his blackmailing first; it was the best way to find out if others were compromised. If we got him first, it might push the others underground. "It's the outcome that matters." I smiled at my little saying. "Okay, I'm sending the payment now."

We all gathered around the phone even though it was projected onto the big TV in the room. Some analysts who helped us find the information were in the room. The analysts had found the information in his email, a hidden account that used his normal email as a recovery address.

"What now?" Aaron asked.

"We wait."

"Oh," Asher said. "Payment failed. Here goes."

I held my breath and bit my lip as I looked down at the little phone.

Asher stared at the program we ran on the computer, "Boston, Financial District, we got a building, right here on Summer Street," he pointed at the map on his screen. My heart dropped. Way too fucking close to home. That part of Boston reminded me of the bombing.

"We have a target?" Aaron asked.

I faked a smile, "Yep!"

17

"Have you seen Jackie?" I heard CJ's question; it woke me up.

"Yeah, she's uh, in here," Aaron said.

"Aaron, I was very specific about this, this is not okay," CJ said, raising his voice. My back was to the door.

"It's not like that." The light from the great room filled the room as the door opened. I closed my eyes. "She's in Asher's bed."

"Why?" I heard the voices get a little quieter; the light was gone. They had stepped out of the room.

"I guess, she said she has been sleeping down here on the couch to be closer to Asher. She talks to him after she has a nightmare, then lays down on the couch. She said it's the only way she doesn't have nightmares," Aaron said to CJ. There was a pause; I strained my ears to hear what I was missing.

"I have seen her sleeping down here from time to time," CJ said.

"With Asher being gone, she asked to sleep in here," Aaron said. It got quiet again and I couldn't hear what was being said. Asher and Mac had gone to help with any support function with the operation going on in Venezuela. The Special Operations team had arrived in Venezuela to find out what the radiation sensor picked up. They were going to make a move as soon as they had an opening, and Asher and Mac knew the area better than them. They would be in the operations room providing oversight, instructions and details when needed. Doc and Lee had already been working on it, but they switched them out.

"She has only been in here maybe an hour," Aaron said.

The light filled the room again and went away again. I thought maybe the conversation was over.

"This is a problem." CJ continued, "Do you know the first thing she says when I pull her out of her nightmares? A few seconds passed, she says to herself, 'He's alive, he's fine.'"

"Okay, what does that mean?" Aaron asked, "I'm missing it."

"Her first two thoughts are of you and if you're okay. He's alive, he's fine. Even before her own safety. Before she even knows where she is or that it was a dream, she tells herself that you are alive, and you are okay. I don't think she is sleeping down here because of Asher; it's you. Knowing you're alive and fine lets her sleep."

"It makes little sense; she largely ignores me unless it directly deals with something we are doing to get work done. I think she tries to avoid even those conversations," Aaron said.

"She told me..." it was hard to hear CJ sometimes, "reality..." his words were inaudible again. "She just had a nightmare, and she said... This isn't safe for the team," CJ said.

My eyes went wide, and my heart raced. If CJ thinks I became a liability to the team, there was a possibility they could send me back to jail. CJ said I had to support this mission because I knew it better than anyone else. He said if I didn't, he would turn me over to the authorities. If I was a liability, how could I support the team? I would need to do a better job of hiding my issues from CJ. CJ saw something in me I didn't even know about. My mind ran through permutations of what they might do, and it made it hard to hear them talking.

"Let's get through the rest of this mission. Whether you know it, you seem to give her peace, and Asher is a great partner. She has a depth of knowledge on the Iranian militia and their influence on the government, and we can't recover that information from files. We also owe it to her to give her a chance to pull it back together after all the trauma," CJ said. I let out a breath. He was giving me another chance.

I heard the rumble of Aaron's voice; I could tell he talked but couldn't tell what he said.

"Don't push these limits. Don't get involved, just like we talked about," CJ commanded.

Aaron again was too quiet. I wish I could tell him to speak up.

"Thanks Aaron, next time, she's on the couch," CJ said.

The light came back into the room. I closed my eyes again, and I heard the door shut. I felt Aaron get close to me. I could tell when he did; he spent too much time waking me up. He wiped my hair out of my face and off my neck, slowly and gently. I couldn't help it. It felt nice, I let out a soft brief moan. He was staring at me; I could hear it.

I thought about what CJ just explained to him, that I was so deeply in love with him I didn't understand my actions. It even felt weird to hear it myself. I would have to push it down. I wasn't getting into his bed, and I didn't want to. I still thought he was dangerous and for anything like that I didn't trust him. We were done, that was clear to me. I finally heard Aaron get back into his bed.

He's alive; he's fine. I thought of the words I didn't know I said, not really. The team, that's what I focused on. They chose me. That's what brings in reality and gives me strength. CJ was wrong.

The person who accepted the payment from the director's phone was in a building on Summer Street in Boston. Armed with that information, CJ decided we would head up there and figure out who was on the other end of that payment.

The last time I was on Summer Street in Boston, the place where we suspected the blackmailer was, I had just finished the deal that would eventually put me on probation. Insignificant to everyone else, I know. It is also just as anticlimactic as it was after I convinced GRE & Associates that they needed my software, the software with the malware that gave us access to Ashenhurst's location, and therefore helped us target our bombs for Operation Fortitude.

Suits and ties covered this part of town, which meant we dressed up too, a new thing for us on our missions. Our team had to recon the fourth floor.

When I got back to our field office, Doc and Lee were already there. "How did it go?" I asked them. The guys looked good all cleaned up.

Doc had a paper cup with coffee, "Empty floor," he said. "What did you find?"

"Mostly empty rooms; I just gave the two names I found to the analysts."

Aaron walked in the room with his tie off and had the top few buttons of his shirt undone, "I don't know how people wear this all day." Aaron looked great in a suit, with his hair in some sort of order and clean shaven; I kept my eyes away from him. He must not have seen himself in the mirror because, well, the suit really suited him. "All I got was five names and one office with no name, but definitely long-term occupied. Hopefully, Asher got some records."

I laughed.

"What's so funny?" Aaron said.

"Asher always get what he wants from women." Asher was all the things women wanted—tall, handsome, a smile that could kill, sweet, and dripping with confidence.

"She isn't lying," Lee added.

CJ and Mac came back together, "I think we got a possible," CJ said. "A high-powered office, Hansen and Anchor, not really sure what they did."

"Super fishy, got little from the receptionist," Mac added.

"Guess we should have sent Asher," Lee chimed in and shot me a grin.

"That boy wishes he had game like me," Mac replied.

Asher walked in with his suit jacket and his tie off. He had a folder with a stack of paper, and a big smile that said he just did something he wasn't supposed to. He dropped them on the table in front of me and shot me a knowing look. He probably took the receptionist he was flirting with into an office and hooked up with her. I smiled. I don't know why it gave me so much joy to see him up to no good. I think I lived through him, with this beautiful wife and revolving door of beautiful girls.

I opened the folder and started flipping through the files. "Are these the sales records for the last month?"

Asher raised his eyebrows and left the room. CJ took the files from me.

"We should have sent Asher to your floor," Aaron said to CJ.

That night, Aaron, Asher, and I went back to that building into its basement. We needed to find where the main network line fed into the building, we could use it to break into any of the systems in the building, and also to block any outgoing messages. They didn't waste money on cameras in the basement. Aaron could pick locks at an alarming speed—I guess I should've known that. He let us into the engineer's office; the light was on inside.

"He's gotta be close, so keep an eye out," Aaron said.

There were some camera feeds on a screen inside. I sat down; the system was in there. It was running primary controls in another room, but the server for the system was there. I plugged my laptop into the server. There wasn't security on the system; I was instantly into the system. I erased the last hour of video and ran a loop from the night before at the same time. Then I went to the system and found floor access, disengaged locks on the elevator and then the doors to Hansen and Anchor.

"Over here," Aaron called.

I unplugged and headed in his direction; he found the network room. Perfect. I plugged into the main router and disrupted the service to the floor. It should prevent any signals out, alarms, phones, etcetera.

"Elevator two, green light is on," I said. We communicated via radios connected to ear pieces.

I stayed in the room and worked on hacking into their network. They had way more security than anything else thus far.

"We're in," CJ called out, he and Mac were in the office.

Aaron flipped the lights off to the network room and quietly closed the door behind him. He held a crack in the door open and looked out. I glanced over to what he was doing and went back to what I was doing.

"Office clear," Mac called out. Doc and Lee would head up there now.

I wasn't getting any crumbs; it let me know we were in the right place.

"You have incoming to the network room," Asher called over the radio.

I closed my laptop and placed it on top of the servers next to the line I was connected to. Aaron came back behind the racks of servers; there wasn't any place to go. Aaron climbed the racks and laid down on the servers. I followed suit on the other side, as the door clicked open, and the lights were flipped on.

I was lying there as the security guard circled the stack. As he came close to our row, I scooted over and on top of Aaron. My face was on his chest as the guard passed and circled around to the end. I scooted back and Aaron rolled on top of me. I smelled him as he lay on top of me.

In an instant, I transported back to the first time we invaded each other's privacy peacefully after he had been in North Carolina and coming around me for over eight months. I was used to him by this time and he kept his distance and didn't touch me.

"Colby?" I heard Ross call out from the kitchen of my small North Carolina house.

"In here," I said and tried to tighten the washer on the toilet.

"You alright in here?" I heard his voice at the doorway of the bathroom.

I rolled my eyes and looked over my shoulder at him. I laid the old innards of the toilet in the middle of the bathroom floor. I struggled with tightening the last few things. I had straddled the toilet backward.

"Does that mean you want to take over?" I asked him, smirked, and tried to get the wrench settled in place.

He smiled and walked up to me and investigated the toilet. "Depends on how bad you screwed it up so far."

He smelled good. He must've just showered before he came over.

He stuck his hand into the tank and took the wrench from me. I leaned to the side and gave him space to see what I had already finished. I removed my hands from the tank and kept my eyes on what he fiddled with and tried to stand up.

"I didn't say you could walk away. Here, hold this," he said and held up the flapper.

I sat back down and grabbed onto it. Our space intertwined, we barely avoided touching. My head was close to his arm. As he worked, my face kept getting in his way. After a few minutes, he stopped and stood up.

"Let me get out of your way," I said and went to stand up.

"Nope, I need your help. You're not getting away with not finishing. It's about time you did something around here. I do everything in this house," he said.

I sat back down. "You do everything in this house?" I asked.

"You heard me right. It's my house," he smirked.

He then leaned down and put an arm on either side of my head to hold a piece and tighten it with the other hand. His deodorant wafted into my nose. He smelled so good between whatever soap he used and his deodorant. This is the closest I had to been to him without fear.

Over time he had gained my trust, and I didn't think he would hurt me. He glanced his head at me and smiled. I blushed and looked away.

"There," he said and stood up.

"What about this?" I asked, still holding the flapper.

He let out a laugh, "guess I didn't need you to do anything after all."

I shook my head and turned myself around to look at him, "Thanks." For a moment we got caught in each other's eyes. I felt overwhelmed and looked down.

"Guess you should clean up 'your house,'" I said and made air quotes.

"So, you don't want those sweet corn fritters I was just about to make? You want me to do this instead? Is that what you are saying?"

I smiled and could feel my cheeks go flush. "I was joking; you're always welcome here. I will take care of this, you take care of that." I had grown used to him making food for me over time, and he was a great chef.

He turned and walked out of the bathroom. I let out a sigh.

He stayed there, with his body covering me. I tried to see what was going on, but it was no use. All I saw was Aaron watching the security guard. He suddenly put his head down and I became invisible under him.

The door opened, and the light clicked off. I didn't hear the door shut. Aaron stayed there on top of me, he must have not heard it either. An eternity passed with Aaron on top of me, distracting me.

"Looks like you're clear," Asher said.

Aaron leaned up, swung his legs off and climbed down. I followed him.

"I need to go up, give me coverage here." I turned to Aaron, "Let Asher in." I went to the laptop and got it up and going. Asher came in and I handed him the laptop, "I am going to break in from the inside; this way will take too long."

"En route," I called over the radio as I exited the room. I went to the elevator and took it up to the floor. As I got to the office I called out, "Entering," on the radio. I headed straight to the back to the big offices. Mac and CJ were digging through everything.

I sat down at the computer and slid in my thumb drive and restarted the computer. I waited about a minute, and I was in. I dug around the system looking for any clues. I found some hidden encrypted files. I clicked on them, and they opened. I recognized them from before.

"This is them," I said.

CJ came over and looked over my shoulder, "How do you know?"

"I have seen this file before, when I was planning my first mission. I saw a lot of files just like this. The formatting is unique. It's the same formatting they used in the blackmail. All I could think of at the time it had something to do with the system they stole the files from and un-encrypted them. It was a security device, but they got through it."

"Who are the people in this office again?"

I rooted around, "Brett Hansen and Dustin Anchor."

"Jack, drop some listeners and let's get out of here," CJ said.

It was nice to not feel like I was going to get shot but the adrenaline of the mission, it didn't get you as high; it wasn't the same. I took some files with me, put in a backdoor to their system, erased what I had been doing, and removed the drive.

"Let's go," I said standing up.

18

I DROPPED ALL I got from Hansen and Anchor with the analysts and headed back to our temporary team conference room in the Boston DEA office. "We have a problem," CJ said to me as I walked into the room. "We missed the shipment in Venezuela. The Special Forces team we sent down there could not find any material and did not pick up anymore readings. Based on the sensor that was there, we think they missed it by a couple days." It seemed to be a temporary staging point. It had only been a few months since we put in the sensor. It appeared CJ had already shared that with everyone else in the room and he was just catching me up. "By the time the other team got into that town, it was gone."

"Fuck," I said. I felt guilty. If they didn't come to get me, maybe my team would have gotten to it in time. "Any idea on where it went?" I asked him and the room.

"We were just discussing that, the analysts think it's headed for the U.S.," CJ said. "They think that staging location is used while they confirm a water-based transport into the U.S. directly."

I took a seat. "Well...assuming they used the same cartel as me, I have some contacts and I know where they transfer to their customers," I said to the room sheepishly.

"What do you mean?" CJ asked with skepticism.

"I mean I helped set up the cartel to do business in a town in lower Alabama." I looked around—it was not something they would typically hear from their colleague. "I know how they move it, the works." I needed explosives for my bombing, but since I couldn't use official channels, I used a cartel to purchase explosives—the same cartel that the Iranian militia ended up using. I was concerned about their security, so I found a town in Alabama for business.

"How?" Mac asked.

I looked at him hoping he would catch the subtext that my previous role had some shadier activities.

Doc chimed in, "You know you work for the DEA now, and maybe you should have mentioned this information at any point when you started working here."

"I can say your intel on the Boston bombing is solid, except to my knowledge the Hermoso Cartel isn't involved. Also, not like 'Jackie' had much room to offer this information." Other intelligence had pointed to the Iranian militia using both the Martinez Hermoso and Jiminez Cartel. The fact a cartel was involved is how DEA got lead in the task force and where we focused our work.

Asher stood up. "You're a total mind-fuck, Jackie." He turned and walked to the back of the room.

CJ stepped in, "What do you mean 'you kinda set them up' in Alabama?"

"Well, I needed a place to make the exchange in the purchase of the explosives. I did a lot of research and digging and found some indifferent cops who were open to bribing. After the exchange, I gave the information to Christian, my contact in the cartel. I think we should start with those cops."

The room fell silent. I thought maybe they would have something to say about my lead. I think that the thought of what I did and me freely talking about it are two different things.

Mac finally cut in, "I'm fucking glad you're on our side and not someone else's."

"Is she?" Doc asked. I shot eyes at him; I wanted to tell him to fuck off, but I was on thin ice with CJ and decided it was best to keep it to myself.

The room filled with tension.

"You guys got a better idea?"

"Hansen and Anchor," Lee said. Lee wanted us to focus on the two people's office we just infiltrated and use them to break down the blackmailing of DIA director.

"Take that interrogator over there and find out what they know," I said and pointed to Aaron. "Asher and I can take Alabama. Lord knows I don't need to be part of interrogation, anyway."

CJ sent Mac with Asher and myself to Alabama to chase our potential lead. Before I joined the team, they were partners. When we got close, I set up a meet with the cop I worked with in the past, hoping we could get intel from him. I pulled into the parking lot alone. There were a few lights in the parking lot. I couldn't see Asher up on the roof of the school, but that meant he was hidden well. Mac was in the tree line bedded down. I parked my car facing out, lights out.

"Cop car inbound," Asher called out. "Appears to be alone."

The car pulled alongside me facing the opposite direction. He rolled his window down; I copied him and rolled down mine. It was the same deputy as before. His uniform was equally disheveled as before and his lack of shave with patchy growth made him uniquely skeevy.

"How you doing?" I asked.

"Been awhile since you've been around," he said. Even his badge was dull and dirty.

I smiled. He had a special creepiness about him, the kind that abused his position. "I couldn't stay away from you too long."

He popped his door open, and I followed suit.

"Come to blow up another playground?" he said as he exited his vehicle. When we purchased our explosives, we tested a small pack on an old worn-out playground.

"No, sir, I'm done with that business." He put his hands on his gun belt and looked me over; it gave me a chill. "Just need information."

"Information doesn't come free around here," he said, raising his eyebrows, hands rested on his gun belt, letting the stench of unwarranted arrogance waft off him.

"Of course." I handed him an envelope.

"Oh, that's heavy," he mimicked like he was having a hard time with the envelope, dropping it low like he couldn't lift it up.

"Any big business come through here in the last few days?"

"Oh." He faked a stumble backward. "That is heavy." He looked me over. "How are you going to sweeten the deal?"

"Not happening." I said with a straight face.

"These people don't like someone sharing their business."

"Fine, give my money back."

He held it back. "You're going to have to take it back." He gave me a creepy attempt at a flirty grin. I smiled and leaned in close. I grabbed the front of his gun belt and brought his face close to mine. "One of two things will happen, one, answer my question, two, I get my money back—if you don't willingly, I will take it back and maybe your life with it." I leaned in close to his ear and whispered softly, "I'm not alone." I leaned back standing up straight. I stepped back and let go of his belt; it fell to the ground. "I want you to keep that money."

He went to bend down to get his gun belt.

"No," I said, "leave it."

He shook his head; he was pissed.

"Five seconds..." his face went straight. "Four..." I said, keeping my eyes locked on his. "3...I'll take that envelope."

"Fine... fuck." Now he was antsy.

"Two."

"Alright, they paid for a wide berth yesterday," he said and shook his head.

"Who's they?" I asked.

"Your friends, the same ones you did business with."

"How wide?"

"Enough for a tractor trailer."

"Who picked it up?"

"I gave them the berth they requested."

"But?" I knew this sleazebag wouldn't be able to stay away.

"Fuck... I got plates."

"And?"

"Some pictures." He hated I knew what he did.

I pulled out another envelope with a smile.

"I fucking knew when you called," he said, looking down and kicking the ground. "After you did business here, I knew I should've taken pictures for insurance."

"Where are they?" I held the envelope closer to him.

"My phone," he said as he pulled it out of his pocket.

"Give it to me." I snatched his phone out of his hand. "Anything else?"

He shook his head no.

I grabbed his shoulder. "That wasn't so bad. I see bright things in your future." I gave him the other envelope.

"I used that money you gave me to fix the park. Well, some of it, and some from him."

"See, bright future."

I got in my car and drove off. He would not stay off law enforcement radar flaunting his money like that.

19

AFTER MEETING WITH THE cop, I knew one of our next best steps was to get in touch with my cartel contact, Christian. Jason, on my old team, took care of all of that, so I would have to find things he used to contact him in order to find out where he was and how to get in contact. After we left, we headed straight for one of my old storage units. We pulled up to a storage unit in Bowling Green, Florida, close to Tampa. It wasn't fenced in, just a bunch of small units on a no-nothing street. Mac used bolt cutters to pop the lock off the unit; the orange door rolled up part way and got stuck. Mac yanked on it and pushed it again, and this time it went all the way up, crashing when it hit the top.

The clang put me back to the first time I visited the goods in this unit with my Fortitude team. "One hundred K," Jason said as he walked up to Furi and me as we lifted boxes out of the back of my truck and placed them in the unit.

"For what?" Furi said after placing a box in the back and then used his shirt to wipe his brow.

"We can't always come to the same place, and we certainly can't leave a trail of our own vehicles coming here," Jason said and stepped into a small unit with Furi and me. The heat caused a sweat without labor, and the shade of the unit was only slightly better than the direct sunlight.

I bit my lip, waiting to see what knowledge Jason planned to drop on us.

"The manager will give us units and access that avoids cameras, and for one hundred K he will move our units around the greater Tampa area or wider, anywhere the owner has a unit," Jason said with a smile on his face and his hands on his hips.

"How many units are we talking about? And does this include the false wall in the back?" I asked and marveled at Jason's genius idea. This was the fourth time we had moved the contents, and this would be a big advantage.

"Up to seven," Jason said.

"How can we trust him?" Furi said, ever skeptical of every single thing we put in place.

"I've been working on him for about six months. This is right up his alley; he fundamentally distrusts people and most of all the government. For the right price, he will help anyone that is in the same vein," Jason said.

I smiled at him, and we locked eyes; he was proud of himself, and it made me really appreciate him as a partner.

"Can you get that kind of money?" Jason asked.

I nodded with a grin and went back into the heat of the day to the truck and grabbed another box.

"I don't think I ever had a key for this unit," I said to Mac after I passed him still messing with the door. It felt really strange to be here with government officials and not my Fortitude team. I went in and pulled out the boxes of random crap and worked my way to the back of the unit. Once I cleared the back wall, I pulled out the false wall. Behind it was a wire cage box wrapped in layers of plastic. I pulled it out, popped it open and pulled out a bag of cell phones. "Hmm," I handed them over to Asher. "One of these will lead us to Christian.

He was the cartel contact on the other end of that Alabama deal that the cop gave us pictures of and should know more."

Asher held the bag open as I dug through them, "none of these are ringing a bell."

Mac commented, "Doc might be onto something."

"What are you talking about?" I asked.

"Are you on our team?" Mac questioned. I couldn't tell if he was messing with me. I shot him a look. They chose me. CJ's words definitive in my mind. They had come pretty far; I didn't think a bag of phones would throw them over the edge.

"Jackie, this is crazy," Asher said. I shot him a confused look and pulled the bag out of his hands. "You pulling out things we consider evidence in an investigation and just using them like they are normal. It's not normal, what you did. It's not okay."

"It's different seeing and knowing about versus using a bag full of burner phones," Mac said.

I ignored their comments. They knew what I did, and burner phones were the light end of what was in this locker; they didn't need to know about the leftover explosives and ignition devices. I pulled out three of the same phones, "Gotta be one of these." I handed the phones to Asher and started putting everything in the unit back together. I put the false wall back in place and moved the boxes back into place. I reached into a box near the door and pulled out another lock and locked the unit. "You guys need to buckle up if you think phones are weird."

My eyes wanted to close as I rode in the passenger seat down I-95. We were chasing our next lead from Jackie's past and headed to find a cartel contact in Miami. For a change, Asher had a turn at the wheel. My phone dinged. I leaned to the side to get an angle to fish it out of my pocket. My wife, Linda, sent me a picture.

"Look at this," I said to Asher as I flashed him the photo of my daughter at his son's birthday party.

"Shit!" Asher said, "I can't believe I forgot, again." Asher slammed the dashboard with his fist.

I laughed, "Every fucking birthday."

"Mandie warned me last week, when CJ allowed me to sneak home for a night. She said, 'Asher, please remember it's Jason's birthday next week.' And I said, 'I will.'" His face snarled.

I pulled up another picture and held it out until he glanced at it. "You didn't?" Asher exclaimed.

"Well, I didn't, but Linda did," I looked back at the picture.

"I don't know what I would do without you two. What did 'I' get him?" Asher asked.

"Let me ask her," I texted back. "Asher wants to know what gift he bought his son." It was the second time my wife had bought something that was supposedly from Asher. She left them in shipping boxes to make it more believable. My wife did stuff like that all the time. I loved it about her. Also, Mandie, his wife, confided in her all the time. And Linda didn't want to hear about this again. She had a soft spot for Asher.

"A VR headset," I read to him.

"Oh, geez. Mandie will be pissed I spent that much. I will pay you back man, send me a bill," he said and shook his head.

"No," Jackie said from the backseat. She had fallen asleep twenty minutes ago, the first time I had seen her sleep in the few days we had been down here. Not surprised she was awake again.

"No to what?" I said, looking down at my phone.

She grunted, then moaned, and I felt her kick my chair.

I tried to spin around to see what happened.

"JACKIE." Asher raised his voice and tried to glance at her. He reached his arm back and grabbed her leg. She screamed and ripped his hand off.

"Fuck, Mac, wake her up," he commanded.

She was mid-nightmare flashback, she had them a lot since we got her from that prison. She went through hell there. Doc told us about her injuries, we saw some, but the nightmares were telling. I actually have more respect for her going through that. I took off my seat belt and twisted in my seat, she had curled up in the seat and whimpered. "JACKIE, wake up." I touched her and she screamed and yelled "No, please stop."

"Fuck, Mac." Asher slammed on his brakes and came to a complete stop and got out of the car. The truck behind us screeched to a stop; Asher didn't even get out of the driving lane. Asher climbed in the backseat and grabbed onto Jackie. "JACKIE YOU'RE DREAM-ING."

The car behind us honked. I got out and jogged around to the other side of the car. I pushed on the back door, but Ashers wasn't in all the way. "Get in and shut the door," I said and got in the driver's seat and screeched the tires pulling out.

Asher pulled the door shut behind him. "Come on, Jackie," he said.

She took a deep breath and stopped the fighting and thrashing. "You're okay," Asher said. I glanced at her in the mirror. She looked lost.

"You're okay." Asher must've touched her.

"Don't fucking touch me," she said.

"Don't get out of the car," Asher said, and I locked the doors. Then rolled down her window. I glanced in the mirror; she leaned her face into the wind.

Asher stared at her. After a few minutes she reached into the floor of the car and pulled out one of the energy drinks she purchased at the gas station. She popped it open and took a sip.

"You shouldn't drink that; you need sleep," Asher said to her.

"Do you not see what sleep does to me?" She said and gazed out the window.

"I see it," Asher said. "It's okay when we are near, right? That's what you told me?"

She nodded and held the can up to her lips.

"Don't drink this," Asher said and grabbed it from her slowly. He put it in a cup holder up front and splashed some on me as he fumbled trying to find it. I wiped my hand on the passenger seat.

"Come here," he said and pulled her into him. I knew Asher and Mandie, they loved each other. But he never was like this with Mandie, calm and quiet. Him and Mandie would be screaming at each other right now. He was different with Jackie. From the second he met her, he was soft and kind or joking. They were very close to each other. She leaned into his chest. He put his arms around her. "I have you." I couldn't explain it. They didn't sleep together nor seemed to want to. Asher didn't have a problem sleeping around, so that wasn't the problem. Mandie hated Jackie and so did Linda. I didn't like Jackie at first, but she had grown on me. Mandie though, she should hate Jackie and would if she saw something like this happen. There was something between those two. Asher leaned his cheek to her head.

He whispered something to her. I flipped on the radio; it was better I didn't know.

20

"There he is," I said to Mac and Asher as a well-dressed man stepped out of a Tesla SUV passenger seat.

"Are you sure you want to go in alone?" Asher said.

"Yes, he knows I work in a team. He'll know you're around. Trust is his number one concern." I took the radio off and turned on the listener on the phone I would carry into the meeting. Mac and Asher could listen in, but not talk to me. "Setting to listen only." I got out of the car and walked toward him. He was outside the restaurant talking to someone. This was "his" restaurant; he acted like he owned it. I put on a big smile and headed straight for him.

"Well, well..." he said as I got near. "If it isn't a blast from the past."

"Good to see you," I pushed my smile into my eyes. I held out my hand as I got near. He shook it as he swung to put his arm around me and to guide me into the restaurant.

"I am surprised to see you," he said as we got to the archway leading us into the back of the restaurant. I smiled back at him. "You understand," he nodded to his guards who frisked me. I held out my arms in compliance with their search. When they finished, they pulled my phone from my hand, and I let it go with them.

"Tell me, how did you get out of all that shit you were in? I need your secrets," he held a chair for me at a table that would put my back to the doorway. Not the best place for me to be sitting.

"Let's just say the right skeletons on the right people can work wonders," I watched him circle the table to his side.

"Are you here for more business?" he situated himself directly across from me.

I smiled, "I have had to remove myself from direct frontline work, but I made an exception for this." I leaned forward and rested my forearms on the table on the table. "We had a shipment problem that I'm trying to resolve." I matched his eyes to impart the seriousness of the situation.

"I haven't moved anything for you lately." He looked down at me from his perch across the table.

"I imagine you think that." I nodded, looked off and brought my attention back to him as I leaned back to sitting straight up. "I was supposed to receive a shipment last night and somewhere between you and me it's um..." I paused and looked up and turned back to him, "Taken a turn," I said. I reached out and grabbed a cigar out of the box on his table. "Of course, as expected." I prepared the cigar, "your job went flawlessly. I am trying to figure out where the breakdown happened. Since my team is trying to hide their fuck up, they haven't even admitted to it. They obviously don't know how deep are the tabs I keep on them." I finished talking and concentrated on the cigar. Finally lighting it and leaning back into the chair. I pretended that shipment that just went through Alabama was mine. It was a big bluff, but I think I could play it off.

"Hmm..." he said, steepling his fingers and pursing his lips. "That's a good story, sounds like your problem though, not mine."

"You're right, it is." I leaned forward. "You and I both know we have more coming, and something tells me you have fail-safes in place for this. Like the ones you put in the YETI coolers in our last package from you." I found a GPS in the YETI cooler from my shipment of explosives.

Christian leaned back and stared at me, trying to figure out the up and downside of dealing with me. I believe he trusted me, mostly. I was arrested and didn't dime him out. We sat there staring at each other. I knew Christian; he was trying to weigh out the risks of believing me, of helping me, and he had to maintain an upper hand. It was very possible that I was on the far end of the shipment he brought in.

"If we had something like that, it would be very expensive. I don't know if you, Ms. Colby James, could afford it, if we did." He puffed on his cigar.

"You underestimate me. What's the price?"

He lifted his eyebrows. "You."

I smiled. "What from me?"

"You, you are the price. There are many people that would pay to have your information, who you are, where you are, what you are up to, and the like."

"Oh, really." I wasn't sure what he meant by that. I guessed that Colby was a suitable target for many people. Also, if I was a part of that shipment I wanted information on, he could sell me out too. He didn't know I was an agent and Colby was behind me. Before I could respond, he chimed back in.

"It doesn't matter, anyway; we don't have that information."

He was stalling. He could weigh these decisions for days. I took a puff of the cigar and set it down in the ash tray and looked out the window.

"Maybe I overestimated you." I played against his ego. Christian didn't know how much time Jason spent studying him before we ever approached him. I kept my eyes out the window, at the palm trees and the breeze fluttered their leaves. I turned back to him and smiled. "It really is good to see you," I stood up.

"Good luck, Colby," he said, but it felt like a warning.

I walked away, then turned back. "Can I get my phone, please?"

"Of course," Christian said as he waved one his attendants to him. He whispered in his ear as I turned my eyes back to the palm tree outside. I tried to catch the movement of the world around me in my periphery. I didn't want to look around too much inside; it would put Christian on edge.

After about five minutes, his attendant came back with a phone, but it wasn't mine. He handed it to me, and I went with it, anyway. I nodded gently with a soft smile to Christian as I walked away.

I walked to the car and tried to get into my new phone, but the screen was locked. I got in the car and drove away. I needed to ditch the car and head back to our rally point. My team would freak out because we had zero comms while I was in there. Hopefully, they saw me leave.

I waited at the bus stop rally point for five minutes and got antsy; something was wrong. If the team knew I left the building when I did, no way they would leave me standing here for this long. I walked away toward a small grocery store. I got inside and got a glimpse of Mac in the back of the store. I walked toward the back, and he avoided me. He knew something I didn't know. I headed toward the back and pulled the phone out. If Christian tracked me, this was how.

I took the phone apart but kept it. I had a feeling the tracking software for the shipment was on this phone. The fact we were being followed and compromised meant that this phone was being tracked by Christian.

A man greeted me near the storeroom door. I recognized the tattoo on his neck and jammed him in the throat hard with my hand and spun and got the side of his knee. He fell to the ground.

I went back into the storeroom and out the back of the store. We would have to fall back to our back-up spot. I ran out the back and around the block.

Then I headed toward Walmart a few blocks away. I walked through the parking lot looking for an excellent target. I found a woman who struggled with her kids and a cart full of groceries. I grabbed her cart as it was rolling away, "Oh, let me help you. My kids make the store impossible," I said to her.

"Mine too," she said as she struggled to get one of them into their car seat.

"Mine are five and three. Anyone who says the twos are terrible didn't have their two-year-old turn three," I said put her groceries in the trunk. I needed to gain her trust and a made-up kid would do just the trick. She continued the kid wrangling into the car seats. "How old are yours?"

"Six and two," she said, standing back up and closing the door. "Thank you so much for helping, really," she said, turning to me.

"Well, that's it," I said and pushed the cart away to the cart coral. I stopped and turned around. "This is going to be a strange question." I looked at the bus stop and back at her. "I just took the bus over here, and they don't have this thing we need. Is there any way I can hitch a ride to the other Walmart across town?" I reached into my pocket, "I got..." I hoped I would pull out a small bill. "Five dollars," I pulled one out of my pocket. "It's going to save me a lot of time on the bus."

She stood there a few seconds outside her car; she looked at her kids then looked up at me, "Sure."

"Oh, my God, thank you!" I said to her.

All my practice with Lars, my lover from long ago, paid off. I had great stories about my non-existent kids we shared and complained about on the ride over. We talked about the struggle of keeping food on the table or even dealing with kids after working all day. Then of course their fathers, who were no help. When we pulled up, I pulled out the five dollars I had promised her.

"Keep it," she said. She might have thought she had just found a good friend.

"Thank you." I got out of the car and headed toward Walmart.

I was still about a mile from our back-up rally point, but it was way closer than I was across town. I took a crazy route in and out of a neighborhood to make sure I didn't have a tail. I was fairly confident I was clear. I walked up to the gas station, and a car pulled up; it was Asher. I jumped in. We drove that car across town and ditched it; Mac picked us up over there.

Mac was immediate with questions, "What the hell happened?"

"This phone happened," I said as I pulled out one of its pieces.

"That's not the phone you went in with," Asher said.

"I know." I looked down at it; and I was sure of it now. "I asked Christian for the tracker information. He said he didn't have a tracker on that shipment. Then said he would give it if he sold me out. I agreed; he denied he had it again, then I got handed this phone. It's on this phone, the information, but it also will sell me out. The shipment has an active tracker on it, and this phone has that location. It comes with a hefty price though, my location and whatever they know about me and can find about me to the highest bidder."

"He said that to you?" Mac asked.

"Kind of. I studied him before I ever met him. It's how he operates," I said. Mac and Asher were skeptical and exchanged glances with each other. "I'm breaching trust, and he has to exert control over that breach." I looked up at them and put the phone back in my pocket. "His actions also told me he was offered a lot of money for information about me, enough that he didn't even allow a counter from me." That told me Christian had already been offered that money by someone. Whoever it was must be looking for me already.

"Well, aren't you going to turn it on and tell us where it is?" Mac asked.

"I have to hack in; it's locked. We have to respond immediately to the location. It could be anywhere in the U.S. at this point. We need a nationwide coordinated event and a sea of hackers and defenders to get into this phone safely and stop the bomb. Not to mention, he is going to sell the location of the phone to whoever is looking for my information, and he knows we are in Miami now. We need to go somewhere else." I also knew that if I spent too long looking into the phone, they might remove the tracker from the shipment.

"How do you even know he knows where the dirty bomb materials are located?" Asher said.

"He put a tracker on the explosives I bought from him; I found that tracker. He confirmed in his way he did the same for this shipment. As long as it is near the container he shipped it in, we have the location. Or at least know it was once in that location, which is closer than we are now."

"What now?" Asher asked.

"Why are you asking me? Mac's in charge," I said back to him.

"Um, because you have been calling all the shots the last few days," Asher said.

"We need to check in with CJ," Mac said.

"Not in Miami, we don't know who's in Christian's pocket down here," I said.

"Back to Boston then," Mac said.

21

BACK IN BOSTON WE debriefed the team on the materials. While we waited for the next steps, I checked in on the interrogations as CJ processed all the intel we dropped off. "Has he gotten anything from them?" I asked Lee as I peered through the two-way glass. Aaron was talking to one of the two guys, Anchor or Hansen. I hadn't bothered to learn which one was which while I was down in Alabama and Florida. Aaron had a notebook open on the table.

"Yep," Lee said. "He's great at that... never really seen it like that before."

I watched him, his mannerisms and intent, and I recognized it. I didn't like it. It reminded me of his interrogation of me. It put me back in that place when the only thing in the world I wanted was for him to believe me and to get out of that room with him. It made my stomach catch on fire. It was a burning and yearning to know what he was thinking, but it was not good. It's like knowing you shouldn't take that pill or smoke that cigarette but wanting to all the same. I wanted to watch him work when I was not the person he was interrogating, but I knew it would trigger some PTSD from his interrogation of me. It was a strange pull toward an interrogation, back to the beginning. I felt like I could almost start over with him. Lee reached over to the box to allow us to hear and clicked it on. I put my hand on his and clicked right back off. "I know he is good at that," I said as my eyes drifted from Aaron to Lee, and he slowly understood. Aaron was not something I needed to explore.

CJ put things quickly into motion. He took the intel we got and organized a nationwide joint-agency effort, with the help of headquarters. The culmination of years of chasing the Iranian militia's plan to get a dirty bomb into the U.S. suddenly kicked into high-gear when we confirmed the materials made it into the U.S. and we had a lead on a location. We went from intelligence collection to action. People packed into the conference room. Besides our team, there was another team, a pile of suits, and some analysts. The chairs around the table were full, and people lined the walls two deep. One of the suits, probably who was in charge of this office, got up. "Alright, do we have headquarters on the line?" We lined up against one wall.

Behind us was a video screen and tiny boxes of video feeds from offices all over the country. "You have headquarters," someone said from one of the video boxes.

"I'm going to hand off to Special Agent Jones to get us up to speed on what we're dealing with."

CJ stood up; he was rarely called by his title and name, at least not by any of us. "As many of you know we've been tracing the movement of a dirty bomb into the U.S. under a credible yet not specific threat to the U.S. by multiple sources." CJ pointed to one analyst indicating he should bring up the slides.

"We have credible sources that show the material has in fact entered the U.S. by way of a cartel and transferred into unknown custody Monday night, a few days ago." The slides flipped over to show the pictures we got of our cop friend. "You should all have in your inboxes pictures of the truck and the individuals involved. They are hard to see, I know, but the plate number is readable. A bulletin is out as a be on the lookout or BOLO on it. The criticality of this threat has become imminent yet not specific. Given the nature of this group, they will move quickly knowing we are close behind and they don't want the materials seized before they can use it."

CJ waited a few moments while people looked through the pictures and the handouts in the room. "Now to the reason we are all here today. We have a credible lead on how to find the materials, but once we open the window, we expect to have ten minutes or fewer to confirm the location, and it could be anywhere in the U.S. I will now transfer to the FBI Special Agent in Charge Reynolds.

Reynolds stepped in, "We need to prepare all locations to be on standby across all major cities. We know based on other intelligence the most likely places for this bomb include the following cities...Washington, DC, New York City, Chicago, Houston, and LA. Because of the potential danger, we are not excluding other major cities, but we will focus resources on those. We will need coordination with Local LEOs, I mean local law enforcement officers, other federal agencies, the works. Due to the source of the information, the DEA will take lead on the initial window while we confirm the location, then we will transfer control to the FBI. We are looking at opening the window around two pm, eastern standard time. Please note, no one is to engage the suspects or materials without the express permission from the FBI. We will be in close coordination with the ATF throughout the operation; we have also activated U.S. Army Explosive Ordinance Disposal teams. We don't know what state of the materials and will rely on the ATF, U.S. Army, and our local bomb experts as we zero in on the materials." ATF is the Bureau of Alcohol, Tobacco, Firearms and Explosives.

The director of the DEA, Ret. Admiral Holmes, cut in, "I want to first applaud Special Agent Jones and his all-star team for the top-notch work on this. I want to express that for your reference we have been coordinating with the President, other agencies, the military, and National Guard. As the DEA, we are going to help find the bomb, beyond that we are going to be at the direction of the

FBI. The FBI has sent out instructions to each agency and will be in coordination for when we kick this off later today."

The big op briefing wrapped up, and the room cleared out. CJ pulled us into a huddle room to cover our role in the operation about four hours from now.

"Jackie, Mac, and Asher, nice job in Alabama and Florida," CJ said to us sitting around the table. I shot a look at Asher. "Mac has advised me not to ask questions about what happened. Showing he was not comfortable with what he saw. So, I am going to take that as, Jackie, we need to talk later." He pointed at me.

"I like the not asking questions idea better," I said in response.

"Chief Steiner has an update for us," CJ said, turning to look at him.

"Not for the larger group?" Mac asked.

"That was a nationwide call, and this is more sensitive," Chief Steiner said. "We have been going through what we found with Hansen and Anchor and specifically the files. We have confirmed the source. It appears it relates to the big OPM hack a few years ago. It was all data previously disclosed to the government and stolen in the hack." The Office of Personnel Management managed all files on government personnel including the highly sensitive materials related to security clearances that transferred between agencies. It meant they had all the intimate details of all the people who held a security clearance in the U.S.

"Fuck, they have our data then," Doc said.

"Probably," Chief Steiner said.

"Aaron has a significant update too," Lee said, patting Aaron on the shoulder.

Aaron leaned forward. "Hansen first let out, and then Anchor confirmed, Ashenhurst is their contact. He calls all the shots. He runs the blackmailing operation." All the compromised cabinet members and Iranian militia exerted influence went through Ashenhurst. He was the one running it.

The news floored me. I completely missed that the first time around. The reason Ashenhurst knew who was being blackmailed was because he was the one doing it. He could take them all out himself. The reason Ashenhurst was paranoid and my bombing made him stop all his operations and clean house, is because he was the one doing it. The buck stopped with him. He wasn't some guy with influence that could change things; he was the problem. I didn't see it the first time around. I knew I could use him; I didn't know he was the one who created the entire problem. I leaned back and rested my head on the back of the chair and looked up. I fucked that up. I got lost in analysis of materials. I did that all on my own. I missed it. I also missed whatever Aaron said next. I had to pull myself back into the now mentally.

Chief Steiner commented, "That has to be enough to bring around the DIA director."

"They have not let loose if there are more outside the DIA director who are still under his influence. I will keep pressing though," Aaron said.

I bit my lip. I was waiting for the comment on how much I fucked up my first mission. I should have taken Ashenhurst out after he worked with the President and removed all the compromised cabinet members. I didn't even realize he was in on the blackmailing and working for the Iranian militia the first time around. No one commented; maybe they missed it.

"What's our role in the open window?" Mac asked, changing the subject to the upcoming operation.

"Jackie is taking point on the phone. Asher is going to back her up," CJ said.

"What about the rest of us?" Mac asked. He was anxious and wanted in on the action.

"Well, I'm going to be calling the shots for the open window before handing it over to the FBI..."

Lee cut off CJ.

"We want out in the field," Lee said. All the guys I ever worked with wanted to be boots on the ground, guns out, in the big events. No one wanted to be in a command center. You felt helpless in a command center. The reason these guys went special operations or ranger is that they wanted to be out where the action happened.

"Alright, we will get you guys out," CJ said while pointing to Lee, Mac, and Doc. "Aaron, what do you have left with those two?"

Aaron sat up, "I need to nail down Ashenhurst, get some solid irrefutable evidence, not just hearsay. I want to pull back that connection to Iran and the hack with the OPM, or at least their source for those documents. That's just where I want to start, I'm sure there is a lot more to unpack with them. Maybe figure a way to pull around the director. Also, we really need to find out if they know if anyone else is on the blackmail list."

I couldn't help but wonder what this room looked like while I was being interrogated. What were the goals they had for my interrogation? What did they hope to get out of me or what did Aaron say he wanted out of me? I know what Chin wanted; he was clear. He wanted to know who was behind the bombing, who I took orders from. He also wanted to capture Jason and Crystal—the only two members of my fortitude team that the FBI had not captured or killed since the bombing. Furi was in jail and awaiting trial. Dan was dead.

"Aaron, I want you to keep at those two. They are talking; we should soak it in," CJ said.

"I'll stay," Aaron said.

CJ nodded, "Let's get on it."

I needed air before I started, real air outside. "Jackie, stay back," CJ said to me as I got to the door. *Fuck*. I thought he was waiting to talk to me after the mission. I turned and went back to sit in a chair across from CJ. Asher patted my shoulder on his way out and closed the door behind him.

"You alright?" CJ asked.

"Yeah, why?" I said, skeptical of such a question.

"The guys said you didn't sleep the whole time you were down there." I was getting really annoyed with them telling CJ what I was doing and thinking. I don't know if they were just giving it to him or if he was asking. It didn't matter either way. I didn't like it.

"It's fine...I'm fine," I said. "I just got my head spinning on everything," I said, looking down at my hands on the table.

"Jackie." He waited for my eyes to float up to his. "You did good work."

"We'll see if I'm right about the phone." I had a good feeling that Christian gave me the tracking information, but if I was wrong, my intel just mobilized many people across the country for bogus intelligence.

"Not that..."

I looked at him confused.

"Ashenhurst," he said to me.

I already turned my focus to the phone; I had let Ashenhurst slip my mind. I shook my head. "I missed that." I bit my lip. "Fuck," I said under my breath.

CJ waited a second then started, "I don't agree with your tactics, but what you did, it worked. Honestly, you did almost all of that alone. Anyone could have missed it."

"If that was true, why did it work?" I said, now confused on how I could pull that off missing such an important piece of information.

"He knew who they were and wasn't making a move. You knew that. He wasn't making a move because he was the one blackmailing them all. He was terrified they would figure out it was him. Which is why when he thought one of them moved against him, he got rid of all of them."

I didn't have the processing power to handle the fuck up of the past at this moment. My mind turned over the information I had on Ashenhurst and missed the detail of him being the blackmailer.

"The phone, Jackie, I need you focused on that," CJ commanded. "Get ready." He had a way of being definitive.

"I got it," I responded as I turned to get out of my chair.

"Jack, look at me." I turned back to him and leaned forward. He was gazing at me. "Any fractured reality today?"

I shook my head no and scrunched my brow. Why was he suddenly asking that? "I'm good CJ, I'm ready." CJ nodded, and I continued, "You've never done this to me before, so why now?"

CJ looked around the room for his words. "You've had a rough go lately, and I need you at one hundred percent." He paused. He was throwing away sentences, I could see it. "The guys said you haven't slept in a few days. You're leading a nationwide op today, and I need to know what is coming out of your mouth is from reality—not something that is going on up there," he pointed to my head. "I believe in you, Jackie; this will all be good. You are going to do great! We are going to find these materials before they are a bomb, and it will be because of your work."

"Thanks," I said and stood up.

"I need you to do one thing before we start," CJ said.

After I grabbed some air outside, I came back in and saw Aaron coming out of the restroom. "Got a second before you go back in?" I said to him.

"Sure," he said, turning and coming in my directions. We stepped into someone's empty office. "What's up?" he asked.

Once again CJ was putting me in a supremely awkward position with Aaron. "Feel good to be the torturer and not the tortured?" I asked to break the ice.

His eyes softened, and he gave a slight smile. "They weren't tough like you. Started talking pretty easy."

In that moment, I realized I missed my friend. I looked away from him and then back. "Thanks for believing me and joining the team."

He nodded, and he was holding something back. He chose me, I said to myself. He's alive, he's fine.

"Is that it?" he said.

I gave a half smile and said, "Yep." CJ wanted me to make sure I registered that with each team member before the start of the op. If things got heated, he wanted to make sure I could at least trust the team.

He reached out and put his hand on my shoulder, stopped a second, then wrapped me into a hug. "Jackie, I'm sorry I didn't join your team sooner."

I put my arms around him but only for a second. It was something I needed to hear, but I couldn't feel it, not today.

I pulled back. "Don't kill them on accident, Aaron, we know you do that sometimes," I said jokingly.

He didn't like it. "Hey, I will come see you in action when it starts."

I smiled and gave him a little push as I left the room.

I walked into the hallway and bumped into Doc; his shoulder hit me hard. "Hey." He ignored me and continued down the hall.

I turned and followed, "Doc, what was that?" He didn't respond.

I picked up the pace, "Doc," I called louder this time, and he still ignored me. "Doc!" I said and grabbed him.

"Fuck off." He stopped, and I came long aside him. He stared down at me and then leaned into my space. "I just want this shit over and then they can do whatever it is they are going to do with you."

His behavior shocked me; I didn't know Doc had a problem with me still. He didn't trust me and didn't care why I did a bombing; he didn't agree with it.

"I heard about all that shady shit you were involved in; it's clear you are not someone I need around me."

"Doc, we are on the same team."

"Yeah, now that it's convenient for you," Doc scoffed. "Do me a favor and lay off this 'we are friends' demeanor, Jackie. I will do what CJ says and deal with you until it's over, but other than that, stay the fuck away from me." He rolled his eyes and walked away.

22

I SET UP IN the operations center; my screen would be broadcast live. I had a team of cyber defenders and hackers to help us protect and attack the other end of whatever would be coming after this phone. "When we open this up, our location needs to bounce around the world. We need to defend this phone and its location. If it looks like a threat, shut it down. That takes precedence over breaking back into their system until we get the location of the bomb. Then find them, throw it all at them," I said to them. They already had a pre-brief, I needed to be sure we were on the same page.

"I will get us into the phone. Once we do, we need to find the app or website or whatever will tell us the location. I have increased the processing power of this phone by connecting it to this computer which should support us." I looked around and everyone nodded. They had been loading things up and preparing for this. "We will probably get less than ten minutes; we will have to be vigilant and fast. Do last checks to be sure you are ready, and we will give a green-light to command." Everyone nodded and turned back around to their computers.

I looked at my toolset. I had stack ranked them based on the device and based on Christian and what we had hit with the cartel in the past. I felt ready; I was ready. I looked over at the phone and wires I had coming out of it. It looked like a patient on life support.

"Asher," I said to call him back from talking to a cute agent. "Focus, please." He flashed a smile back at her as she left.

"Maybe that's how I focus," he said, raising his eyebrows.

I rolled my eyes, "You have all the fun."

"Don't be jealous, Jackie," he said, walked up next to me and bumped into me.

"You know me…" I said and stopped when I saw CJ headed our way.

CJ walked up, "You guys all set?"

"Just waiting for last checks to come in," I said, checking that my apps were up and ready.

"We are at about twenty minutes out," CJ said. "Pulling things in from around the country."

I decided to get my last bathroom break in and coffee before the operation started. I went to the breakroom and got a crappy cup of coffee. Dear God, grant me the serenity to accept the things I cannot change, the courage to change the things I can and the wisdom to know the difference. I felt the need to connect to what really gave me solid footing. I saw a metal folding chair in the breakroom and decided it was exactly what I needed—metal chair moment. I dragged it into the operations room with my coffee. I pushed my rolling chair out of the way and sat it down.

"Everyone's ready," Asher said.

"CJ, we're ready," I said to him. He nodded as he talked into a phone he had already up to his ear.

"Alright, folks, bring up the national line," CJ commanded.

The call where all the events would be called out came up and beeped loudly. "FBI, DEA Boston is ready," an operator said over the line. "FBI is ready to go," was called back over the line.

I looked at CJ and he said to me, "Ericcson, let's do this." I nodded, and Asher turned the phone on.

The lights flashed on it. It was an old phone. We all watched as the phone took its sweet time cycling through its start sequence. "Get us our location lock," I said to one our defenders before it finished its boot sequence.

The phone needed a 4-digit pin. I loaded my first brute force hack and bit my lip. Sometimes waiting is all you could do. It crashed. *Fuck*. I pushed the next one.

"We have hijacked the location; it's bouncing around the world," said the defender.

The phone unlocked, "We're in, go!" I said to the team that was supposed to help me find the location of the bomb somewhere on this phone. I searched for hidden files and services.

A text came in. I opened it, a link. I didn't click on it because links are easy ways to transfer malware and viruses. I transferred the link to a secure system to isolate anything dangerous. The link went out to a GPS tracking software; the link required a username and password.

Asher called over his shoulder, "Can we contact the company and also push for an emergency warrant?"

Someone called back, "On it."

I scrolled down my lists of hacks and picked one pre-baked easy password hack. No need to get fancy, Occam's razor and everything. I hit execute on it, and the site locked up almost immediately. That wouldn't work. Fuck. I sent the link to a different system to try something new and tried another simple hack, same thing happened again.

Another text came in, "Must use the phone." If I stayed on the phone, it would mean I was with the phone, which is what was needed if he sold me out. Then whoever bought my information would get the complete picture on me and my location.

Asher pointed to one of the team, "Find out where these text messages are coming from."

I took a deep breath, Christian and I had some level of trust, or he wouldn't have given me this phone. Would he have me go this far and destroy the phone? I took a big breath and then clicked on the link in the text, bringing the GPS tracking software website up on the phone. I also didn't think them knowing my location could be that dangerous.

Another text came in "Username: ColbyJames2."

My eyes went wide. I looked over at Asher, and we locked eyes. Christian used my real name, and dozens of federal agents were watching. I plugged it into the browser that opened on the phone. I loaded a new hack through the phone and let it run.

New text: "The deal Colby, you tell me where you are, and I tell you where it is." He would not give away the location of his shipment without making sure I was exposed. We didn't even know if the dirty bomb materials were still in the shipping container the cartel used. We were just hoping they were, or at least the container was near the people that received the shipment. The other potential issue was that if I did what he said, there was a remote chance that I unintentionally would trigger the bomb with the information he gave me. Then this would be my fault. I am Colby James the Boston bomber after all, and what a perfect way to screw me over and get what they wanted at the same time.

I looked over my shoulder at CJ. I did not like my name being broadcast like it was right now. I was Ericcson to everyone here, and my original name was messing with me. CJ did not give away anything with his face, a phone to his ear.

"Can we confirm the phone has been isolated on the network?" Asher called out.

"Confirmed. It has its own."

"Let's drop the masking to one location in Columbus, Ohio," Asher called out to the defender. He picked a random city and hoped it would trick whoever was on the other end of the phone.

"Updated," he called back.

My system trying to hack the site crashed. I switched to another machine.

New text: "Nice try..."

"Any update on the sender?" Asher said.

"Negative."

I decided that the risk was worth it, and I had to find this material. We were on a clock now, and the longer we waited the closer that dirty bomb material was to exploding and spreading its radiation materials.

"CJ, I gotta go outside with the phone put it on an actual cell network," I said to him waiting for permission. I couldn't be in a government office when I opened my location. Christian did not know I was government. If he saw I was in a government location, he would block the information. The phone needed to be on a regular cell phone network.

"It might get you killed," Asher said quietly behind me. We all knew that Christian demanded my head as a price for the location. If whoever he sold it to had my location, they might try to kill me. If it was the Iranian militia, especially, they would love to know the location of someone who dropped into their operation. Christian probably gave them everything else he knew about me. Even if where I was right now wasn't where they could reach me, they knew where I would be and could set up a trap.

"I know," I said back to him.

"Asher, Aaron, suit up, go with Ericcson, we will have a car ready for you downstairs," CJ called out. Aaron had been watching from the side. He put down his coffee and ran out of the room.

"Shut it down," I said as I picked up the phone and its attached laptop and shoved it into a bag. Aaron came back in with gear for me and Asher, handed us bullet-proof vests, radios, and weapons, and we headed to the elevator.

"Do we really want to be so obvious we are DEA right now, when we are about to expose our location?" Aaron said. He was nervous with what Christian would do with our location too. It made sense, but we would have to expose ourselves to find the materials. I was more worried he was tricking us into setting off the bomb.

"It's fine, he's in Miami," I said, psyching myself up. We were in Boston, far from him. People like Christian had reach and who knows who he sold my information to, I had to push that to the side and focus on the task at hand. We hurriedly put on our gear as we went down the elevator.

"He is, but who is the highest bidder?" Aaron asked. Christian sold my information to someone; they could be anywhere. Given the government corruption that accompanied this investigation, we could expose ourselves to an agency with reach. I picked up the bag that sat at my feet and waited for us to reach ground floor.

There was a black Yukon waiting for us outside the door. We ran and got in, and the driver took off. We needed space away from the building. "Going live in two minutes," I called out using the radios we put on. I watched out the window at all the people on the street going about their lives, blissfully unaware that somewhere in America a city or maybe several cities might have a brutal attack killing hundreds and probably way more depending on what the dirty bomb contained. I needed to focus on that; I could die for a worthy cause like that.

I turned my attention back inward and pulled out the phone and laptop. I checked the comms we were still sending images from my laptop back to the operations room.

"Thirty seconds," Asher said over the radio. Then he turned his attention to me, "ready"

I nodded and clicked on the phone again and waited for it to start up.

New text: "Where ru Colby?"

I had to ignore my name, my infamous name, being broadcast to federal agents. I scrolled up in the text exchange and clicked on the link and typed in the username: colbyjames2.

Text: "Welcome back."

I typed a message back: "U can see me now, what's the password?"

Text: "Boston... interesting."

The typing bubbles came up then disappeared... and then again...after a minute a text finally came through, "Remember where you and I got close?"

"Yes," I quickly typed back.

Text: "The first part of the password is that place."

Text: "The second part is who we bonded over."

This was definitely something only Colby would know, maybe Crystal and Jason too. Christian and I jumped Senator Brickman in a park near his house together, that is how I gained Christian's trust. I didn't know how I would explain knowing this. Fuck it. I clicked on the browser and typed in the password.

A map came up with a message and a little spinning globe. "Tracking your shipment." It zoomed in. "Northeast," I called over the radio. The cartel seemed to use trackers on shipments covertly. They did it to my shipment from them, and the hope is that they did it this time. We hope that the materials were still in the packaging the Cartel used to transport them, and therefore still had a tracker. If not to the materials, to give us new information about where they were last and maybe who had them. "New England... Massachusetts... Boston... West Boston... Fenway area." The little spinning globe froze.

Aaron turned to the driver, "Turn the car; take us to Fenway."

"Browser is frozen," I called out. I tried to open another tab in the browser. The phone was legitimately frozen. I was expecting too much from it. I unplugged all the cables, freeing them from the computer. I closed all the apps but the browser and waited.

The map updated again, "Parking lot between Boylston and Van Ness," I said over the radio as I switched back to the laptop. "USPS sorting facility off Ross Way," I said as I got dizzy and had a hard time breathing.

"Aaron." I turned off my mic. He turned around. "That's across from Van Ness garage," I said as terror coursed through my veins.

I turned to Asher, "It's a trap. I'm being set up."

"Why do you think that?" Asher said.

"It's uh…" I froze, I couldn't say the words.

Aaron jumped in, "Boston bombers used the same staging location."

"Christian figured out I tried to trick him, and he sold the information back to the Iranian he actually worked with on the shipment," I said, and no one acknowledged it. If he sold it back to the Iranian militia, that meant they knew I was coming, assuming they didn't figure out I was government. They also could have set me up to make it look like I was behind the shipment of the dirty bomb, why else put it so close to the staging location of my own bomb staging location.

CJ radioed, "Local LEOs are almost on site. The whole team is enroute."

The sirens on our vehicle were loud, and our driver cruised through the roads out toward Fenway. *Should I call it off?*

"Local LEOs have identified the truck with matching license plate," an operator said over the line.

It's too late. I turned on my mic again, "Shutting down the phone," I said back. I took it all apart and put it and the computer back in the bag and tossed it into the back of the Yukon.

"This is Special Agent Reynolds; the FBI has taken control of this operation."

As we barreled toward the USPS lot where the truck that had materials was located, I could feel panic creep into my bones.

Aaron turned around again to meet my eyes, "maybe they are just trying to make us think it's the truck, but they really are doing exactly… ya know… maybe it's in the garage." He understood me. I staged my bombs for the Boston bombing in that same garage across the street from that parking lot. If they wanted me to take the fall for the materials coming into the country, why not put them in a place I had used before.

"If it's a set-up, that would make sense," Asher said. If they knew I was after the material, they could get it pinned to me if they could get me to go to the same location. It made even more sense that they chose a location I had used in the past. So even if the materials aren't there, people will suspect they were linked to me or at least linked to Colby James. Then they would go looking for Colby James and found she dropped off the face of the earth. Then my cover as Jackie Ericcson would be blown.

We all switched our radios to the team line. We were going to clear the garage and needed a clean line without other chatter. Asher started, "We want to search the garage across the street, let's rally by the building and clear it together. If they are copying the Boston bombers, the van is in the garage, not in the parking lot," Asher said it all for me. It was still all messing with my head. I was being called Colby, in public, in front of federal law enforcement, and no one was blinking, not yet anyway. Now they were copying my modus operandi. If anyone made the connection that I was actually Colby James and that the materials are staged in the same place I staged my materials, then I would be blamed for transporting these materials. I didn't think the materials were there anymore, I was being set up. Christian just made it seem like we were following the materials, they weren't there. It was making me sick. I put my hand over my face and took some deep breaths. I was terrified of what it might mean. I was being set up, and I was being driven right to the scene. I felt my unhealed mental fracture ache; I knew I was losing reality.

"Ash, they are setting me up; we shouldn't go," I said, desperate to stop the chain of events. Asher had to do it; it couldn't be me. CJ would know my mind fractured again. "I shouldn't go. They are luring me there to blame this on me, or to die, or something else." I also thought if they got me to go there and they killed me, they killed two birds with one stone. They blamed me and got rid of me.

"Jack, it's alright, they don't know you brought the entire U.S. government with you." Asher reached out and grabbed my arm.

Aaron turned around and looked at me from the front seat of the Yukon, "Look at me, Jackie." I did. He was worried. "We chose you," he said. Our driver had the lights on and was driving furiously, but few cars were getting out of our way. "We aren't taking you into a trap."

I smiled, my affirmation. CJ must've told him; it calmed me.

"We have no better source having you," Aaron said reassuringly. He implied that if they copied me, then I knew better than anyone what they were copying.

I nodded. "Take us to Van Ness and Kilmanok. We can enter the garage there," I said to the driver, while keeping my eyes locked on Aaron. I took my M-4 and strapped it over my shoulder now that my laptop was out of the way.

"Van Ness and Kilmanok," Asher repeated over the radio to the rest of the team.

23

When we pulled up to Van Ness and Kilmanok, the rest of the team was already there. I got out and ran straight toward the door that would take us down to the garage. We stacked outside the door.

I called out to everyone, "Inside to the left we have two elevator doors, followed by the door to the stairs; straight across enters the building. We want to go past the two elevators to the door on the left and down the stairs, one flight, down to the first door. When you go out that door, the vans will be to the left up near the entrance, but on the other side of the garage. I don't believe there is a line of sight from the door to the vans."

"Everyone ready?" Mac asked. We lined up on both sides of the door to the garage.

Everyone nodded.

Mac entered first, and we flooded in behind him. Lee went for the stairs and we followed him down. Doc looked through the slit of a window from the stairs into the garage, and we lined up to go out again. He pushed the door open, and we spread out around the cars. I pointed toward where my vans were in the garage.

Mac, Doc, Lee, and Ty, the driver from our vehicle, crossed to the other row of cars. Asher, Aaron, and I moved along the wall. As we got toward the end of the row, near the entrance, a white van came into view.

"We have a possible," Mac said over the radio to CJ.

I felt a pit drop in my stomach. They were copying what I did exactly; this was going to be put on me. I couldn't look at the van; what if that is a bomb? I took a knee behind a car. I couldn't breathe. I had to put myself back together. I felt my reality cracking, like when I saw Ross alive outside the prison with Chin. The van, the method was exactly the same as me. *Did I do this?* Maybe I was so cracked out on reality that maybe somewhere in the midst I did order this bombing, or I asked Jason to. I didn't know what to believe anymore. I didn't trust myself in this moment.

I told Ross when he interrogated me after my bombing there were four vans, mine, the one that went off, the one they found, and another. I was messing with him, *wasn't I? Was there another one?* The lines of reality were so blurred. If I did this, *what was I doing on this side?* I slid onto my butt behind the car. I couldn't look over at the van. It was fucking with my reality or bringing it onto me. Either way it was making me sick, and I shook from the confusion.

"Jack," Asher whispered to me from his position behind the car next to me in the parking garage. I opened my eyes and looked at him. "Are you alright?"

It snapped me back out of my mind, which was lost in trying to figure out if I put this in motion. I nodded I was okay. I wasn't though. *Was that one of the bombs my team built that we never got to use? How did I get here; how did it get here?*

Mac and Doc climbed over the small wall between our part of the garage and the van's.

I had a good position, so I trained my weapon on the van from where I was.

"Two males, possibly Caucasian, maybe Middle Eastern," Doc said. "Dodge Promaster, white..." Doc continued to detail the scene over the radio. It was too close; I thought maybe Jason or Crystal would show up based on what was happening because it was the same as my bombing. They were on that team, and they were out and free. They could be the perpetrators behind this. Maybe they hated me so much they were doing this just like our last one, to blame it on me. My heart quivered. *Was Jason putting a deadman's switch around someone else?* Jason was the final steps before I drove the van to its target; he activated the bomb and the deadman's switch.

"I'm going to go up and cross and come back down," Mac said over the radio, quietly. Lee climbed over the wall to take Mac's former position.

They chose me. I had to keep it together.

"Crossed and coming down," Mac said.

The van turned on. "Van is on, potentially moving out of the garage; we need containment," Asher said over the radio. We weren't getting responses from CJ or anyone.

"Jackie, Ty, get us transportation," Mac called out. I glanced at Asher and fell back. It was better I got out of this garage, anyway.

I met Ty at the stairs, and we ran up together. "You wait at this door; I will go over to the garage entrance," I said to Ty.

I jumped in the other Yukon and pulled it up to the corner.

I felt better being out of the garage, not looking at the van that looked like the one I used in my bombing. I was waiting for instructions on the corner outside the garage. Ty was back at the door we had entered. I wanted to know what was happening in that garage. I also could feel I knew what was happening. I remember pulling out with my bomb, the adrenaline of it all. It waned as I drove downtown.

Then a screech over the radio. "They spotted us and are peeling out. The garage needs to be blocked off," Mac called out over the radio.

I ripped around the corner in the Yukon toward the exit. The local police were all still across the street focused on the USPS parking lot, and it didn't seem right. "There aren't any cops at the exit, why aren't they containing the scene?" Gunfire erupted to the left of me. I heard them hit the Yukon. I looked over; it was two cops. "LEOs are firing at us, get them to stop. Friendly fire."

I pulled up and Aaron was on the ground, not moving. I didn't think—I just jumped out and ran down the ramp to him. By the time I got down there, Asher had pulled him up and behind a column. "Take him," Asher said as he threw Aaron's arm over my shoulders. The rest of the guys were climbing into the Yukon between the sporadic gunfire.

"Get the local idiots to stop firing at us!" Mac yelled over the radio.

"We gotta go. Jackie, take him to a hospital—we don't have time," Asher said as he ran for the Yukon.

"Ty, wait there, I'm coming to you," I said over the radio. Aaron slumped when he threw his arm over my shoulder. "Come on, Aaron," I pulled on him. He was walking kinda. "Almost there," I said. Stairs were out of the question; I pushed the elevator button.

I pushed Aaron up against the wall in the elevator, "You alright, Ross?" I hadn't called him that in a while; it just slipped out.

"Yeah," he said.

"Good." We got out of the elevator and out the door. I loaded Aaron into the back of the seats of the Yukon Ty was driving. I pushed him in, and he laid down. I climbed in behind him.

"Beth Israel Hospital is just down the road," Ty said as I climbed in.

I reached in the back and grabbed some clothes that were back there and pressed them into the side of Aaron's stomach as Ty took off. "It's gonna be alright, Ross," I said, trying to sound confident looking into his face and using my name for him.

"We're taking gun fire again, what the hell is going on?" Mac yelled over the radio.

"Wait one," CJ said.

"The van turned down Boylston toward Charles Gate," Lee said. The bomb headed toward downtown Boston.

"Can someone please tell us why some cops are firing at us?" Mac said.

"Colby," CJ finally said. "There is a BOLO out on Colby. They are reporting she is behind this. The team is burned, all DEA has been pulled off. They know Jackie is Colby."

"FUCK!" I screamed and ripped off my DEA hat and ripped the DEA emblem off my vest. I turned my attention back to Aaron. I had to focus on my task, or the fracture in my mind would bleed causing the lines between reality and whatever I thought was mixing and not make sense.

"Do they know we are chasing the bomb?" Lee said.

"They are only after you; they think you seized the opportunity to grab the materials," CJ said from the command center. He was in the middle of it; I imagine some level of chaos in that operation center as me being Colby came out.

Shots rang out, and Ty swerved and slammed us into a parked car. "SHIT! What the FUCK?" I said after slamming into the back of the front seats. Aaron moaned and held his stomach. A few more shots came in, and Ty's head exploded onto the passenger seat.

"Ty's dead, exiting vehicle." I opened the door and got out in between two parked cars. I pulled Aaron out between them.

"Ross, are you hit again?" Calling him Aaron just didn't make sense to me.

"No," he said. He clutched his stomach where he was bleeding.

"We can't shoot back at LEOs, they are friendlies. I will not kill a cop, no way." Asher said over the radio, "What the fuck are we supposed to do?"

I leaned up against one car and pulled Aaron into my lap. I looked down at him, his beautiful eyes and his gorgeous hair. The bullets stopped.

"Go to them," he said.

I shook my head no, "I can't leave you."

He reached up and touched my cheek, "It's okay, Colby." When he used my real name I could feel the tenderness between us.

"I can't leave you; I can't kill you, not again," I pushed down on his stomach with my trembling hand. I thought they killed him in the prison because of my actions and that pain was near unbearable until I found out it was a lie. If I left him this time, he might actually die. I didn't want to feel that again. Lie or not, I broke down when I thought he died. I would break again if he died.

"You never killed me, Colby. I am going to be okay. Go to them; they need you." He assured me I fell for a trick and didn't need to worry about him.

"I need you, Ross," I said as I looked at him and ran my fingers through his hair. I didn't know until that moment how much I needed him. My heart ached for him even though everything else told me he was a traitor. The thought of him dying pushed it all aside.

"You'll never be able to live with yourself if you don't go to them. I know you, Colby, go."

Tears welled up in my eyes. "I can't live with myself if you die again."

Aaron looked up at me from my lap. "I don't deserve your forgiveness; they chose you. You need to choose them."

I leaned down and kissed him.

"I'll be okay," he said. "Go."

"I love you, Ross." I said it out loud for the first time, and it made my heart flutter.

"Your mine, Colby," I kissed him again. "Jackie," he said, "stop doing what Colby would have done and start doing what Jackie would do."

I nodded and laid him down and pushed him under the car in front of me to protect him from the fire I was about to draw. I walked half a day with a gunshot wound, and he is stronger than me. "I'm leaving Aaron here; get him help," I said to CJ. I wiped the tears from my face, but it just meant I wiped his blood across my face. Maybe it was Ty's blood.

24

THE GUNFIRE WAS SPORADIC. I think for even the local cops it was hard to shoot at the DEA agents. Maybe even messed them up blowing Ty's head off. They were probably mostly in pursuit of the rest of the team, not realizing I got left behind. I had to take advantage of the chaos of the situation. The mission changed halfway through, and with so many agencies local and federal involved, I'm certain no information came out right. Orders went sideways. The SUV that sped away from the garage was the most likely target.

I slid around the back of the Yukon, staying low. I clicked open the back but didn't let it open very far. I heard another shot and ducked down. I reached in and pulled out the bag with my laptop and the phone in it. I went behind the car that Aaron was in front of, then bolted for the barbecue restaurant next to us. I ran through it to the back and into the service area. The lock was engaged on the door that connected it to the apartment section of the building. I shot it and went in. There was a West Elm on the other side of the building. I knew the area well from my previous bombing. I headed straight for the store.

"You guys, get a tracker on that van and break contact."

"Aaron already did; that's how he got shot," Asher said.

"CJ, do you have the location?" I asked. I pulled my hair down. I was trying to look like I should be there, the blood probably didn't help. I tried to wipe my hands on my pants.

"Yes, we have it here," CJ said.

"Break contact. They want to blame the bombing on us, me, and if we get away from the city before they get to the target, they won't be able to blame it on us," I said and used my shirt to wipe the blood off my face. "Head north or west," I said as I tried to shove my equipment into the bag and hid my M-4 between the bag and my body.

"CJ, disconnect my laptop from operations?" I asked.

"How do I do that?" he asked back.

"That place where the phone was with all the cables, there is a box there, unplug it and unplug all the wires," I said as I entered the West Elm and plopped the computer on a desk to work.

I pulled out the phone and turned it on. "Christian, I miss you. This was special. Can I make it special for you?" I sent the text.

"It's done," CJ said over the radio.

I turned on the laptop and started my location spoofing program. I programmed it to use driving directions to take me to an airport and then take a common flight to Miami. I connected it to the phone and let the program run. It didn't fool Christian or whoever was on the other end of the phone, but maybe it would fool law enforcement. If they tried to use the phone or laptop to find where I was, I would give them a false trail to follow. Even if they found the phone and laptop, it wouldn't be with me. I couldn't hold on to the laptop and phone; it was too dangerous. I needed a place to stash it to let the program run. I found a large armoire closet with drawers on the inside. I then went around and found a box and I emptied the contents. I put the phone and laptop in it and then put it in the back of the bottom of drawer of the armoire and closed the drawers and doors. This should provide me crucial time to get away. Even if it was only thirty more minutes, even if it's all I got, it was needed.

"We've bailed out, Lee's cruising north out of the city," Doc said over the radio.

"If you guys are free of LEOs, follow the bomb," I said to them.

"Where's the bomb?" Mac said.

"Looks like it's slowed down, pulled on the side of the road," CJ said. "Parking lot, Martha and Charles."

"That location is really close to the last bomb," I said to them as my brain was freed up to think about where it was. It was close to downtown and all the tunnels underneath the main parts of Boston.

I headed out and tried to casually cross the street to a garage that had valet parking. A valet was unloading a car; I jumped in and drove off.

I was hoping our ploy would work. Did we stop them from the bombing because we stopped following them?

"They are setting a blockade for Lee, bail from Twenty-eighth and don't get on Ninety-third," CJ said about the roads leading out of the city.

"I got a bike," Asher said as the scream of a motorcycle came into our ears.

I was going to find out what this car could do. "Three minutes out."

"I have eyes on the actual bomb," Asher said. "They are just sitting in the parking lot."

"Probably awaiting instructions. If they think I'm headed west and the rest of you are headed north, they are losing their scapegoat. Don't expose yourself," I said.

"We're on scene," Mac called over the radio. "And we have eyes on," Doc said.

"The van is moving," Asher said. "East on Martha."

"SHIT, they are going through with it, stop them." That road will take them right under the city, into the heart of it.

Doc cut in, "Asher is in pursuit."

"Turning left on Nashua," Doc called out.

"That's where the underground city tunnels are." I was so close.

"They are out of sight," Asher said.

"West on Twenty-eighth," CJ said. "Moving away from down-town."

I let out a sigh of relief.

"If they continue on that route, they will run into the roadblock intended for Lee," CJ said. "Never mind, they are now heading south on Edwin Boulevard."

"I'm in close pursuit," Asher said.

I pulled up to the parking lot to pick up Doc and Mac. "I'm at the parking lot, red sedan that just screeched in." I saw Mac running in my direction and I jumped over into the passenger seat. Mac and Doc got in.

I pointed, "Cut across that way, over the bridge," I said to Mac. Mac pulled into oncoming traffic because of the one-way road and headed straight across the bridge. I looked at the hand I pointed with, I was covered in blood, Aaron's blood, from pressing into his stomach. I closed my eyes.

"Where now, Jackie?" Mac asked.

"Left at the light and then listen to CJ," I said. I was feeling sick. My crack in reality was no longer healed. The way I felt when I knew my perception was altered in the prison, is how I felt now. I didn't know what was real anymore. I was making judgement calls, but I didn't know how much of it was based on what was actually happening and how much was made up in my head. It made everything so hazy like a dream. God help me. I focused on my gear. I strapped my M-4 back on. I pulled my hair back up. I glimpsed myself in the side mirror. Aaron's fingerprints were on my left cheek. I focused out the front windshield. I didn't have time for anything else. "I'm glad they are headed away," I said.

"Just crossed the river," CJ said, "headed to Mass Ave."

"I got them in sight," Asher said.

"Back off, Asher, you might scare them back into the attack. We have a tracker," CJ said.

"Roger," Asher said.

"They are getting on Ninety West, leaving the city," CJ said.

25

WHEN I WAS IN high school, I went on a mission trip with my mom. "Colby, go through this drawer and take out all the pictures," my mom said to me from behind the mask and goggles that protected us from the mold and other airborne contaminants.

"Mom, we were literally told to throw everything away," I said back to her in protest.

"That man's wife passed away, and he just lost everything in the hurricane. We're going to save the pictures."

It was hot and humid enough, but having to wear long sleeves, pants, boots, mask, goggles, and gloves made it even hotter and a little claustrophobic. I pulled on the drawer, and the handles and front panel pulled off; the soaked plywood was paste. I reached in and pulled out some boxes of pictures and some binders. I piled them up and brought them outside to a table out by the road. The old man who lived in the house was sitting out there. He wasn't able to do the work; that's why the church sent us. I set the pictures on the table and took off my mask.

"I suspect we should dry these out and try to keep them." He covered his mouth, and tears ran down his face. It made me well up too.

"Thank you, Jesus," he stood and hugged me. It made my tears run. "My girl, my baby, I thought she was gone," he carefully pulled apart some photos. "You know her dying was worse than losing every-thing—believe me. You remember that, young lady,"

I smiled at him.

"Oh…" he said, "this is our wedding album." He put his arm around me as he flipped through it. "I'm going to pray for you," he said to me.

"Shouldn't I be praying for you?" I questioned back.

"Honey, we all need prayer," he said, looking down at me. Then he gave me a squeeze as he pulled me into him. "Lord, bless this young lady…" He stopped and looked down at me again, "What's your name, honey?"

"Colby," I said back as he closed his eyes again.

"Lord, bless Colby here. May she value what is good in life and you being the most of those things. Lord, help her value love and goodness. May she know those she loves are precious and should put you and those things above all else. For the mighty hurricane by your hand may take the materials, but those things burn in her. You are most precious of all. In Jesus name, Amen."

I sat on the floor and leaned up against the wall. My knees bent. Aaron's blood soaked into my now dry pants. I couldn't think about it. *How did they figure out I was Colby? Did their trap work? Was I going to be blamed for this?* I leaned my head against the wall and closed my eyes. It all felt so unreal. Not much had felt real since I left the company of Chin, this was just especially unreal. My body wasn't giving me as many signs of being hurt. I felt weak, but on the way back to me. The reminders of life I got from pain were gone.

In that moment, I somehow finally felt I could sleep. Maybe when I woke it would all make sense. *What happened? Why was I set up? By who? Leaving Aaron was so hard. Is he okay?* We didn't stop the bomb or the materials, but it had not been detonated. I had to sleep. I could feel it all over my body; I couldn't fight it anymore.

I jolted awake with a kick to my foot, "Jack?" I looked up to see Doc. My eyes couldn't focus; I rubbed them. "Yeah," I said.

"Did you hear anything we said?" I looked over at the last of us. They were sitting on various things they had found in this abandoned store in this forgotten part of town. I shook my head 'no' as I leaned forward and pushed my feet under me.

I found a five-gallon bucket and flipped it over, dumping its contents, so I could sit near everyone.

"You're covered in blood. Are you okay?" CJ asked.

"If you are asking if the blood is mine, the answer is no. It's Aaron's and Ty's. Am I okay?" I chewed on my lip and shook my head 'no.' "How is Aaron? Did he get picked up?" I asked CJ.

"He's at the hospital. Last I heard he was alive; he made it there alive," CJ said.

"But?" I asked.

"Jack, that's all I know," CJ said, shaking his head.

"The bomb?" Mac said.

"Last I knew, they tracked it to Providence, Rhode Island. Things went sideways with the news of your identity. The FBI couldn't get their arms around the operation. It was chaos. Soon after you all left the area, the FBI finally got their arms around everyone, took over, reeled in the cops, and then took the tracker information from me too. They kicked me out of operations. Kicked all the DEA out. They said a separate investigation would open up for us, but they would continue chasing the dirty bomb materials." CJ said.

"Because of me?" I asked. Everyone looked at me. I knew the answer was yes.

"How do they know?" Asher asked. We all wanted to know how they suddenly found I was Colby. Then a thought snuck into my mind. Christian could have sold me out to anyone or multiple someone's. Maybe the government lies in that chain too.

CJ shrugged his shoulders.

"They didn't know before I was Colby, so how did they find out?" I knew my team chose me, but I didn't want this for them, to be under investigation because of me. My heart became heavy. I knew what was going to happen next. They had to turn me over to whoever was investigating what went wrong on this operation. It was the easiest way to move forward. A tremor worked its way into my lungs, and the thought of torture brought water to my eyes, and my ears rang out in high-pitch.

"Do they all think we are like Colby? That we are all terrorists who perpetrated a bombing? That we would want to do it again, with her?" Doc pointed at me. It hurt, but I deserved it.

"I don't think they suspect anything from me. They are probably on the fence with the rest of you," CJ said, keeping his eyes on me. It made me sick. The fracture in my reality was wide open now turning the world hazy. I could no longer trust my judgment. It all started with that text, "ColbyJames2." I closed my eyes; *was Aaron really hurt? Did my team think I did this? Did CJ just lead the FBI to us, to me?*

I rubbed my face as I stood up and walked away and had to fight an ever-increasing vertigo. One moment I was in the garage with Jason going over the deadman's switch and I blinked I was pulling Aaron out of it. The two realities clashed in my mind. I went to the old counter in the back of the store that probably used to host the cash register; my world spun.

We are in the middle of a shit storm, and you're right in the center. CJ's words screamed through my mind. I leaned forward putting my elbows on the counter and held my head up by putting my forehead in my arms. I rocked forward and back on my feet.

The sleeves of my shirt were covered in Aaron's blood. I hated how much I loved him. I used to think him being dead would straighten my brain out; I wasn't sure now. "God save him," I whispered.

Chin was right, I destroyed everything around me. Chin told me in the prison it was my fault my parents' lives were ruined and that at the time Ross was dead, even though it was fake. He said I destroyed everything around me. That's what I did. My stomach turned over, and again. Nausea climbed up my throat. I went behind the counter and puked. I kneeled down, still holding onto the counter with one hand trying to stop the spinning. Nothing made sense.

Someone pulled me up, toward my feet, and I couldn't hear anything, I hadn't slept in days. The fear of the nightmares was greater than I could face. I didn't feel safe. Now, I would be sent back for more.

Doc slapped me and I was suddenly back in the abandoned store with its faded reddish pink carpet stained with the foot traffic around what most likely was displays.

"I need sleep," I finally said. Everyone had come back to where I was. Doc kept ahold of my arm; it helped with the spinning.

"We need to move anyway," Mac said.

"What's next?" Asher asked.

"We don't know what the depths of the corruption are. We assumed she got out all the other corrupted officials with her bombing and only left the DIA director. But maybe there are more people involved than that. Maybe Ashenhurst has new people on the payroll. Perhaps others who are maybe not at the top of the chain wreaking in the system as well. Jackie helped root out the last group of corrupted officials, and we don't know if there are new ones. We need to figure out what's what before we allow them to detain our team," CJ said. He already determined that before he got here.

"Look, I think they are focused on the bomb. We still have Chief Steiner on the inside. You guys go back to the cabin. We'll go from there," CJ said. He wanted to protect the rest of the team from whatever went wrong. Once he got a better handle on who is who and if there were other corrupt officials to worry about, they would most likely turn me over to whoever. He didn't want the team to get mired by the entire sequence of events too. Them chasing the dirty bomb materials was the perfect distraction. CJ could also go in and talk to

DEA leadership and see if there was another plan of attack to get us out of this situation.

I wanted to see Aaron, be with him in the hospital, by his side as he went through whatever he was going through. The way Jessie was for me after my car accident, the way the team was for me. I knew that was out of the question. Somehow me focusing on anyone but all of us made me feel better.

26

I SLEPT IN THE cargo space of the Suburban all the way back. I woke up as we pulled onto the gravel road. I sat up just in time for us to pass the house with the women who saved me before. Just seeing their house, their flags, I was filled with hope. When I saw the blood soaked into my clothes, that hope ran away. It snapped me out of whatever good feeling I was having from actually sleeping. Dawn peaked when we pulled up to the house. I needed to shower, but I also needed a long run. It had been a few weeks since I was freed from the prison, and a lot had happened since then. If I went for a run this time, it would differ greatly from the first one I did up at this safe house.

The place had been cleaned and put back together like we weren't all living there for the last few weeks. It messed with my mind. I headed straight to the supply closet and got what I needed. It was restocked too. It was unsettling. Maybe it was always like this, what did I know? I couldn't trust my memory. After my shower, I went into the room that was... I guess mine. I couldn't do it. I couldn't sit down in that portal to my nightmares. I went down the stairs to Asher's room. If I was going to sleep more, it would have to be in this room, near Asher. Asher made me feel safe. I knocked softly and cracked the door. Asher was out. I went in and shut the door behind me. I climbed into Aaron's bed and went right to sleep.

I woke up in the late morning and for a moment, just a moment, it was all a dream. It was the second time in a row I had slept without a dream, a new streak. Then it all flooded back. It was growing in me; I knew what I had to do, but I didn't want it to be true. I rolled to my side and looked over to the windows, to Asher who was still asleep. My team chose me, but that choice became destructive. They were now all under investigation for something I did before joining their team. Then whoever set me up in this most recent bombing attempt also put dirt on them too. I snuck out of the room.

By the time CJ got there that night, we were all dying for news. We had all electronics off for safety since we left Boston. I was mostly holed up in my room, keeping my distance from everyone. I heard his voice downstairs, and I put my boots on because I did not know what would happen and headed down. I went straight for the coffee pot and poured a cup and sat down at the table with everyone else.

"They got the bomb; it was materials really. The bomb was very crude; they aren't even sure if it would actually detonate. It appears it was thrown together pretty hastily by people who didn't know what they were doing. Initial speculation is that they jumped the gun because they figured out someone was on their tail, but thank God they abandoned that plan when they thought they got away," CJ said.

"It should've been us," Mac really wanted our mission to culminate in us being the ones arresting people.

"Any news on Lee or Aaron?" Asher asked.

"They're still holding Lee," CJ said mainly to Doc.

"What for?" Doc asked.

CJ looked over at me. I knew he meant me. I could feel all eight eyes on me, CJ, Mac, Asher, and Doc. They were burrowing into me. They were all asking themselves if they made the right choice. They were burning into my soul.

"How did you know it would be Boston?" Mac asked.

"Excuse me?" I said as rage unexpectedly climbed up my throat.

"None of you find it strange she goes in to see that cartel guy ALONE and then has a magic phone and wants to go to Boston of all places?" Mac said. He implied I knew the materials were in Boston and that is why we were in Boston, and that perhaps Christian had told me that in advance. He tried to say I was in on everything that happened in Boston.

Rage pounded in my head. "Go fuck yourself, Mac. You were there for all of it, and we went to Boston because the team was there."

The eight eyes were burning into me again.

"This is..." I stopped and looked up and shook my head. I couldn't tell if my reality fractured or if... did they ever choose me or was I right from the beginning to think that this was always a trick? Or did they choose me and now they were done? I couldn't expose myself to them anymore. "I was set up. Anyone who studied the Boston bombing could've looked at the Wikipedia page and copied it," I said to CJ then looked over at Asher. "I was set up. They wanted me to go there to get my fingerprints on those materials. I don't think they anticipated us finding the actual materials, just the shipping container. They probably didn't expect me to have the government in tow." That is what I said out loud; it was the most likely explanation. Although I didn't know who. I just spent most of the day trying to figure out how and why. "If my fingerprints were on it, it would pull it away from those who actually did it."

No one talked. I could feel my stomach being ripped open as the silence ate at me. They were out of words, but what they weren't saying was loud and clear. They made a mistake and were done. They clearly believed I was involved but didn't know how.

"You guys are the only thing I have left, I would never..." a wave of sadness doused over my anger. I remember when I saw Aaron outside the jail, smoking, fine with Chin. The moment I knew they faked his death. This moment felt like that moment. This time I wasn't weak; I would keep it in. I would not show them or anyone. Hold it in. Anything you do or say will be used by the team to bury you.

CJ broke the silence, "Ericcson, the FBI wants to talk to you."

"How's Aaron?" I needed that answer before I could process what was next.

CJ shrugged his shoulders and shook his head. He didn't know.

"How do we know they aren't corrupted?" I asked.

"We don't, but we also can't hide from the FBI," CJ said definitively. "They have good reason to want to talk to you. That doesn't mean we will stop our mission. We still have to figure out who else the Iranians compromised and what else is planned. We stopped that one shipment; it doesn't mean they don't have more planned. We won't stop working on all of this." The team would turn me over and continue their mission without me.

I nodded to agree and looked down. It was turning on that strength I get when I'm alone. If I was honest, I would say it started with that text from Christian or whoever was on the other side of "ColbyJames2." When I felt my mind fracture, I knew it was a set-up, I knew this was coming. "I guess I can't outrun Colby anymore," I said, meeting CJ's eyes. I looked around at each of them. I'm Colby James. The acknowledgement to myself meant it was time to take responsibility for what I did. "Thanks for, at least for a moment, believing in me," I said to them as I reached out and put my hand on Asher's leg; he was right next to me. "I didn't do this, for what that's worth." I could feel the doubt in the room.

Asher reached down and squeezed my hand and looked away at the same time.

I took a deep breath. "Let's go," I stood up. Someone set me up, and they did a good job, so good that I wasn't sure I wasn't involved. Maybe Crystal and Jason from Fortitude team did it, they had good reason, and they knew me better than anyone else. Crystal and Jason showed they never wanted to deal with me again the last time I saw them. They were still free and had not been caught for the bombing. They were another set of folks who would have a motive to set me up, plus the knowledge of just how to do it, not to mention connected to Christian.

"Will they let Lee go when we bring her in?" Mac asked.

My mind snapped, Mac is a fucker, he always was. I had to prove myself to him and I thought I had. I was wrong. He and Doc seemed to be on the same page now, united in destroying me.

CJ slowly nodded, "I think so."

"We should make sure. Give them Colby, release all of us from this shit. Not just Lee," Doc said. The words cut; he didn't know it strengthened me.

I bored my eyes into Doc, "all of you with Doc on this?"

I heard enough, I scoffed, "Let me know when you're ready, CJ," I said as I walked over to the stairs.

I looked out the window in my room when CJ came in. "Jack," he said.

I glanced at him over my shoulder at him. "Call me Colby. Jackie is dead," I turned back to the window. I wanted to cry but also knew I wouldn't have time for tears soon. For now, just dealing with reality.

"She isn't," CJ said back.

"You're about to turn Colby James into the FBI. Everything I was or wanted to be as Jackie Ericcson is gone." Colby was about to pay for what just happened. Jackie wasn't in consideration. The FBI was a better option than going back the DIA prison with Chin. Given the public nature of what just happened, I don't think the DIA could get me into their prison if they wanted to. Chin, though, could get access to me in FBI custody. The possibility was something I didn't want to prepare for, but I would have to.

He came alongside me, looking out the window too. "They are going to straighten it all out and you will be back in no time."

I rolled my eyes. "Even if they let me go, which they won't, these people will never want to work with me again, especially Doc. I don't know if I want to work with them." I paused for a moment, thought of each one of them and confirmed they would all feel that way. "It's okay, it's time for me to atone for being Colby."

"I believe you, Jackie." he emphasized the 'Jackie,' and putting his hand on my shoulder. "I don't think you had anything to do with this shipment of dirty bomb materials or this sad attempt at a bombing."

Even if he told the truth, I couldn't tell. It was all a trick to me. Maybe it wasn't a trick. Maybe I did those things, or I ordered them long ago. It was so blurry. I looked at him with a half-smile. "Doc is right, use me to get all of you out from under this. I'm done being the middle of your shit storm." I shirked his hand off me.

"They just want to talk to you," CJ said, trying to reassure me, I think.

I started laughing; I turned to look at the windowsill. "You know the last time I was in FBI custody, my shoulder was dislocated, my arm was broken, so was my nose, and my face was fucked up, and that was just what happened the first night I was in custody. This will probably be the same. Me in prison taking another beating. I obviously don't have top coverage anymore. Any protection I had from the DEA has evaporated." I felt it course through my veins, my strength. It crowded out the weakness as the hope of this life left me. "I am sorry, sorry I put all of you through this. I didn't do this, but I'm going to pay for it. It's going to be pinned on me this time. I can't stop that, I know that. I just hope I can stop it from hurting all of you. That's all I care about."

"Jackie, without you we wouldn't have gotten the bomb at all. We had no other leads on the location of the bomb. Without you, Boston would hurt today."

"Well then, you are the only one who thinks that." I don't even believe I wasn't a part of the attempted bombing.

"You have saved hundreds of lives, maybe thousands. We stopped that bombing, and you gave us enough leads we can stop any that are planned next."

"I should've saved Aaron's life, then maybe I wouldn't be going to prison for something I didn't do." I was flippant and dismissive of CJ. I didn't care what he said; it didn't matter, and I let it come out in my tone and my face. I had nothing to do with this attempted bombing. I had to hold that line to CJ even if I wasn't confident of my own mental status.

"You've lost it!" CJ angrily turned and left the room.

"Did I ever have it?" I asked.

He slammed my door on the way out.

Aaron would have my back; he would know if I was lying. He is the only person who would believe me right now. He would also know that if I talked to the FBI, I was never coming out. If I talked to the FBI, there would be too much to unpack, and they would get me for at least the first bombing. That would be the only way to get out from under this attempted bombing. I couldn't convince them of the truth unless I laid it all out there. I couldn't do that without top cover. Aaron might also be my only hope of getting a grip on reality. He broke me; he could help put me back together. Maybe if he dies that will help too. One less person to mess up my perception on reality.

For a moment I thought back to my Fortitude team, Jason, he would know what was real right now too. I missed him and wondered where he was. Where did he and Crystal go? Were they like me and just blocking out the consequences for our actions? They hated me for Dan's death. Maybe enough to frame me. Maybe I told them to do this, or they misread something I did.

It didn't matter at this moment; it was time. I went to my door and listened; I heard the front door slam. CJ went to go call in to make sure they had a deal before they turned me over, he had to drive away to make sure he didn't expose our location. No one would want to see me in a while. This was my chance.

I climbed up on the ledge of the window, curled up, window size. I pushed the window open, slid to the other side and closed it as quick as I could. I almost fell, but I got it closed. I waited and there was no alarm. Perfect. I jumped down and ran. My go-bag was stashed about ten kilometers away. I took off running at full speed. I wasn't talking to the FBI. I had to find out who did this to me. *Who copied my bombing to set me up? Who purchased my information from Christian? Were they the same people? Was the Iranian militia involved? Was it Crystal and Jason? What parts of the government were corrupted enough to toss me under? How did they figure out I was Colby James? Was Aaron going to be okay? What other things did Ashenhurst get involved in? What was the end-game of the Iranian militia?* At the very least, I would not subject myself to another beating, more torture, or another interrogation. I couldn't do it again. I wouldn't ever, no matter the cost.

Part III: inculpatory (adj)

/en kol pa tor ee/

a) lending to inculpate

b) placing of blame or guilt

Similar: denunciative, incriminating, recriminatory

27

I OPENED THE DOOR that adjoined my motel room to the one next to it and picked the lock to the other door. I walked into the back to check to see if I could get out the window and out of there. I went to the front and peeked out my new window, standing far back in the shadow. The man in the sedan was showing the back of the camera to someone else, someone familiar but I couldn't place it. They laughed, and the guy in the sedan got back in his car and drove off. Maybe I was paranoid. No maybe, I was paranoid. I have been on the run for a long time. I should leave anyway. I went back to the other room and took off my shirt. I slid on my bullet-proof vest and put my shirt back on. You can never be too careful. I headed for the adjoining room when I heard the crack of a bullet hitting the TV.

The first place I went when I left the safe house was back in North Carolina. I knew it was stupid to come here, but I had to. Sometimes what puts you together is knowing what broke you. I entered during the day. I went through the back door into the garage. There was a big, black pickup inside, it confirmed it. I knew that truck—it was Aaron's. The door from the garage to the house was unlocked. It was a bigger place than the one I had down here and a lot newer. No one had touched it in quite some time.

The garage door led into the kitchen. Through the kitchen toward the front of the house was an office. Both the kitchen and office came off a large living room. I went straight into the office. There were pictures of him in uniform, military haircut, with other guys. He looked completely different. No wavy red hair, big smile.

On one shelf the pictures were all laying down, one with a shot glass upside down on the back. I pulled them up. It was him on his wedding day. He said he was divorced. I didn't want to know what else was in the other pictures, but I kept looking anyway. She was truly breathtakingly gorgeous. I, of course, hated her on sight.

There was a binder of pictures on the shelf. I pulled it out. There was a woman's handwriting. She made this. I flipped through their memories, with people I assume were family, people who looked like they were in the military, at the beach, out camping, up in New York City, in the backyard here, in this house. Near the back I found one of him, just him, his beard, his wavy hair, T-shirt, laughing. I pulled it out and put it in my pocket. I didn't consider that this was what I wanted here, but I would take it.

On a different shelf were all kinds of books: French, Arabic, and Korean dictionaries. Piles of study materials for those languages. I didn't know he spoke other languages. He had all kinds of military books, a collection of Chuck Palahniuk, and random military manuals.

I found a folded flag in a case with an engraved knife. Maybe someone he knew who died. His name was on the plaque, Jack A. Ericcson.

His laptop was on his desk. I flipped it open; it turned on. No password. Hmm. I would be back for that. I could always use more computers.

Time to find what I was here for—materials for my next steps. I knew Aaron had all the gear that I needed and that he wasn't home. I crossed the living room to the hallway that led to the rooms. The first room was full of military gear neatly arranged into piles of like items. I went in and found a pistol. I took it and slid it into the back of my pants. I took stock of the rest of the gear in the room. I grabbed ropes, first aid kit, bullets, night vision goggles, sights for weapons, tape, and a holster. Then I found a bag already packed, probably a go-bag; it was a great place for me to start. I pushed everything into that bag. I found a rifle case and picked that up too. I wanted to see what else he had available. The second room was empty.

His bedroom was the last room. I suddenly could feel his presence; I could smell him. He had old baseball caps all over his dresser. Most of them I knew; he always had one on his head. I took a black one that he wore often. It had a blacked out military unit patch. He had quite a few things with that unit patch on it. I needed to research it. I slipped it on my head.

Next to the hats was cologne; I picked it up and smelled it. I had never smelled that on him. His deodorant, Old Spice, was next to it. That was him. I took a moment, and his memory became fresh; I could almost touch him. It made me smile. I put it back down.

Since I was in here, I would grab something else for a memory. I slid the top two drawers of his dresser open, nope. Next two—left drawer was full of T-shirts. I pulled out a pile and set it on top of the dresser, nothing gray in the pile or in the drawer, all military brown and white ones. I slid the bottom two drawers out, more T-shirts. It made sense that was about all I had ever seen him in. I dug through the drawer, pulling the shirts out and setting them on top of the dresser. Finally, a gray shirt. I pulled it out and unfolded it. It was the one. The side was all stretched out with the rips. I smelled it; it smelled like him. I threw it over my shoulder.

His bed was a gray comforter covering gray sheets. His bed was messed up; that wasn't like him. He was always neat and orderly. Lee and Mac probably caught him at night. I leaned over and smelled his pillow; it was him again. On his nightstand was a book he had borrowed from me. Under that book was a leather-bound notebook that was worn and bent like it had a lot of use. I opened it, nothing to note on the first few pages. On the fifth page scratched across the top

"Colby James 3/31." That was my first day in his custody. I thumbed through it. Lots of notes on me. I took it too.

I headed back to get his laptop. Flashing on the screen was a Skype message: "Jack, it's Ash. I know it's you." My breath left me. I hit the airplane mode button. I shut down the computer, grabbed the cord and picked it up. I looked for something to carry all these things. Aaron had a backpack in the office. I took all my new things and shoved them in. It was time to go; if Asher knew where I was, they did too.

After I left North Carolina, I headed back to Tampa. My Fortitude team had a lot of extra supplies and meeting places. If I wanted to launch an operation of my own, I would need more than what I got from Aaron's place. Also, it would be a good place to start if I wanted to find Crystal and Jason. I walked down the bike trail through the park, it would take me to the back side of the business park I wanted to visit. I knew few people in Tampa, yet I still felt like I might run into someone I knew. Whoever that person was, they knew I was the Colby James who did the Boston bombing, the scandal of the town. I pulled Ross's black hat down to cover my face. I also had on big sunglasses. When I reached the back of the business park, I left the trail and walked around to the front gate. I punched in the code, and the gate popped open.

I walked down the left side of the road, where the cameras didn't reach. This business park was used more as workspace and storage, and not for businesses where customers visit. The unit we rented had a big garage door and an office space. I checked everything I could on the internet, and I don't believe the FBI found this place. We used it to build our bombs and to make that safe we altered their software to create blind spots in the security system.

I got to the door and punched in the code; it didn't work. I tried it again, and the door lock popped open. Just inside there was an office, and someone had been there. The trash bin overflowed onto the floor with bottles and food wrappers around the base. Someone had been here.

"Hello?" I called out. "Jason? Crystal?" I flipped the lights on and walked into the garage workspace. "Anyone here?" Our work bench was trashed. I looked in the bathroom, and no one was in there. Someone had been here, probably lived here for some time. They had the same idea as me; this was a great hideout.

I went back into the office and looked at the desk. There were piles of newspapers, a couple with my picture all beaten up from Ross. I pushed those to the side to see the dates on the papers. It looked like they were put here around that time I got arrested by the FBI the first time. The couch had a blanket and pillow. I went back into the workspace to see what I had for tools. I found a box of our plastic explosives that we definitely didn't keep here. If the FBI had found this place, this would not be here; that was a good sign. It also meant that Furi was not the person to stay here. He seemed to give up information since he got arrested and this would be a perfect place to give up. Maybe there was hope for Furi yet.

I started with the trash in the office and pulled some of it from the floor, the expiration date on a milk jug was from over a year ago. I think that is from when whoever stayed here, and also Crystal didn't drink cow's milk, so this had to be Jason. I took a deep breath; I didn't spend enough time wondering what happened to them. I went and lived my life and left all of them in the dust. I knew I couldn't contact them; it would put them in jeopardy. It would give a trail for them to be arrested. Instead, I just grabbed onto the new life the DEA gave me and let whatever happen to them happen. I threw them away like they were just tools to reach my goal. I should feel guilty for that, and I didn't.

I sat down on the couch, and a little metal box slid out from under the pillow and into my side. I opened the box, and inside there was a bent burned spoon and a rubber tourniquet. "Shit," I said out loud. Jason was using again. I picked the spoon up and looked at it and the sight tied my stomach up in knots. Wherever he was right now, he was struggling. I wanted to hug him so badly. Why wasn't I brave enough to love him out loud? We were the best team, and we had a chance at real love, maybe we had it in our way. I had left this bombing behind, got a great new life and he is on the run and on drugs. I am on the run now; I would have to avoid the drugs. I blinked, and some tears fell from my eyes. I stood up and went to the workspace and tossed the spoon onto the workbench. I grabbed a large trash can and set it next to the bench and took an armload and pushed it into the bin. I needed to erase this workspace so if the FBI found it one day, there would be no trace of who was here. Especially not Jason.

28

I HAD TO FIGURE out what happened in Boston. There was only one person who knew was involved, it was way too much speculation on my part to figure it out. I pulled up to the restaurant and got out. I went to the trunk and pulled out some gift bags. One bag ripped and the boxes from inside the bags went everywhere. "Shit," I said as I bent down and picked them up. I handed the key to the valet and went into the restaurant and sat down a bag in the coat check closet, which was empty. I headed straight for the back to the room where I met with Christian last time. He was in the middle of talking to some men. They looked a lot rougher than Christian, like they were from the street. They had that same neck tattoo of that person I ran into last time I saw Christian.

"Christian, honey, I've missed you," I was stopped by the guard.

He waved the other men out of the room. "Colby," he motioned me in to take a seat.

"Strange," I said.

"What's that, Colby?" he asked back.

"I didn't take you as someone who would cooperate with the feds," I said with a smile.

He laughed, "You're a fed, Colby."

I laughed now and leaned over the table. "Yes, because you often find feds on the run from the FBI and wanted for questioning in connection with a few bombings, some of which killed almost forty people."

"Why are you here?" he said, getting serious.

"Aren't we old friends?" I asked and shot him a flirty smile.

He smiled.

"Don't we go to friends in times of trouble?"

"Once again, your problem is not mine. That last deal was a one-time deal," Christian said.

"I've been puzzling it out, you see," I leaned back in my chair and crossed my hands in my lap. "Why would my good friend Christian deliberately give information to a federal agent about an old colleague who has kept her friendship with Christian a secret?"

"You burned yourself when you came here," he said in response.

"Christian, I just didn't take you for a rat nor someone who wouldn't know who he was dealing with."

"Strong words for someone who came here alone," he said, shooting a look at one of his guards.

"Always underestimating me."

"You are in grave danger of not walking out of here alive," Christian said as a warning.

I frowned, "Do you know the time?"

He looked at me for a few seconds and looked down at his watch, "Ten thirty-two."

I got out of my chair and laid down on the ground on my stomach and put my hands over my head. "I suggest you do the same."

An explosion rocked the room from somewhere behind the restaurant. Then another, somewhere on the roof of the restaurant; it was loud and alarming but did nothing to us in the room. Christian stood up. I crawled around the table and pulled Christian down to the ground, as his guard came running in. The main entrance to the restaurant blew; you could feel that one shoot through the room. The debris and dust fill the air. One of my gift bags had gone off. The guards dove to the ground.

Christian pulled a gun and put it to my head, "What the fuck are you doing, Colby?" He didn't know I would rather take that bullet than go back into custody by anyone. I wasn't afraid of dying, I was afraid of living and going back to a prison hell. "Make them stop," Christian said, grabbing my hair.

"They will stop when I walk out of here, upright and alone. Otherwise, we will get buried in here together," I said calmly to him.

Another explosion went off behind the building, loud, from under the dumpster.

"What do you want?" he demanded, pulling my hair and screaming with the gun now between my eyes.

"Who's the contact? Who did you sell my location to?" I said, looking at him calmly.

The sprinklers went off and soaked us with water. Another explosion, this time more directly above us. I made them to be loud, not too damaging, more of a flash and burn than a bang and shrapnel situation. I also didn't plan to be there long, so pulling in the local police and fire department didn't bother me either.

His angry face was terse.

"I'm dead without the contact's information, so shoot me and die here and get buried with me. Or tell me, and I walk out, and all this stops." An explosion went off in the room, spraying shrapnel at us, hitting us both. I did not plan that bomb well. It also caught some curtains on fire that separated this room from the rest of the restaurant. The bombs made it seem like I was with other people and not alone. I timed them to go off, without me being involved. I thought it would be the fastest way to get what I needed from Christian. I reached up and felt the blood on my face. I smiled. "Shall we get buried together," I looked at the blood on my hands. "My friend's patience seems to be running low." I hoped he was buying it; I was running low on charges. The police and fire department had to be there or be there pretty soon.

Another explosion went off in the room. This time I ducked. I knew it was too close. "Who did you give the phone info to? Who did you sell it to?" I asked from the ground. Even laid down on the ground now.

"Fucking bitch," he said.

"I have made my peace with dying, have you?"

The smoke grew thick.

"Here's my phone, you figure it out."

"Fuck your phone, we aren't playing that game again."

He unlocked it and showed me an email address. I stood up, and another explosion went off somewhere out back by the dumpster. I ran through the flames and out the front. I covered my face as I coughed my way past the fire department.

I glanced back as Christian got out of the restaurant. The package I dropped under his car went off. I used the scuffle of the last explosion to duck into a business and out the back, away from the scene.

29

I TOSSED AND TURNED and couldn't sleep. I needed sleep, but I didn't know what to do next. Aaron's face came to my mind when I closed my eyes. Sometimes it was his face as I pushed him under that car. On the patio behind my North Carolina house. Sometimes it was after I told him I loved him for the first time. In bed he pushed me into the pillows and kissed me. In the office before the op. In the room with the tape. His face was ever present, and I had no way to make it go away. The nightmares still loomed; there was no CJ or Asher to pull me out. Luckily I could probably literally murder someone in this motel, and no one would call the police.

I gave up on sleeping and sat up. I pulled out my laptop and used it to protect my connection to the Internet. I would use it to block my location and secure the other laptop from attack. I chased the email address I got from Christian. I got to the site, and it required a token to log in. I had a hack for that, safely stored at work on the server. I wouldn't be able to recreate it. I needed the off-the-shelf solution. Instead, I traced the server that was hosting the account, hoping they weren't on the cloud somewhere. It traced to the Capitol Hill area of Washington, DC, but I wasn't getting a more specific location.

I was exhausted, but I needed more answers before I could sleep. I had to find out if Aaron was alive or dead. It plagued me. I connected Aaron's computer. I disabled Skype before I connected everything to the internet. I dug around. Maybe I could find information about if he was okay or not.

I opened the browser and clicked on the bookmark for his email. It opened, password saved. He has piss poor security habits on his computer. I found an email about health insurance. I clicked on it, and it took me to their website. I used his email address for a login, then clicked "forgot password." It offered to send me a one-time passcode to his email, so I clicked on that option and logged into the health insurance site.

There were a series of charges from different institutions: ER BIDMC, MEDSURGE BIDMC, ICU BIDMC, all with a slew of charges under each that made little sense to me. I wasn't sure what they meant. I knew the hospital he went to was called Beth Israel. Maybe it meant Emergency Room Beth Israel, I wasn't sure of the rest. All the charges started the day he was shot, and the last one was from a week ago. There was nothing else in there. They could be running a week behind; they could have transferred him to a different hospital, maybe a military hospital. He could be dead. I couldn't find anything in there about any of it. After clicking on everything and Googling weird charges, I was nowhere closer to having any answers. The more I clicked the more the tears came. I clicked over to his email. He hadn't touched it in weeks, nothing helping me there. I stopped and laid down and stared at the laptop, willing answers out of it.

Skype was pinned to the task bar. How did Asher find me on Aaron's Skype? Aaron has to be dead or in the hospital or anything that would prevent him from using his Skype. My heart told me Aaron was dead, and Asher knew I was looking for that answer. He knew I would hack into his things to get answers. Maybe it was the FBI. I stared at the Skype icon.

I didn't have a next move.

I went back to my laptop to make sure I had a good firewall up; I used a VPN to bounce my IP around the world. I also set up an alarm to have the virtual machine running my internet self-destruct if it was being traced or breached. I sat up all the way and leaned back into the pillows. I opened Skype.

"Messages received while you were offline," I clicked on it.

"Jackie, I'm on your side. You're not alone."

I didn't believe it. It was a weird account. I had to find out if it was Asher. The account was marked as "away." "How do I know it's you?" I hit send, and my heart raced. I stared at the window, nothing. After five minutes I laid down, exhausted. I stared at the window. After about twenty minutes, the other account turned green and typing... appeared at the bottom.

I quickly sat up and held my breath.

"Remember, we chose you." I waited; that wasn't enough.

Typing... It popped up again.

"Even if you aren't a desperate, thick girl,"

I smiled, it was Asher, but he was trying to tell me someone was looking over his shoulder, the words were just off but just right. I used to say the girls Asher cheated on his wife with were desperate girls. Him saying 'not desperate' meant as yes it's me, but beware I'm not alone.

"How's Aaron?"

"Touch and go."

"Lee?"

"Let him go."

"Still after me?" it was a while before I even saw typing...

"Yeah."

"I didn't do it." I had to make sure he knew I wasn't involved in this dirty bomb.

"I know, Jack."

"Can you help me prove it?"

Typing...

The virtual machine shut down. They were watching over his shoulder and trying to find where I was at the same time. I don't think they found me, but I would not stick around to find out. It was time to go back on the offense. I had enough lying low. I needed progress.

30

I NEEDED TO GET near DC to plan my next move and do what I could to find out who was behind that email address. If Asher would really help, I would need to find another way to contact him. I staged in Manassas, Virginia. I kept the phone on while I drove and kept checking the app. It was a risk, leaving the phone on, but contacting Asher was worth it. I knew from the Skype it was him, but I also knew he was warning me because his words were his, but off from how we talked to each other. That told me something. If I could contact him in a way they didn't know about, then he might help me. Not like he would likely tell the FBI his favorite thing to do at the end of the day is work out, sleep with a random girl or at least flirt with that idea, and then go home. I got on the Tinder app and got near him and swiped until I found him.

I checked into a rundown hotel and went into my room. I sat down on the bed and opened the phone, clicked the app, still nothing. I opened my bag and pulled out that picture of Aaron. It was strange to look at it. I couldn't feel the ever-present hate and anger I had for him. I think it's because I prepared myself for his death or in the least of never seeing again, or it was my mind protecting me from all the things I had to deal with. I think the thought of him being dead was putting me back together, and if he died, it would fix so many of my issues. Still his face calmed me. I loved him, even if that was the most fucked up kind of love you could find. Maybe he was just a reminder that I could be whole again. I was once whole before. I didn't know. I wiped my finger over his face and sat it down next to me.

The notebook, his notebook. I hadn't opened it. I had let it fall from my memory in the midst of all I had been doing, also somewhat afraid of the contents. I pulled it out and cracked it open.

Colby James 3/31

I wiped my finger over my name, his name for me. It was his for a while; I was his for a while, before all of this.

Little girl in video, find out who she is.

That was one of his first entries. That must be the Kool-Aid smile girl that haunts me. She died in the bombing. He found out who she was and used her picture to tear my soul out. Deserved, yes. I flipped forward a few pages.

Jessie = FBI Informant–If she blames her, she talks more

I skipped ahead a few pages.

Extremely intelligent, calculated with all responses

Why give up the van???

I flipped toward the end, to find the last time I saw him before it all fell apart. The last time we saw each other he found me in DC between my team's missions in Venezuela and Nicaragua. We spent the weekend together and had a big fight at the end of the weekend because he wanted to know more about my involvement in the bombing and I refused to tell him the details. Maybe I would find out what he was looking for when he found me that time. Maybe he put in details of why they put me back in his prison for the second time. What did he write about his last visit to DC or him visiting me in the hospital after my gunshot?

The last comment was about a ruck march, where you pack on a lot of weight and hike 10 or 20 miles. The last time I did that or at least talked to him about it was in North Carolina. Somewhere in the middle of my training. I flipped backward to find the date he found me there. I was so confused. His notes on me had ended somewhere in the middle of my training. We spent all our time together, and he just stopped taking notes on it halfway through. There was nothing else in the notebook. He kept it on his nightstand, why would he do that if he was not taking notes on me? Was he looking at it when Mac and Asher found him? I was so confused. Why would he stop writing things down about me? Maybe he wasn't lying, and he got too close to me. Maybe I didn't tell him anything worth writing. Maybe he started taking notes somewhere else. I flipped backward in the notes.

Condo for sale. All that's left is a table, two chairs, blue bowl. From last time I was there.

That had to be when I left my whole Colby James life in the rearview and moved to Fayetteville and started my life with the DEA.

PO–Transferred control to Fayetteville??

That must be about my probation officer.

Unable to locate PO in Fayetteville that has heard of her.

I didn't have a PO in Fayetteville. That is when they helped me disappear off the map.

There were lists of names, maybe probation officers he had contacted. He also had my Tampa-based probation officer in there. I didn't miss that guy.

A few pages later at the top was a heavily underlined statement.

She's not afraid of me anymore, she feels protected by someone.

That must be the day he came into my house in North Carolina, for the first time.

Need a new approach

The words made me sick. It confirmed the parts I ignored. When he found me in North Carolina, it was deliberate. But saying he needed a new approach confirmed that his decision to act kind and helpful to me was a manipulation, an approach, to gain my trust. After a year with him, they were the parts I didn't want to be true. I knew he was bad, but I fell for him. Everything he did for me, I thought that maybe somewhere in there he cared about me. Even if the reason he was there was not genuine. I pushed it aside and ignored it. Then in the prison for the second time, he told me he loved me and he did all these things for me. I believed him then. I didn't know until I saw him outside the prison alive and fine with my interrogator that he was full of bullshit. That is what it took for me to understand that he was a master manipulator. Here I was again, manipulated by him, and with this note in the notebook realizing I fell right into it, again.

The phone dinged with a Tinder notification.

"Desperate heap?" It was Asher. I took the pictures of him he used on his profile. He is extremely good looking, but also, he looked like trouble. Tall, athletic, strong, dark hair, and a debonair smile.

"Yep." I sent it back. "I need your help."

"Of course, what?"

"Can you get one of your other thick girls to agree to a threesome so I can talk to you IRL?" I wanted to meet with him in real life but I used the acronym IRL. He called me a thick girl in his Skype message so I played on it.

"You finally want a piece of me?" I felt human. Talking to Asher, the way he was an ass to me, and I was to him. It was our language, and I liked it.

"RME" I sent back shorthand for rolling my eyes.

"When?"

"ASAP"

"Oh... I don't know if I can get away from everyone."

"Please, you hooked up with a girl in the parking lot while we were in a training op."

"She wasn't good."

"Focus!"

"Where?"

"Are you thick now? At the desperate chick's house!"

"Hey..." he paused for a long time after sending that.

"Yeah?"

"... Nothing, I will let you know when I get an update."

I looked over at Aaron's picture. I wish I could find that picture on Tinder and find out if he was okay or if he was dead. Aaron wasn't the tinder type. At least not the Aaron I knew. I guess I didn't really know him at all.

Back in his notebook I found a new note.

Ashenhurst. It had a box around it. *President's inner circle. Cabinet just had major change. Is the President the target?*

Aaron had put more together than I realized. He knew the cabinet shakeup might have been connected to Ashenhurst. We targeted Ashenhurst in our bombing, and I told him we did. He knew Ashenhurst was in the President's inner circle. At least when he wrote that note he thought the President was the target. I was impressed he pulled that together, I didn't think anyone would correlate those as a direct link. They might have thought there was a shakeup because of failures, not that the targeting of Ashenhurst caused the cabinet shakeup.

I laid down, I needed sleep and had not had real sleep since I left the cabin. Just like that I fell into a memory of Aaron right after he found me in DC. Aaron leaned up on his elbow and leaned over to kiss me, while my head was in the pillow. His hand was on my cheek. He pulled back and smiled. "I'm so glad I found you," he said.

"Me too." I reached up and ran my fingers through his hair. I pulled myself up and kissed him again.

He pulled away, "I better feed you. I know how dangerous it can be if I withhold food from you."

"What if you withhold something else I want?"

"You're fine, for now," he said with a smile and sat up on the edge of the bed. I followed behind him and wrapped my arms around him, his bare skin. I ran my fingers through the hair on his chest. "Are you telling me you're not hungry?" he said over his shoulder at me.

I let him go and laid back into the bed and watched him dress. He put on his T-shirt, then his jeans over his boxer briefs. He left his hat as he left the room. I didn't know how much I missed him until he showed up on the other side of my truck. It was like a piece of me was missing—the new me, anyway.

I showered and headed downstairs, wearing his hat. He was out on the deck messing with the grill. I sat on the counter next to him where he was making dinner. I took his cup and smelled what he was drinking—water—good. He usually had a beer or two while cooking or with dinner. He came back to the door and smiled when he saw me.

"What brought you up here?" I asked him.

"You," he walked up next to me. I didn't believe him, not really.

"How was your trip?" I asked.

"Alright. Missed you mostly. Got used to seeing you and then I go on one little deployment, and I got nothing from you, not even a postcard," he said with a sullen face.

"You are full of it, Ross," I said back to him, and he shot me a smile. Then leaned over and kissed me. My heart skipped.

"What have you been doing?" he went back to concentrating on the food.

"Had a few tours of my own, shorter than yours though," I said.

"Chasing after former mayors again?" he said, not even breaking his eyes from what he was doing. Ashenhurst was a former mayor.

I scowled and jumped off the counter and walked away.

"Oh, I'm kidding, Colby," he wrapped his arms around me from behind.

"What are you chasing?" I said to him over my shoulder.

"No one as difficult as you."

I woke up. "Brickman," I said out loud. The one Aaron was always after and didn't even know it, the man who hired me to root out the depths of corruption in the government. I protected Brickman from everyone, didn't even tell my DEA team. The country should show gratitude for this man, and they don't even know why. He seems to do things because they are right, doesn't even use them for re-election. No nightmare this time. Little victories. I would have to spend more time with Aaron's thoughts on me in the future.

I knocked on the door and a girl answered it. "Courtney," I said with a big smile.

"You must be Ashley," she said.

"Yeah," I said. "Call me Ash, though." Of course, he gave me his name. "How are you?" I asked her as she walked me toward the living room.

"Good, you?"

"Excited." I raised my eyebrows and feigned excitement.

"He's so hot, right?" she said. "Want a drink?"

"Sure," I said. Asher better show up soon because I didn't know how long I could handle talking to her. I just didn't have the patience for it today. She went to the kitchen and came back with a White Claw as there was a knock at the door. Thank God.

"Sorry, I got caught up at work," Asher said in a soothing sweet voice that I had never heard from him before. She giggled and came back now raising her eyebrows at me. I smiled back at her.

He sat down next to me and put his hand on my leg as she went into the kitchen, "You okay?" he asked.

I shook my head no. "Get me these," I said and handed him a list. I knew she distracted him and would forget it if told him.

"What for?" he asked, looking at the list in his hand.

"If I'm going to get out from under this, I have to prove who is behind it," I said to him.

"Come back with me, let us help you," he squeezed my leg.

I put my hand on his cheek and spoke low and quiet to make sure she couldn't hear us from the kitchen, "I'm not letting you guys hand me over to the FBI. I can't go through torture again. I won't make it," I looked deep into his eyes, but he didn't get it. How could anyone who had not been through it?

"We won't."

"You won't," I said, dropping my hand. "CJ has to, and Mac wants to. Doc wants me dead. He only went along with what the team wanted for a short while. He will not want me around after all of this." I tried to catch his eyes again, but he looked at her. I could feel her eyes on us. I turned my head and looked at her through the kitchen window. She was doing something at the sink. I smiled at her; she was nervous and dropped the cup in her hand.

"I will come with you, then," Asher said.

"Okay, Ash, but get this first," I looked down at the list in his hand.

He looked to me for a moment. "Jackie, do you know Jason Rasmussen?"

The comment stopped me in my tracks, "Yes, he was on my old team, Boston. Why?"

"He's turned himself in, at a consulate in the Dominican Republic." He glanced over at her and back at me. "He said he has information about your involvement in the bombing."

"This one or the ones I did?"

"This one," he said and turned back to watch her move around the kitchen.

"That makes little sense, how can he have information about something I didn't do?" Asher wasn't paying attention to me. My time with him was running short. "Any word on Aaron?" I asked, finally getting to the piece of information I had been dying to know.

"As sexy as advertised," she said.

"Aaron," I said in an annoyed tone and shaking my head; he told her his name was Aaron. He was into her, checking her out. He wanted her. She was cute but reeked of self-loathing. I kissed him on the cheek. "Please," I gave the hand with the note a squeeze. He looked back at me and shoved the list in his pocket and put his eyes back on her.

"We can't meet this way next time," I said to him.

"Next time just meet me at Meghan's house then," he said, speaking of his long-time side piece.

"Oh, now you want me to know about her?" I laughed because he used to pretend he didn't have her on rotation. I could tell though, when I met her at the coffee shop near our gym that there was something more to their friendship. She lived in an apartment behind the coffee shop. "He's all yours, Courtney, I can tell."

She beamed. I left.

31

I waited for the Senate to go on break and waited in the basement between the Senate subway and the elevator he would most likely take to get back to his office. I pretended to type on my phone as I leaned up against the wall. I saw a hoard of people coming in my direction from the subway. I saw him in the sea of people walking in my direction. His staffers surrounded him, some of them furiously typing on their phones and another telling him something he listened to intently.

I waited for them to get a few steps from me, and I stepped out running into him, and dropped a phone into his pocket and made eye contact with him.

"Watch it!" one of his staffers yelled at me while the realization of who I am washed over his face.

"It's fine," he said as I passed him breaking eye contact. He recognized me.

I left the building and headed straight toward Union Station. As I was crossing the plaza, I called the phone I dropped in Brickman's pocket.

"Hello?" It was Brickman. He was the one that set my mission, Fortitude. He handled all the money and gave me the clearances I needed to get my mission done.

"It occurs to me that only three people knew the password to find that bomb given the clue and you have more to gain than the other person." I referred to the password I used which contained the location of the dirty bomb materials, he would know the answer too.

"Umm..." he said. "Give me a minute," he said, half-mumbled, not to me. "Just give me five minutes," he said again. Then there was silence on the line. I kept moving quickly through the plaza.

"Ms. James, I'm assuming this is you and, I don't know what you are talking about," he finally said to me.

"I've been through hell protecting you, never once mentioning your name. I suggest you figure out what I'm talking about. I'm guessing though, you already know," I said to him. Everyone wanted to know who in the government backed my bombing. From the FBI to Aaron to Chin, Brickman was the name they wanted. Even the DEA wanted it, and I never once let it go. All the torture would have ended if I just said Senator Brickman.

"I certainly don't."

I hit "play," Brickman's voice started talking, "Did you study Latin, Colby? Fortitudo, what do you think it means?" I hit stop and waited for him to talk. I recorded all our conversations, but this was from our first one, where he recruited me.

"What do you want, Colby?" Brickman said.

"Figure out who is setting me up for this dirty bomb and why my cover is suddenly blown, or we can go down together." Even if Brickman was behind it, which I could not imagine, everyone else had betrayed me. He still had enough pull with any agency to get more details. He could get details my DEA team and Asher couldn't get because they were partially under investigation. He could get me insider information from the investigation. I threatened to expose him in order to get him to help me. I knew I had to draw a hard line with him, he was clear he would not help me after the bombing. I should never contact him again; he would deny knowing me and everything in between. Once the mission was done, the corruption was pulled out of the government, our connection was done, permanently severed.

He made that clear when I asked for collateral damage clearance for the bombings. I could not contact him, and he would not help me. The phone went silent as I entered Union Station and headed toward the commuter trains in the back. "You have twenty-four hours."

"Do I call this number back?"

"I will contact you," I hung up. I removed the SD Card with the recording and dropped the phone into a commuter's bag who was on the way to Charles Town, West Virginia.

It had been twenty-four hours, I kept hitting "refresh" on the browser, waiting for it to show-up, a new review for Luhmann and King's Trust and Power 1st Edition on Amazon. I had used an app to request someone take a copy from the Library of Congress and drop it in his office. A note accompanied it that said, "Technically, this book isn't supposed to leave the library, return before the twenty-four hours is up." In the back was an old library check out card. I wrote Amazon review in the first open line. It was entirely possible he missed the clue. He was supposed to talk to me in the Amazon Review section for the book.

I grabbed a coffee and sat back down. I needed patience now. I waited for a few more moments and hit refresh again. It popped up.

"I think that prison took more from you than reality." The comment was from a user called anonymous.

I was confused, it was clearly a message intended for me, but I was missing it. I added a comment "?"

"Tell me, Colby, since you left have you done anything for your country? Or has it just been for you?" The words were biting.

"My country is against me," I retorted.

"I thought you had fortitude, is that what they took from you in prison?" Brickman was a mirror I had not looked in; he convicted me at my core.

"Is this all you have for me?" I zipped back.

"Who you seek is after Amazon Review in what I just returned." I would have to get the book again and read what was written under what I wrote in the checkout card. That could be potentially tricky to go to some place someone would expect me.

"One more thing... what you'll find will only serve you."

Brickman pointed out a character defect that I had listed long ago along with so many others, in the days when Narcotics Anonymous was what I lived by. Selfish. I wanted so much to be anything but that. I thought I had fortitude. Brickman warned me this would happen. He told me I would have to have a stronger conviction than they could break out of me. He was right, they broke me. I lost it in prison.

Step 10 of Narcotics Anonymous: I will continue to take personal moral inventory and when wrong promptly admit it.

I looked back at the words again. They made me sick, *what had I become?* All I had done since I got out was trying to survive and clear my name. For a moment, I tried to do that by convincing the DEA to keep me then I almost lost all of that because of Aaron. Now, all I could think about is who was framing me for this thing I didn't do. I wasn't doing what I should do, which was figuring out how a bomb almost detonated in Boston and stopping any that were planned to come behind it. I was failing myself. I lost my fortitude, and I was failing my country. I closed the computer. I would need a really long run to reset where my brain just landed.

32

I TRIED TO FALL asleep, but I couldn't. I don't even know the last time I slept longer than an hour at a time. I was falling apart at the seams. I gave up on sleep and got up. When I got to the foot of the bed, I noticed something. There was a line of black tape across the floor. I reached down and touched it; I didn't remember it before. It made me dizzy bending down, and I felt nauseous. I stood up and laid back down on the bed.

"Colby," I rolled over. It was Aaron, he was in a hospital bed. He had all kinds of tubes and wires coming from him. He was on a ventilator, and it was pumping up and down. Everything had noises and hissing and beeping. I leaned over and kissed him and laid down next to him in his bed.

"Ross," I said to him. "Don't die on me again." I didn't expect Asher to tell me he survived. I really thought he was gone. Maybe he was just waiting for me to say goodbye. "I will not say goodbye," I said to him. I ran my fingers through his beard.

He turned his head to me, "Colby," he said. I looked at him and his machines beeped louder and rang out. I got scared and stood up. Did I break something? Where were the nurses, why weren't they coming? Why weren't they stopping him from all the beeping?

"Ross!" I was flooded with being upset. "Come on!" The machines started ringing out again. It made me more upset, and my heart was now racing. They did it again, and I woke up. It was all a dream. The phone was ringing. It was 4 pm. I slept. The phone, why is it ringing? It scared me. I got up and got dressed. I shoved all my things in the bags. I did a quick final sweep and peeked out the window. The phone kept ringing. No one was outside. I went to the back and looked out the window. No one was there either. I had to get out of there; it was probably the cops. The last time I answered a hotel phone, the police tackled me. I opened the back window and dropped out my bags and climbed after them. I don't know what that phone wanted, but I didn't need to find out.

This time I waited outside Meghan's apartment for Asher. He left me a note telling me to meet a few hours after work. We had communicated on Tinder too much, so I was nervous of the possibility someone figured it out. I got there really early and scoped it out. There were no signs of surveillance.

When Ash pulled up, he seemed purely focused on his look. He kept fixing his hair. He got out of his truck and did a bunch of push-ups. I rolled my eyes and watched him grab a bag and head into the townhome. I continued to observe the world, looking for any signs of surveillance before I finally headed toward the door.

Asher opened the door, and his shirt was already off. "Couldn't wait for me?" I asked him, giving him a frowny face.

I heard giggling come from the home. I followed him in. "Ooh," I said. I walked up to her and kissed her. She kissed back, and she was good. We kept kissing, and I spun her around so I could catch Asher's eye. He was not happy with me. I stopped kissing her.

"Something wrong?" she said.

"No," I said. "I think he maybe just bit off more than he can chew."

She giggled. "I've seen you with him. I didn't know you were into this."

"Give us a minute," Asher said.

"I'm going to head to the bedroom," she said.

He immediately turned to me, "What's wrong with you?"

"She's hot, one of the good choices you have made," I said, then leaned into his ear, "other than your wife."

"Just take the bag, Jack," he said, annoyed with me.

"Thanks," I headed toward it. He walked back toward the bedroom. "Ash, wait, what's going on in the office?"

"Nothing really, we're under investigation because of you, and CJ's dealing with a lot with the FBI. So, we just mostly support the investigation." He walked back toward me. "Jack, it's not looking good for you. They haven't told us everything, but I mean it all lends itself to you being very involved in this dirty bomb. They think you organized the transport and that meeting you had with Christian was worse than it was, like you organized something with him. There is also other evidence coming and witnesses that all point to you. I believe you though, Jackie. It's just not looking good. I'm worried about you," he said. It was genuine. He had dropped the joking and playful manner we usually had with each other.

"Are you guys coming or what?" Meghan called out to us.

"We're headed your way, but we aren't coming without you," I called to her, still with my eyes on Asher who looked genuinely worried about me.

"Jackie, it's going to take a lot to get this off you. It's not good."

"Someone is planting this stuff, Ash. And never mind that, what about the other bombs? We had all this intel saying it would be multiple bombs. There was one crappy one. Are you chasing that?"

"No, I mean, kind of, we are just hamstrung right now. I'm trying anyway." He was sheepish, again something he wouldn't do in front of the others.

I nodded and walked past him toward the bedroom. He grabbed my arm. "Jack, seriously?" he said, exasperated.

I laughed and wrapped my arms around him. "Thank you for believing me, it means a lot and for helping. I don't know where I would be if I didn't have you in my corner." I let go of him and stepped back. "Ash, she is probably fun, but one day when your wife leaves you... because she is going to leave you... ask yourself if you would give up this day, and all the days like this, to keep Mandie and the kids with you. Don't wait for it to be too late to know what you love and want to keep it close."

I picked up the bag he brought for me. He watched me walk to the door. As I pulled the door open, he stopped me.

"Jack," he called. "Aaron's back in the ICU."

I nodded but didn't look back. It was already too much not being able to go to him. I felt his hand on my shoulder, and I turned to him. He wrapped me in a hug.

A moment passed, and I felt unexpectedly choked up. "I will always be here for you. No matter what happens, always." He squeezed me tighter.

"I'm so lucky to have you," I said, as I processed what we told me—from whoever framed me to Aaron taking a turn for the worse. I stopped myself from feeling it, though I couldn't process it. I had to focus on the task at hand. I put my hands on the back of his head and pulled back, smiling softly. I did not know how to get out of this mess, but it was good to have an ally, someone I could trust.

33

I opened the laptop; the list was closed in it, and everything was checked off. Asher could be so meticulous when you got him to focus. He added his own items to the list. I spoofed my location to Asher's house and logged in with his credentials. I knew having those would come in handy one day.

Asher downloaded the backdoor I had left into Hansen and Anchor's system. He also loaded links to the systems that we had dropped down range in Columbia and Nicaragua. I could tell Asher had been messing with them, looking for something. Brickman was right; I was so focused on me that I was missing things. I instantly felt guilty. I was letting everyone down around me out of selfishness. Asher downloaded the token hack to break into the server of the person who purchased my information from Christian, as requested. I had to push it to the side.

"I would be so wrong to use that," I said out loud to myself. I would heed Brickman's warning. I still wanted to know, but I had to turn this around and serve my country before myself.

It was 4 am, so I put on another pot of coffee. I felt exhausted but felt like I was getting somewhere. I had piled the data into our system and was sorting through it line by line. Hansen and Anchor did a lot of business with a government contractor, Top Hat. It was their number one source of income. From what I could tell, Top Hat provided interpreters in Iraq and other third country nationals for jobs like truck drivers and cafeteria workers. I wrote it down; I didn't know what it meant.

Somewhere after reading the word 'interpreter' a few more times, I remembered a lead Crystal and I got on the Fortitude team, but we never could track it down. It was the only time we forayed into talking to people. Crystal and I met a lead, with Jason doing the lookout for us, but it proved to be too dangerous without the proper backup.

Crystal and I had tracked down a former US Marshall. He left the Marshall service after a series of events including his partner, Agent Vernon, dying under suspicious circumstances. It was clear the Iranian militia got involved but was not clear why. We decided the best way was to talk to Officer Hartford because we could not find any other official records. He was a police officer now.

"I can't help you," Officer Hartford said and threw his bag into the trunk of his police cruiser, then slammed it shut. "I need to go, anyway." He walked toward his driver's side door, but Crystal stood in his way.

"We just need to know what you found out." Crystal looked him in his eyes with intention. "Agent Vernon knew something, we know it, but all his files have been deleted." Agent Vernon was his partner who died.

"I'm not a Marshall anymore, just a local cop," he said, defeated.

"Why is that, anyway? Who leaves US Marshall Service up in the Northeast to be a local cop in a suburb of St. Louis?" I asked him.

"You don't know who you are messing with," he said with hands resting on the weapons that sat on his gun belt, he already resigned to not telling us anything. "They killed Agent Vernon, his wife, and his sweet little girl," he looked over, clearly choked up.

"Murdered?" Crystal questioned. "I thought they got in a car accident." We suspected it was murder, but all there was left in any files we could find was an obituary that said car accident. We knew it was more because of everything around it.

"You think a few days after we were threatened, we get a major break in the case, tell our leadership, and then boom, he is suddenly dead. Then all the case files go missing. You think that is a fucking coincidence?"

"What was the major break?" I moved past his comment, hoping his amped up attitude would cause details to spill out.

He shook his head, "Not happening, nope."

"Help us get them. We want to figure out the corruption, not the case. We want to know why certain cases stop and what it's related to. We can't do that without you. We can get them, find out who did this to your partner and his family."

He looked down at the ground and shook his head.

"Can you do it for him, for them?" I asked.

"I already did it for him. When our leaders told us to stop, he didn't want to," he sneered slightly. "We kept pushing, then we get a few bullets left on our windshield, a few bullet holes in our front doors. Vernon said, 'We are on the right trail, that's why they are threatening us.'" He stopped and took a big breath.

"What trail? What were you investigating?" Crystal probed. I could tell we pushed too hard.

"I left that life. I would appreciate it if you let me leave it in the past," he said, and the radio on his shoulder squawked. He held up his finger and leaned his head toward his right shoulder. "Bravo Thirty," he said.

"Go ahead, Bravo Thirty," dispatch said.

"Coming into service, responding to Lewis Ave. Ten mikes out," he said. He just got himself a reason to get away from us by calling himself into service and indicating to dispatch he was responding to a call.

"Did you get thrown out of the agency?" If he left out the case he investigated, maybe he would discuss why he left.

"No, but in no uncertain terms my career got thrown in the air. I wasn't safe, neither was my family. I got out before it was too late for my family," he stepped toward his car door, Crystal remained in the way.

"Please tell us," she said, inches from his face. "We can stop it, but we need to know what we are up against."

He grabbed the door handle and stared back at her. She stepped to the side, and he opened the door and sat in the seat. "I swore to protect my family, and I will," he slammed the door. He drove forward about 10 feet then came to a stop. Then reversed and rolled his window down.

Crystal and I stepped toward the window to find out what he finally wanted to say.

"They will do anything to keep you from stopping them. Are you sure you can pay that price?" he said with his gaze squarely out his windshield.

"Yes, I will," I said to him.

He looked over at us and his eyes bounced between us. "Did either of you serve?" he asked.

"I'm a vet," Crystal said. "Multiple tours in Iraq, Afghanistan, and Syria." She stepped forward and slightly in front of me.

"You know all those interpreters we used over there?" he asked rhetorically. "It's a shame they are just letting them into the country. They know nothing about them."

"What?" Crystal asked.

He put his car in drive, flipped his lights and sirens on and sped off.

"Interpreters?" I said out loud to no one in particular and watched him speed through the parking lot and out onto the street. As he left my sight, I turned and walked toward our car.

"Am I counting wrong? Or are we at eight dead people connected to four agencies? All dead for investigating a different part of this." I fiddled with my keys as I turned over the details in my mind. Jason came over to his from his car where he provided over watch on the situation.

"Nine," Crystal said. "What about you, are you really going to keep following this?"

"I have nothing to lose," I said.

"Your parents, your brother?" she said and tried to catch my eyes.

"We will find a way to stop them." I had confidence in my mission, but I also knew the importance of not showing weakness. Especially if it got dicey.

"Iranian militia group, bombs, dirty politicians, corrupted agencies, dead agents, dead children, what makes you think we are so special?" She grabbed my arm and turned me toward her.

"There is no way every agency got corrupted. We will find the one that isn't. We can do it. We don't report to anyone, they won't see us coming."

"Colby?"

"I'm not giving up like Officer Hartford there. Some things require more fortitude than people have. If you want out, get out. This is what I'm doing. I'm going to do everything in my power to stop this corruption and this Iranian militia and whatever it is they have planned."

"Can we even be successful?" Crystal said.

"We have to try. Nine, right, nine people died just for looking in, that we know of. It's worth finding the bottom. Someone has to try. Vernon and Hartford were good agents, which means there are more good agents out there. Probably way more good ones than corrupted."

"Given Hartford's story, he told his leadership and suddenly Vernon is dead. Then someone in the Boston Marshall office or in their leadership chain is definitely corrupted. We don't know where it starts and stops, just like what we found with the Coast Guard down in Miami," Crystal said. "This is not the first trail of militia influence we found in Boston, but the real question is why Boston, why Miami?"

Jason added, "I know this much—we will not stay off anyone's radar if we keep poking the bees' nest. We need to pull back, stick to the computers and surveillance. We don't want to come across an Officer Hartford who has actually flipped who will tell them we are onto something." Jason gave us the strategic view on what to do, and we would not have made it without him.

"We will probably only get one shot at this. If they find out we are onto them, we will end up in a ditch somewhere too," Crystal said.

"Initial success or total failure," I said, repeating the explosive ordnance disposal (EOD) motto to her, the motto she had as an EOD officer.

She nodded. She understood. "We find the right way, strike first and hard, and they can't come after us."

I nodded and unlocked the car with the key fob and headed for the door.

Crystal reluctantly nodded in agreement.

"Your list though, Iranian militia, politicians, etcetera, you forgot interpreters," I said to her and got into the car.

She got in the other side, "Great, another thing we have to track down."

If Hansen and Anchor were linked to the interpreters that Officer Hartford was chasing as a US Marshall up in Boston, then there had to be more in the money trail. Top Hat was a big part of it. I couldn't find anything else that jumped out at me.

I switched the money trail and switched to all the things we got from Columbia. We broke into the home of one of the accountants for the drug cartel. We had been watching his work, his money laundering and the like through spyware on his systems we had installed. I looked through his transactions to see if anything lined up.

Hours of numbers and spreadsheets and... wait... I've seen that name but in Hansen and Anchor's files or somewhere else. I went back and searched Isfahan Royal. I used some Boolean logic to get around misspellings. Then it popped up Esphihan Royal Star. They system didn't catch it because it transliterated from Farsi with different spellings. Isfahan had made a substantial payment to a consulting company supporting Hansen and Anchor and a sizeable payment to a Columbian Company that the accountant did work for.

Holy fuck. I had tied Hanson and Anchor to a company that was doing business with the cartel. That might have been the payment for the explosives shipment. I had a good feeling Isfahan was the front for Iranian Militia Group. That is a solid lead the team could put the forensic accountants on.

My eyes burned. I had to get Asher his laptop back by morning, before he went into the office. I quickly pulled out enough info to make a report, but I didn't write it all. I knew they could tell from the report it was me. I put an extra item at the bottom of the checklist. Found it with a check mark and FINISH REPORT without a checkmark. I also wrote, "Look into Top Hat, there has to be a connection."

I drove to Asher's house. I used his truck keypad to drop the bag in his truck.

I twisted down hard on the tourniquet around the young Turkish man's arm. He worked in this chow hall as a server. I saw him every day; I didn't know his name. His arm was mangled, and I don't think doctors could save it. He looked so scared and, in this moment, English clearly made little sense.

"Put pressure here," I said to the soldier that helped me. I checked the man's body. None of the other injuries seemed as severe as his arm.

"You are gonna be okay," I said to the server.

I looked up and surveyed the chaos, and it was just that. No one had taken charge of the situation.

"You got this. Stay with him," I said to the soldier who pressed down on his arm.

"Yes, sergeant," he said back to me.

I got up and assessed who else needed help. It seemed the ones with the worst of the injures, the life-threatening type were under someone's care, almost all people from my team who saw to that. There were three obviously dead bodies, one appeared to be an Iraqi, and two were U.S. soldiers. The Iraqi was most likely the suicide bomber who perpetrated this lunchtime massacre.

"You three," I called out to some soldiers who looked shocked but not too terribly injured. "You alright?" I asked.

"Yes, alright enough," one of them replied.

"Good," I said. "You see these injured folks back here? It's gonna be real hard to get them out. I need you to move over some of this debris so we can get stretchers back in here and get them out. Someone's gonna be coming in that door, so we need to make sure they can get in." I was certain that people who responded to the blast tried to clear up to us. We were in the thick of it, but the serving lines and such were partially blocked off by a wall. Most likely on the other side of that wall were a ton of people who would try to come back to us.

They immediately went to work pushing the largest debris to the side as they worked the way to the door.

"Any of you three have a phone?" I asked.

"I do, sergeant," one of them said.

"Give it to me," I said.

His face was covered in dust, blood hung on his cheek, but I don't think it was his blood. He handed it to me.

I swiped the camera on and filmed a video. They would need it for the investigation. I first detailed the area they cleared. Then turned and gave a wide view and headed toward the others. Especially the suicide bomber. That was ground zero for the investigation. Details were already lost when we treated the wounded; we didn't need it to be worse.

"That Iraqi," said a lieutenant leaned up against a serving trolly flipped on its side. He seemed alright, with some shrapnel but shook up real bad. "He had a suicide vest." He was in shock, more than he realized. Help was moments away, and I knew it. "He..." the lieutenant paused.

"Sir?" I asked him and snapped him out of his daze.

"He was my interpreter," he said. I knew that would hit him hard in the coming weeks, and probably for the rest of his life. If I was his unit commander, I would be seriously concerned about suicide and put him on watch.

Three minutes ago, I had just loaded a big plate of food after being out most of the night and morning on a mission. I didn't even get out of the serving area when it exploded.

34

I HAD NOT HEARD from Asher in three days, and he had deleted me from Tinder, so I had to pursue other avenues. I don't think Asher turned me in, but he was smart enough to remove traces of our connection if someone was getting close. I hired Peter through a college message board to go to the Library of Congress and retrieve the information Brickman left there. I couldn't stand being stagnant. I told Peter I was in New York and needed the information desperately as part of a scavenger hunt. In reality, I went to DC, and I didn't want to be too close to the Library of Congress when this went down. I needed to have an avenue to take what Peter found if needed. Chinatown was busy enough to keep me hidden, but close enough I could respond. Peter said he would get there around 3:30 after his last class. I waited impatiently at the Chipotle.

I never understood DC's Chinatown. This Chipotle was dead in the center. Sure, it had a sign with Chinese writing, but it was just Chipotle. Same with most of the stores and restaurants in this area, same as just about anywhere else you go. It was nearing 4:30 pm, and I was getting anxious. Luckily everyone in Chipotle was just as in a hurry and impatient as me. Finally, my email dinged; it was a picture on the back page. Under 'Amazon Review' it had:

"Choose a path; Top Hat or Penn 701, CV-67, VT-24, VF-34."

Fuck. What the hell does that mean? I wrote back, "Anything else written in there?" Top Hat, again. Brickman knew there was something there, or he heard after the report I helped Asher put together.

"No," Peter typed back.

Peter sent another email, "Is that an address? 701 Pennsylvania?"

I Googled it, Navy Memorial Museum. "Could be, can you go?" I knew I picked Peter for a reason. He was smart.

"Sure."

I wasn't far from there. It was in a basement. I couldn't go into that place. This would be an excellent opportunity to see if anyone was following Peter. The National Archives were across the street, and I could watch from there. I packed my things and moved in that direction.

There was a line of tourists waiting to get into the National Archives out front. I needed to get in much quicker before Peter made it over to the Navy Memorial. I looked at their website and found a business entrance on Pennsylvania Avenue. I found the name of an archivist as I walked up to it. At the security check, I emptied my pockets into the basket and pushed it in to the x-ray machine. I walked through the detector, and the guard said nothing to me. No need to lie, great. I headed up the stairs. I needed to find an overlook. I climbed up to the third floor. I pretended to know where I was going. It worked. I saw an open conference room along the window side overlooking Pennsylvania Avenue. I went in and pulled out a camera and hid it behind a curtain. I aimed at the plaza, giving me a view of the Navy Memorial and the main entrance to the museum. The plaza was a huge oval with a sailor statue in the middle. It was lined by a bench. Behind it all was a sidewalk and a building; in one of them, it led to the basement museum of the Navy Memorial. The camera captured a large portion of it. I wanted to see what tails Peter might have, and I needed more than one angle. Also, it would be better for me to be farther away in case they were people laying a trap for me.

I had to go; staying there would raise too many questions. I went back down the stairs and back out the entrance I came in. I crossed the street and headed down into the Metro.

I found a bench near the trains and pulled up the feed from the Archives of the plaza on my phone. I watched, waited for Peter to show up. I saw it then, something was wrong, wasn't it? No, I was seeing things.

I glimpsed Peter, coming off the Metro. He didn't know what I looked like, so I didn't have to worry about that. I kept my eyes on the phone, on the plaza. Peter emerged at the top of the escalators into the edge of the plaza and headed toward the museum. I kept watching; I could feel it again—something was wrong. I couldn't place it. I stood up and stepped into the waiting train. I didn't know what it was.

Then I saw it—an SUV pulled up slightly out of frame; three people got out and spread out. FUCK! I dismantled the phone. FUCK. I couldn't check that email, not again. I also needed to get out of the Metro. Too many cameras in here.

The next stop was Gallery Place; it was usually a busy station. It would be perfect. As I exited the train, I dropped a piece of the phone in the crack between the train and platform. I threw another in a trash can and dropped the rest in a homeless man's cup with some change.

As I approached the escalators to the next level, I noticed a cop at the top. I tried to keep from looking over at her. As I reached the top, she grabbed for her gun. She yelled something that was inaudible with the noise of the crowd and train. The gun, however, parted the masses and backed people up onto the escalators. She wouldn't fire into the crowd. I slowly moved toward her with my hands up. The crowd surged with me, and I grabbed her hands, pulling her toward me and sweeping her legs and taking the gun as she fell to the floor. I took the gun apart as I ran. I dropped it on the ground. I didn't need to be shot in all of this for holding it, DC has strict gun laws.

I headed toward the stairs to the surface; the crowd was so thick I had to wade with them. It was insane. There had to be an event at the arena with the number of people that were in the Metro. Capitals game...I saw the sea of red as soon as I recognized one jersey. I saw a hat sitting in someone's purse; I snatched it and put it on my head. I kept close to a group of rowdy college kids, smiled and tried to make it look like I was with them.

As I approached the surface, I saw one of the big dark SUVs. I averted my eyes away from the SUV. Someone grabbed my arm through the crowd from behind me. I pulled my arm out of their grasp and threw the student next to me at them. I was grabbed again, this time by two arms around my body. I slammed my head backward into his face and grabbed his nuts at the same time. Then dropped my legs out from under me, freeing me from his grip. He leaned forward, and I used his momentum to throw him forward into the crowd.

I got up, pushed my way into the crowd, snatched a jersey off someone's waist and threw it on. I found a drunk guy and put his arm around me. He was talking to me, and I was watching the world. We got near the mall doors before the Arena, and I turned out from under his arm and went into the mall. I passed the first store and went in an unmarked side door for the service hallway. I ran for the stairs and went down to the service basement and started an all-out sprint to the other side of the mall.

"Have you seen anyone run by?" I yelled at the lone janitor in the corridor, as if I was chasing someone. He stared at me in stunned silence and leaned against the wall. I went around him and continued my sprint. At the far end of the building, I climbed up a level and went into the back of a Chinese restaurant and out to the street. I saw a cab coming, and I jumped in. That was too fucking close. I would have to find another way out of this shit storm. Of course, Brickman set a trap. "God damn it, FUCK!" I said out loud.

"You alright back there?" my cabbie asked me through the mirror.

I looked up at the driver, "Fucking lying man," I said. "No offense." He smiled back at me through the mirror. I had to leave DC.

"Why are you fixated on Top Hat?" I asked Asher.

"Mac, how many times are you gonna ask? They just have a lot of business with Hansen and Anchor, the blackmailers who worked for Ashenhurst." Asher said and focused on his computer.

"I have known you a long time, and you are not acting normal right now," I said to him.

Asher shrugged his shoulders and continued whatever he did on his computer.

"Didn't you just go see Aaron in the hospital, right before he got discharged?"

Asher didn't reply.

"Did he talk to her? Is that where this is coming from?"

"I don't know what in the fuck you are talking about," he said and continued what he was doing.

I rolled my chair up to him, "If you or him have been talking to her, you need to fucking let us know," I whispered into his ear.

He looked at me, "Talked to who?"

"I fucking knew it." I knew by the way he responded he had talked to her. All we talked about around here was Jackie. What we did wrong and what she did. There were no other women for us to talk about. Jackie was the center of everything going on in our professional lives.

"Mac, what are you talking about?"

"Are you going to stake your career on her again? What did she tell you?" I lowered my voice, and we made direct eye contact from our chairs.

"She didn't say a word to me," Asher seemed confident in that statement, maybe that meant they were sending messages to each other somehow.

"If you know how to find her, or contact her, this is the time to say something." He turned away from me and went back to his computer.

"Those guys we caught up in Boston confirmed that bombing of hers was a part of their plan." I said to him. The would-be bombers caught with the materials for the dirty bomb said that Jackie was in on their bombing. She actually ran her first few bombings as a test run for them so they would know what to do when they finally got the dirty bomb material into the country.

"That it isn't true. She told us what the bombing was and gave us all the details. She is one of us," Asher said.

"She was duped, Asher. She was too stupid to see she was being used."

"Go to hell, Mac," Asher said.

Doc walked up, "What is going on?"

"Asher has been talking to Jackie," I said in a normal voice and leaned back in my chair.

"What the fuck, Mac? No, I haven't," Asher said and turned his chair around.

"I swear to God, Asher, if you have been talking to her and not telling the FBI, I'm going to kick your ass," Doc said. "She is a fucking terrorist. When are you going to get it through your fucking skull? Just because you want to fuck her, doesn't mean she is worth shit. How can you look at the mountain of evidence and witnesses and say you know better than all of that? She is a terrorist. She bombed her country before, and she was happy to do it again."

"Don't talk about her that way," Asher said, stood up, and got in Doc's face.

"Whoa, whoa, you two, calm down," I said. I wanted to fire up Doc, but I forgot he had gone down the "I told you so" route.

Lee walked up, "What is happening?"

Doc and Asher were in each other's faces, both with fists balled up. They were within a foot of each other.

"This fucker is a traitor," Doc said and pulled his hand up to just in front of his face and pointed at Asher.

"Fuck you, Doc," Asher said and lurched forward.

Lee jumped between them and pushed Asher back, "Not worth it, stop, stop."

Asher took a few steps back.

I grabbed Doc, "Come on, man. We can't fight in here." Doc turned to leave.

"Don't come near me again, Doc," Asher said from behind Lee.

35

I did something I had not done in a really long time. I got ready for the day, heels, nice outfit, make-up, curled my hair, and even put on lipstick. I looked in the mirror, and I wasn't recognizable. I could walk right in front of anyone, and I would not be Colby or Jackie to them. I had a big bag with boots, just in case, and so I could throw in whatever I found.

I took a Lyft, because that's what a normal person my age does in the city, especially in heels. It pulled up outside the building, and I got out. I was a little unsteady in the heels, but I would struggle through. I walked through the door, and an employee greeted me, "Welcome to West Elm, can I help you find anything today?" I stopped here on the day we chased the bomb. Except I came through the back entrance from the service hallway. If I were investigators, I would expect me to come back here.

"I will let you know," I said with a smile. I headed straight for the back corner of where I was before. I found the armoire and opened it, pulled out the drawers, nothing. Damn.

I stood up and looked around for a second as another employee came up to me, "Do you have any questions about the armoire?"

Then I saw two of the same desks sitting next to each other. "Do you have another one of these?" I asked him.

"I think so, we have one in clearance," the employee said. "It's right upstairs, I can show you."

"Thank you." I didn't remember being upstairs when I was here. I followed the employee up the escalator as he pointed it out.

I looked at it for a second then went to look at the other things in clearance, waiting for the employee to walk away. Once he did, I went up to it. There were smudges on it, brown, spots... blood. It's probably what got it kicked up to the clearance section. I closed my eyes as I remembered my hand pushed into Aaron's stomach, the blood that covered me that day, the blood I didn't get to scrub off until the following day. This was the armoire; I knew it. I opened it and saw the smudges on the bottom drawer. I pulled it out, and the box was still in there; it was covered with smudges too. I pulled out the phone and my work computer and slid them into my purse.

I shut the drawers and the door, and I said goodbye to the smudges of blood that belonged to Aaron. If Aaron was still in Beth Israel, it was less than a mile from here. I was very tempted to see him. It hurt to know I couldn't. As I was going down the escalator, I pulled out his picture and looked it over. I didn't think he was going to make it, and I wouldn't even get to see him before, if it hasn't happened already. I could feel it in my soul that he was leaving. I almost needed it to put myself back together. Him dead solved so many of my problems.

36

OVER THE LAST WEEK, I used tools I could pull off my laptop and information I found on hacking message boards to break into the GPS tracking software that had the location of the crude materials for the dirty bomb. Christian used the software to track the shipment, and something told me he used that software before. It would be difficult to prove though. Even with the tools I could pull off my work laptop I found at West Elm, I still had to find help elsewhere. I spent more time on hacker message boards looking for tips.

While on the message board, I saw a post from someone named C_S3PS; I recognized it, but the name was spelled differently, probably to avoid detection. The name was the same as someone I had run into the past, Zeps. You had to read a different language in these chats and message boards. I opened the message posted by C_S3PS. The message included a challenge to find the real-life location of the person in the picture.

When I was in college, I used to spend hours on different sites trying hacking challenges. At one point, I saw a message board, "1000 dollars to the first person who breaks into this app."

I was hard pressed for cash, and it was a lot better than all the hours I would have to work minimum wage to get that kind of money. I click on the link and accepted the challenge. I spent the better part of my spring break breaking into the app. I probably didn't sleep with all the Adderall and Monster Energy drinks I was addicted to. I was so worried someone else would beat me to it, I really wanted the money. Once I finally made it in, I confirmed on the message board I made it in. I found the post and submitted proof I made it into the app, just as he requested.

Just then I got a private message from the man who posted the challenge; his name was Zeps. "How did you do that so fast?"

"I was worried I wouldn't be first," I said.

"Oh, you were first, and many have been trying."

"That's great to hear. How do I claim my prize?" I replied, eager to get my money.

"First, send me a way in," Zeps typed back.

I realized then that maybe Zeps had a target, and he tricked me into doing his work. I went back to look at the app and actually take in what it was. It didn't look like much, a non-profit for something that made little sense to me. I realized then I had been tricked into committing a crime. I didn't think straight on the Adderall. I just saw money and a challenge.

"Forget it man, I don't want your money, and I'm not giving you that." I dismantled what I did and backed out of breaking into the app. I also had destroyed everything related to what I just did.

"Don't go. We could use someone like you. I have asked everyone in the alliance, and no one was able to do that, and you did it in a week."

I was intrigued, "What alliance?"

"Cordyceps Alliance. We fight to uncover the injustice in this world, seek justice for the weak, and hold the powerful accountable."

I freaked out. I accidentally contacted some of the most powerful and infamous hackers. They popped up on the news from time to time for their vigilante justice work. They would break into systems, release the information to the right parties or destroy systems of the corrupt. The last time I heard about them, they broke into a government con-tracting company and released information about government contracts coming up. They were internet vigilantes, good intentions or not, and they were operating illegally. I wanted to have their skills, but I had no interest in jail. I destroyed everything that night, including that computer.

Now looking back, I got it—they used it to recruit.

I got into the GPS tracking system two days ago; I had been dumping logs from over 2,000 users who had GPS tracking in the greater Florida area. Tonight though, I took it all and loaded it back into one login–so I could find trends. The GPS tracking data didn't really work in another pieces of software so I had to use their software to go through it. It was easier all the data was in one place though.

I used the shipment that we used to track the materials in Boston to set a baseline of what to look for. I traced it backward to Alabama, to my favorite cop, and then back to Florida where the signal originated. After some time, I found a unique set of trackers that originated in Venezuela. Out of all of them, only one ended in the area where the dirty bomb materials shipment started in Miami, about a week prior. It would make the most obvious sense; this was most likely the materials for the dirty bomb. This gave me a complete trip for the container.

I knew the cartel was not the only company using this software, so I had to find patterns that mirrored what I just saw. I had to filter out the legitimate use of the software, which I guessed was 99% of what I was looking at.

I looked for similar patterns: Originating in Venezuela, then a new tracker starting in Florida within two weeks.

By 2 am, I had established an easy way to pull patterns, and I found a consistent pattern of a few a week. I had gone back in time about five months when I got an alarm on my virtual machine. Someone was attempting to breach my firewalls. I hit download on the materials. They were attacking from the GPS tracking software...SHIT. I don't know if they were government or just cyber security for that GPS tracking software company. I booted up my old work laptop. After a few minutes, I was kicked out of the tracking software. It seemed to me then, their cyber security team figured out they had someone in their system. I had enough details though, to make a case for further investigation.

I needed to connect my work laptop to the internet to pass this information over to my old team. If they had their ducks in a row, the FBI and DEA would be waiting for this missing laptop to come online and should even let me connect. That would help them find me. I had no other way of contacting them. I didn't trust other agencies.

I knew this was going to be the final stop, and then I would say goodbye to everything. If I got out of this shit storm or not, I was going to say goodbye to it all. I had to let it all go—that is what I was good at. That is how I moved on.

I tried my old credential to login, but of course, that didn't work. I used Asher's credentials, and I was in. I started to transfer the materials from my virtual machine to my work laptop, and I then had to get it uploaded into the DEA servers.

A work chat window popped up, "You're not Asher." It was from Mac. When I logged in as Asher, it probably kicked Asher out of his profile, if he was on that late. Mac must have noticed it, or Asher said something to him and sent me a chat message. I guess he must have known that Asher was not logged into the system, and how strange it was to see him log in. A green dot would have popped up next to his name. Also, they probably were watching Asher after I fed him intel before. It would make sense if they considered his credentials compromised.

It gave me an idea. Instead of just uploading the data, I could talk to CJ. I clicked on CJ's profile and typed him a message, "I can't prove a negative, but I can prove whose side I am on and will always be. I'm putting it on the shared drive. All the data on drug shipments coming through Florida in the last six months and how to find more. If I'm right, there might be more materials inbound from Iran. In the very least, you will find a lot of drugs and might dismantle the cartels' operations in the U.S."

The transfer to my work laptop finished. I then started the upload to the work servers what I learned from my analysis of the tracking software and what I suspected linked to the cartel. It would take additional research to find out what were drugs versus other shipments for the Iranian militia. They would have to do that with the additional manpower and follow up with on-the-ground investigators. I had to give it over to CJ because I knew he would dig into it, where potentially it would be buried with another agency.

Whoever figured out I had breached the shipment tracking software, knew my location, and so I had to move quickly. I watched the data as it uploaded; it was a lot, so this was going to take time.

The virtual machine on my other computer continued to send me more alarms; they had broken through my first line of defense. They had breached some of my walls and were bringing down the software hiding my location. I knew then it was not just cyber security; someone who wanted to find me was tearing through my security. That took expert level hackers that the government employs. I couldn't stop them; I had to get what I found uploaded. I had to stop additional bombs. My research showed them how to find the materials. We knew intel said there would be multiple bombs, and to me that meant, we only stopped one in Boston.

I stood up. I watched the progress bar. A new alarm came up; they had breached another layer. My VPN had gone down—my tunnel to the internet no longer protected me; it also meant they knew where I was. All that was left was my last firewall, and they would be into my system. I had to let it happen; I just needed the data to finish uploading.

I checked the cameras in the building and in the hotel, so far nothing out of the ordinary. I went to the door and turned to watch the progress bar; it was so close to being done. I needed the progress bar to say "complete" and then disappear, and I would do the same. It was hanging. I went back to see what was going on. I glanced over at my VM; my protection was gone. They could see my computer, my IP, everything, and they were on the inside. Hopefully the upload would finish before they stopped it. They knew where I was now. "Come on," I said out loud to my work computer.

I went back to the door and looked back at my set-up. SUVs had pulled up outside. I opened the door; I had to go. I stepped outside, turned and ran back in. I couldn't leave Aaron. I ran back in and grabbed his picture. I was going to leave it too, but when it came time, I couldn't. Whatever we were, it was over, but his picture brought me comfort. My IP should put me in the real estate office, not the hotel, which would give me precious time to get out of here. I was in a mix-use building in New York City that had a hotel and some commercial offices. Earlier I found my way into a real estate office and connected to their Internet. I ran a direct line to my hotel room.

I had preset a route to get out of here. I ran to the far side of the hotel and went down the stairs. The stairs connected me to the offices on the opposite side of the building. I went down a couple flights and through the door I had taped open; I removed it as I went through. I ran to the service doors in the service hallway. I ran across the building and down the stairs to the service entrance. My bags were stashed in a service closet just outside the bottom of the stairs. I grabbed them and went into the back of a restaurant. I pushed my way into the crowded bar. I got near the windows and peered out but stayed a few rows into the crowd. There were SUVs out on that side.

I opened my phone and ordered a Lyft. I knew Aaron's military backpack would be a dead give-away. I took a knee and moved what I needed into my other bag. The Lyft pulled up. I quickly typed to him, "Be right out."

I looked around the bar and saw a woman leaving. I stopped her, pulled $100 out of my pocket and waved it in front of her. "A hundred dollars if you do something for me." She stared at me, suspicious. "My ex wants this bag back, he's... look can you take it and drop it at that building over there, just outside the apartment doors," I said, pointing down the road and across.

"One hundred dollars for that?" she asked, still suspicious of me.

"You ever date someone you swore you would never see again?" I asked her.

She took a second, "Yeah, okay," she said. "Give me the money." I handed her the money and the bag. She walked out the doors and lit a cigarette and walked up the street. I texted the Lyft again, "Coming out now." I waited until the men from the SUV spotted her and followed. When they passed, I went straight out to the car and got in. We drove off, and I tried not to look out the window. I don't think they saw me. We got about ten blocks away, and I got out and hailed a cab, more anonymous.

"Sulaiman," I called out as I saw him cross the street into the park. I suspected his route home from his office would require him to walk through Tudor Park on his way to Grand Central Station in New York. He didn't love cities that much, and he loved birds. He used to say, 'what I wouldn't give to not know what we were dealing with.' This park had those things. I pushed myself up with my arms; I had not quite recovered enough to be out running after a source. Asher had been tracing a lead from Colby that linked Hansen and Anchor to Isfahan Royal Star. She also had him looking into Top Hat's connection to them, a contractor that supplied interpreters to the U.S. in Iraq. The trail went cold, and no one would help him. No one wanted to take Colby's lead about Top Hat.

Sulaiman turned and took a minute to recognize my face.

"Ericcson," he said, "almost didn't recognize you without your beard," he said and came in for a hug. I gave him a hug and tried to hide the pain of him running into my recent injuries from my gunshot.

"Glad I caught you," I said.

"Why did you catch me?" he said, and his eyes darted around.

I walked in the direction he headed before I derailed him. "I'm glad to see you doing so well. I always thought you would set the world on fire. Interpreter at the UN is a big deal."

"I haven't seen or heard from you since Iraq, two, three years ago, maybe more. Something tells me this isn't a social visit." He didn't mince words—he never did—even when he worked as my interpreter.

"I wish it was, but I need help."

"If you didn't save my life more than once, I would say fuck off," he said and let out a laugh. "Is this about that attempted bombing up in Boston?"

"What are you talking about?" The details went out to the public, but the news didn't really pick up the story. No one cared about the thing that didn't happen. I wanted to sus out what he already knew.

"Don't play dumb with me. Iran had a successful bombing a few years ago, and rumor has it they almost did it again, but it would have been much worse this time."

"Iran was involved before?" I asked genuinely. Jackie never mentioned that part of the story. I was honestly shocked; with everything she talked about, she never alluded to that. Of course, why would she? Maybe she is playing both sides so well, we missed it.

"You and I both know Iranians are involved, hardly a hidden fact," he leaned toward me. We both descended the stairs to the main road as we continued toward the train terminal. "Although, no one really knew that previous bombing was Iranian, but it makes sense that information is coming out now."

"You aren't supposed to play intelligence agency," I said to him.

"It's not my fault interpreters are involved in every meeting of consequence across the Middle East, especially ones that require high levels in English, Farsi, and Arabic, and somehow people forget we exist. What do you want, Ericcson?"

"What can you tell me about Isfahan Royal Star?"

"They supply interpreters, just like Top Hat, my old employer," he said.

"Same thing?" I asked again.

"Same company essentially," he pulled me aside. "Iranians need interpreters just like Americans, same skill set. Just different brands for the same group of people. Isfahan in Iran and other middle east countries, Top Hat for the expat countries. I only worked for Top Hat, but I know many interpreters who have worked for both."

"So they supply both sides?"

"Wouldn't you? Then you are always employed. Also, gives them insight into what is going on, especially in Iraq and Iran."

"To what end?"

"Look, Top Hat, Isfahan, they have one goal, always have," he looked around.

"Which is what?" I asked.

"Establishing the true Kurdistan across Iraq, Iran, and Turkey. They serve no other purpose. They use the interpreting contracts to get money and to gain intelligence on what is going on. It's why I left them; once I reached a certain level, it became obvious that is what they wanted to do. My leadership asked too many questions about my actual work. They asked about my last commander's missions and priorities; I did not feel comfortable with it. The higher-level person you worked for, the more you were pressed. That's all the leadership talked about. That's why I left them. I'm not Kurdish, I don't need to forward that agenda."

"Is this related to the attempted bombing in Boston?" I confirmed the information I denied before.

He gave me a knowing look, "I don't know. I'm not in that business anymore, but if they were, it makes sense. If they could lure the U.S. into war with Iran, Kurdistan would have time to break free and establish their own country."

"So this is an Iranian Kurdish thing, not an Iranian special interest group?"

He gave me a knowing nod and then descended into the subway.

37

"Hey, Stacey," I said, walking in as I tied on my apron.

"Jackie," she said and didn't look at me. She was checking someone out and God forbid they gave her cash because she had a tough time making the change.

I walked into the back and clocked in. The old man that ran the place still used an old punch clock. Can't hack an old punch clock, not the way I would. I would like to take it apart one day though. I washed my hands and headed back out. It was a small restaurant, but it stayed pretty busy. There are only a few restaurants around here and on the weekend, this place had a steady crowd. Between this job and the maid work, I was doing alright for the last three months. The first couple months were dicey until I found this place. They didn't ask many questions and most importantly they didn't ask about my lack of documentation.

It was after lunch, so the place was having a momentary die down in traffic. I grabbed a bin and went out to help clear some tables. I kneeled down on the bench of the corner booth. It had a big round table, and some kid always left a syrupy mess somewhere and I wanted to find it. I pulled all the dishes in and wiped the table and the booth down. I put everything back in its place. I turned with the bin and looked at the three other tables that needed my attention. I wasn't watching where I was going, and I crashed right into someone.

"I'm so..." I stopped breathing when my eyes met his. I dropped the bin on the ground. "You...?" I said as the world collided on top of me. His eyes pierced through me. I saw a knife on the table I needed to clear. I backed up, reaching my hand out for it. "Why are you guys here?"

"Just me, Colby," he said.

I had the knife in hand, "I saw Asher, earlier, when I was running. I thought I was seeing things."

He put his hands up, palms facing me, "It's okay, we aren't here to get you or anything. I just... I had to see you."

I was shaky as the periphery of people around Aaron came into view. One cook had come out of the back and stared at us. I breathed out through my mouth. I let go of the knife, opened my eyes, and ran into his arms, wrapping my arms around his neck, "You're alive..." I said in utter disbelief. In my mind I decided he died. It was how I dealt with the trauma. If he were alive, I had to deal with my feelings for him. If he died in that hospital, then I could close that chapter and let him go. When I got a chance, I tried to find information about it or him and couldn't find any. I made my peace with myself; to heal from the trauma was to just assume death. The last update I got was he was back in the ICU.

His arms closed around me, "I told you I would be okay." It felt so good to be in his arms. His beard felt so good against my face. He smelled like him; it sent goosebumps all over my body. I pulled back to see his eyes, and my eyes filled with tears, my stomach flipped, and my heart raced. I kissed him, and he kissed me back. I got weak. He stopped and pulled back out of my arms. He reached for my hand and pulled me out of the restaurant.

It was then I noticed the whole place had stopped and was fixated on us. I turned red as I followed Aaron, my Ross, my ranga, out of the restaurant into the rain. Once outside, he wrapped me in his arms again as the rain soaked us, unwilling to let each other go.

I woke in the middle of the night. When I opened my eyes, I was in disbelief. There he was my Ross, my ranga, Aaron. He lay on his side facing me. I rolled onto my side and looked at him, every piece of him. His chiseled face with his two-day-old beard. I reached out and felt his face; he moved to my touch. He didn't even open his eyes; he just reached out and pulled me into him. He wrapped his arms around me tight, and it felt so good. I missed him.

After a few minutes, he fell back to sleep, and his grip around me loosened. I slowly rolled out of his arms. I went over to my dresser and pulled out some clothes, put them in my bag and got dressed. I put on our gray shirt, threw on pants. I looked around the room; my bag was pretty much always packed; it would be enough. I grabbed it and my shoes and went out to the front porch. I sat down on the stairs and tied on my shoes. I stood up and walked down the street.

I was only a house away when I heard, "Jackie." I turned, and there was Aaron in his black boxer briefs. "Where are you going?" he asked.

"If you can find me, they can too; it's not safe for me here anymore." As I said it, I was unexpectedly choked up. This place was good, and it was good to see him, but I…

"Come on," he waved me back, "come say goodbye to me."

That warmed my heart, I walked back to him. He was still as sculpted as I remembered him, but you could tell all the time in the hospital took its toll. I wrapped my arms around him and felt his chest on my face.

He took his hands and cupped my face. "Colby James, I love you." When I first met him, before I even changed my name, I told him my name belonged to him. It was inextricably linked to him and our relationship. Ross held the same meaning.

I went flush. I leaned up and kissed him; those words were harder for me to say because I loved him so much, but I…

"I asked Asher to come by in the morning; don't you want to see him?"

I wanted to see him, but my safety, my freedom, was paramount.

"I will make breakfast, and we will get all caught up."

I stared back at him conflicted on what to do. I would love to sit there with them and start life over, start my life with Aaron, to catch-up with Asher, but I was afraid of prison, his prison, any prison and it collided with it all.

He wrapped his arms around me again, "I promise you, Jackie, no one followed us. No one wants to; you're safe here. I will make sure it stays that way if something changes."

I nodded. "Asher's coming by in the morning?" I questioned him.

"Yep."

"That confident you would get laid, you sent him away yesterday?"

He smiled and chuckled a little. "Maybe. I needed you to myself," he grabbed the side of my chin with his finger and thumb. "Stay just a little longer?"

I nodded yes. I wasn't questioning the sanity for my love of him anymore, I accepted it. I knew about the albatross that was undertow leading to our drowning, my unrequited love for my country would mean we would never work. He was still property of the United States Government, and I was wanted by that same government, and I would have to keep running. Our worlds wouldn't be able to merge.

Since he found me in the diner, we spent the day wrapped up in each other. Talking about his recovery, his time in the hospital. My adventures of trying to make things work, being wanted, and not having any documents and running low on money and everything in between.

I didn't tell him I took one of the C_S3PS challenges to find a person, who I found out was involved in child sex trafficking. I found his location in Madison, Wisconsin, and the bitcoin they gave me for that helped me get through. I also didn't mind helping track down a predator like that. I thought perhaps this might be a good way to go in the future; it would give me freedom. Given the fact the FBI was looking for me, a savvy investigator might find me through something like this. So it would be best I didn't show up too much in that realm.

Somewhere between talking in bed, he made me dinner. The entire time I knew there was a clock running on the time, the one that said the longer I lived in the moment, the higher risk there was of me being dragged out to sea. I knew if I tried to leave while he was awake, I wouldn't be able to; that's why I chose the middle of the night. I knew when I turned and saw him on the sidewalk in front of my temporary home, I wasn't leaving.

I walked into the house and kicked off my shoes and sat down on the couch. This one-room house was all I had. I couldn't get invested; I needed to leave at a moment's notice. It was around 3 am. Aaron went into the kitchen and made coffee. Maybe he knew that if he fell back to sleep, it would be the end. I had functioned on little sleep, occasional naps. Between the nightmares and the fear of getting caught, I could never sleep, not for real.

I leaned up against the arm of the couch; he came sat down across from me. He pulled my feet into his lap and rubbed them. I put my head back and for a moment imagined our life together if... just if...

"Is that my shirt?"

I turned red and picked my head up, "Maybe."

"I knew you ransacked my house, but I was confused by the dresser. Now I get it."

I smiled.

"What else did you take besides a bunch of my military gear and guns?"

I leaned over and picked up my bag. I pulled out two laptops. "This," I said, showing his of the two.

"Find anything in there?"

"Only that you have piss poor security habits."

"That's it?" he said skeptically.

"I can't tell you everything." I set the laptops on the ground and reached into my pocket and pulled out his picture and handed it to him. It was beat up from always being on me. He looked at it and back at me. He scooted toward me on the couch, pulling my legs over him and reaching his hand out to touch my face.

"I thought you were dead," I said.

He wiped his thumb across my cheek.

"I guess it's a theme with us, me thinking you are dead," I said with a chuckle.

"What else?" he said.

"One of your hats, a black one."

"Where is it?" he asked.

"You can't have it back," I said.

"Okay," he said with a smile.

"I keep it in a safe spot with some other things I don't want to lose. This stuff headed there soon, too."

"Is that it?" he asked.

I shook my head no. I reached back in the bag and pulled out his notebook on me.

This time he went flush and pulled it out of my hands. "Have you read this?"

I didn't answer. I read it, poured over it. I tried to connect each note to me, to us, to him. How rare it is to get a glimpse into someone else's point of view on you. I wanted to fill in the gaps between what he wrote, what happened, and what he thought and didn't write.

"You still want me after reading this, after what I did to you?" he asked.

"You still want me after what I did?" I asked, knowing how much he despised my bombing, and the notebook confirmed it.

He thumbed through it. "I was ruthless with you," he shook his head, and his eyes went wet. "Something about you triggered me. You hid so much, and I had to find out the details, and I would stop at nothing to get it."

This time I scooted toward him and put my hands on his face. "It's okay, I understand, I forgive you." One thing I learned in Narcotics Anonymous was holding onto the past could kill you. Living the way I was at this time I would have lost my sobriety. I also would have lost my mind if I didn't forgive myself for falling for him. Before I could forgive myself, I had to forgive him. Since I did all of that, I felt so much better.

He shook his head and pushed my legs off him. He went into the kitchen and stood at the sink with his hands stretched out on the counter, staring out the window. I watched him as he went over to his pants and pulled out his dip, put it in his lip and went back to the sink.

I got up and went to him in the kitchen. "Aaron," I said as I got near him. He didn't look back. I leaned up against the counter and looked over at him. "Somewhere between 'you're dead,' needing to move forward, needing my nightmares to end, my sobriety to stay intact and loving you with every part of me, I had to forgive you, and I did." The loneliness of being on the run and losing everything was too unbearable to carry additional guilt. I understood Aaron and why he did what he did. We are completely and utterly the same person at our core. We will do whatever it takes to get the mission done, and giving up every part of ourselves and those around us seem to go with the territory.

He got out the coffee cups and set them in front of the pot.

"Aaron," I said, putting my hand on the back of his arm.

"I can't believe I did those things to you." He met my eyes and held his emotions back, then looked away. "I can't believe I did those things, and you still want me."

"Really, it's okay. I would've done the same thing if the roles were reversed." He still didn't look at me.

"Ross," I said, trying to get him to look back at me. "I love you. I forgive you. I need you." I reached up and put my hand around the back of his neck. He shook his head and went back to fixing our coffee, just the way I liked it. "It's okay to forgive yourself."

He sighed and closed his eyes. He turned to me and put my head in his hands. "I love you," he said and kissed me, and my knees went weak. He pulled back. "Have you forgiven yourself for what you did?" he asked.

The words hit me hard. I pulled back and bit my lip. It swirled in me, and I looked up at him. "I guess... some things only God can forgive."

"Have you asked him to?"

I didn't know this ranga... all this time I never broached the topic of faith. It's just an unspoken rule in our world, our community. I prayed every day for my sobriety especially as I became increasingly alone. The last time I talked about faith was somewhere in the time of when I was still Colby in Tampa, somewhere in the time of NA every day.

He grabbed my hands, "Would you?"

I shook my head; I was lost.

"Pray with me?"

My breath left me. I was overwhelmed in a good way. I didn't think of this from him, and I wasn't ready for what he knew I needed to ask.

38

I was curled up tight in the tub waiting for the bullets to stop. I didn't have a gun. I had to get out before they found me. There were men yelling, and the bullets slowly ended. I don't think bullets, gun shots, are that loud. I have spent a lot of time at the range. Something about them being destined for you made them louder. The bang, crash of them embedding into walls and furniture is so much louder at this end when you are not pulling the trigger.

My ears were ringing. I had to go. I waited a few breaths longer to make sure no more bullets came my way. My window to leave was getting short. I peeked out the bathroom window, and it looked clear. I slid the window open and got on the toilet to shimmy my way out. I was about halfway out balanced on the sill using my hands when I saw the barrel of a 9mm inches from my head. I looked at it, and I couldn't look past it. My body froze, all of me. I stopped breathing, moving, I stopped coming out of the window, and my heart felt like it took a break too. It was just me and the barrel of a 9mm suspended in time.

I woke up on the couch while Asher and Aaron talked in the kitchen of a tiny one-room house. It was late, the sun baked the leaves through the window as I blinked myself awake. I sat up and breathed in the moment. I had slept for a long time; someone new arrived, and I missed them coming into the house. I don't even remember the last time I slept like that—safe, secure, deep, and free of dreams.

I got up and went straight to Asher; I missed him, even though all I had on was Aaron's gray shirt. I put my arms around Asher.

"Hey, Jack," he gave me half a squeeze back.

I headed back toward my pile of clothes by the mattress on the floor. "I can't believe you're here," I pulled on a pair of pants.

"You must be exhausted; you've been sleeping for hours. It's almost noon," Asher said.

I looked at the clock and thought, Fuck, I'm late for my shift at the diner. I guess I'm done with that now. I would not go back to the diner, and today would be the last time I was in this house. "I've been sleeping with one eye open for so long, I finally felt safe enough. My soul was at rest enough to sleep for real." With Aaron there, I didn't feel responsible for my security. I also didn't have a nightmare either. I looked over at Aaron, who leaned over the stove. "I wish I could have more of that." I brought my attention back to Asher, "How have you been, Ash?"

He shook his head, "You were right."

"I usually am. What are you talking about?" I lifted myself up onto the counter next to where he leaned.

"Mandie left me," he looked straight ahead.

"Ash, I'm sorry," I put my hand up on his shoulder.

"She deserves more than me," he shook his head.

Asher took her for granted, and I saw how badly he treated her. He didn't need to hear that from me. I laid my head onto his shoulder, "Should have listened to me a lot sooner."

Asher turned his body, so my head fell off his shoulder, "You?" he said, shocked. "You helped pick girls out for me."

I smiled and laughed, "Ah... those were good times."

He shook his head at me and rested against the counter.

"How is everyone else?" I asked after the team.

Aaron interrupted and handed me a coffee, just the way I like it. He was really good at that. "You guys want to sit down?" Aaron asked.

I wanted a nice CrossFit gym, a good workout, and a long run. This town didn't have that kind of gym, and the run would have to wait. I walked back to the couch and Asher pulled over a chair.

"So, this is what you ran off for? It's a real beaut, Jack," Asher said as he scanned his eyes around the room.

The last time someone touched up this old rundown house was sometimes in the '80s. I put a mattress on the wood floor. Someone a long time ago painted the floor white, and the years of stress had slowly sanded the paint away. I had dragged in a dresser I'd found in front of someone's house down the street. I had one dilapidated dining room chair I found in the backyard. The old couch came with the place. I put a blanket over the couch to hide its stains from my brain so I could still sit, and apparently sleep, on it. The house's one room contained my kitchen, living room, and bedroom, and a bathroom sat in the back corner.

"Thanks, it's everything I have ever dreamed of," I said with a smile draped in sarcasm. "You didn't answer, how is everyone?"

"Well... I uh... I got a three-month suspension for helping you," Asher said with a grimace.

I sucked in air through my teeth. I felt bad. I guess I didn't think about that when I asked him for help. Also, it's how they knew Asher wasn't really logged in when I logged in as him to upload the data.

"CJ knew you did the intel work on that report, but he couldn't prove it," he caught my eye.

"How did he know?" I knew how he knew. It wasn't a good time to tell Asher.

"I don't know."

"I'm sorry," I took a big sip of my coffee.

"It was worth it to me," he said. "Although, it's probably what did Mandie in, me getting suspended for you and being okay with it."

She really didn't like me, but she didn't know she had much bigger problems with Asher.

"Lee's finally marrying Dale. Doc's divorce is finally over. Mac is still an asshole," he concluded everyone's life in such a short amount of time. "We got some solid leads thanks to that last report you turned in and really tore apart the cartel's operation."

"And CJ...?" I asked.

"Here's the thing..." Asher started.

I looked over at Aaron who had sat down on the couch with me. I was instantly pissed off. I didn't think there would be a "thing."

"He believes you, Jack, we all do, even Mac." Asher leaned toward me.

"But..." I waited for the other side of this equation.

"No 'buts,'" Asher said, sitting up straight, "everyone wants you back. We see now you were set up. And you did good work even when on the run."

I shook my head, "I don't believe it." I looked at him and back at Aaron. Then looked back to Asher, "Just like that the FBI is done?" It made me antsy; I needed to leave. I did not like the direction of the conversation.

Asher and Aaron looked at each other and back at me.

"But is the bomb still on me?" I asked Asher. Nothing mattered if the bomb was still on me.

"No..."

"No... no, what?" I waited for the next part.

"The records from the DEA had you covered," Asher said.

"So that's it? It's over?" I asked and didn't believe the chain of events.

"They just want to talk to you," Asher said and leaned forward and opened his hands.

"That's not an option." I got up and walked into the kitchen area.

"It's okay. We're just passing a message," Aaron said. "You don't have to."

"Jack, what are you going to do, keep running, living like this?" Asher motioned around the room with his hands.

"How did you find me, anyway?" I questioned them.

"Jack, there was an 'anonymous,'" he put up air quotes with his hands, "detailed report on the movement of drugs in the next major town." He paused for a second until my eyes met his. "Everyone knew it was you."

I did that. In the running from the law enforcement coupled with lack of sleep, I nearly lost it and my grip on sobriety. I found places to buy drugs. It soothed me to know where they were, and it went that way for a while until I bought some. Back in my car I stared at the little bag of pills that sat on the passenger seat the whole way back to the place I stayed. I came very close to using those drugs. I tossed them and did something with the information to hold myself accountable. I had to remember me and not let the drugs back in to ruin my already ruined life.

"Once I had an area, I got Aaron because I knew he could find you."

I looked over at Aaron; he knew me better than I knew myself.

"Come back, talk to the FBI, and then we talk to CJ and get you back on the team. Put our team back together," Asher said with his eyebrows raised. He was always more optimistic than anyone I knew.

My anxiety shot through the roof at the thought of submitting to questioning by anyone. "Did CJ send you?" I questioned.

Asher shook his head no.

"Then why are you here?" I asked back. CJ had to approve my return to the team.

"Jack, you're out here living this life, and you don't have to. This is Colby's life; come back to Jackie's life," Asher said.

I mulled over the idea of finally escaping this life and weighed it against the fact this could align better to an elaborate trick. The two people here, would they do that to me? Maybe not knowingly. I wanted out of this life, but I didn't want to be interrogated. I hated interrogations. I had been hurt in FBI custody before, but not by them.

"There are other options," Aaron said. I stopped and looked over at him. Asher looked at him too, equally confused. "I know people who would like a chance to talk to you as well."

"About what?" Asher said defensively.

Aaron shrugged his shoulders, "They didn't say, will only say it to Colby... well, Jackie."

After Asher, Aaron, and I spent the afternoon together, I had to leave that tiny house and life I built. By them coming there, I no longer could stay. If they could find me, anyone could find me. I also had to digest their offer before I decided.

"I will meet you guys... here," I pointed to a map of Dallas.

"That's a big place, Dallas," Asher said.

"Somewhere between the Cotton Bowl Stadium and the Aquarium or somewhere around there," I said.

"Three days?" Aaron questioned.

"Three pm, three days from now," I said.

"Okay," Asher said.

"I need to think, arrange a few things," I said to them. What I needed was time to figure out a potential exit strategy. I needed to make sure I wouldn't lose what I gained. I also needed time to make sure this wasn't some elaborate trick; I had trusted no one or anything since the prison stay.

"Are you sure you can't just come with us now?" Aaron said.

"Yeah," I said. Truthfully, the thought of surrendering to the FBI terrified me. I didn't want to go to jail for that bombing. I mean maybe I could handle prison; I couldn't let my team down. I didn't want them thinking I did that. I know it didn't really matter, but it did to me. Also, what if Chin got access to me like Ross did last time I was in FBI custody?

"Can I go with you, help you?" Aaron asked.

"No, it's okay," I gave Asher a hug.

I went to Aaron, hugged him and rested my forehead against his and closed my eyes. He whispered, "Remember, you're mine, Colby," and it made me smile. I kissed him. I pulled back and got one more good look at his face; I needed it. I slowly let go and walked away.

I turned around, "If you bring anyone with you, you won't ever see me again." I looked at both of them in the face one last time.

I turned back to my path. I knew I would most likely go through with it. I just needed to be sure my emotions didn't cloud my decision-making process. The FBI could have sent the two people I trusted most in the world. It could be a ruse. Seeing Asher and especially Aaron, I knew my emotions definitely could be a factor and likely caused me to make a questionable decision.

39

After the three days passed, I went to Dallas to meet up with Asher and Aaron, just like we discussed. Asher was on a bench overlooking the pond. I couldn't find Aaron. I put a couple cameras up yesterday to watch the area. I don't know what I was looking for or if it even mattered. Maybe it was trust. If I was still wanted, the FBI would be there. I checked all their sites; I wasn't on any list that I could find. They knew I would check though.

It was nearing 3:30 pm, and I could tell Asher grew agitated. It was well past the time. I put the phone in my pocket and walked out of the aquarium, toward Asher. "God help me," I said to myself as I saw the back of him in real life.

"Ash," I said as I got near.

Asher turned around and saw me. I went and sat down next to him.

"Hey," he said.

"Where's Aaron?"

"He couldn't come, got pulled into something and said he had to go. He thought you would understand. He said he will see you later."

I glanced around hoping to catch him. I hoped I would say goodbye to him today.

"So?"

I nodded, "Let's go before I change my mind."

We pulled up to the gate of the Dallas field office. Asher had called ahead, and when we got to the gate, he showed them his badge. We pulled through the gate and Asher stopped the car at the sidewalk in front of the building. I got out of the car; Asher flanked me. I looked at him and then darted my eyes around the parking lot again for Aaron. At this point I had to trust them and take them at their word.

An agent met me outside. "Hi, Colby," the agent said. I was anxious, but I guessed whatever would happen I was done running from it. "Are you sure you don't want a lawyer?" she said as she put an arm around me to guide me into the building.

"Yeah, I'm sure," I said to her as I peered into the office building in front of me. This might be the last time I'm free for a long time, if ever again. Once inside the door, I saw the place was trained in on me, every security guard, staffer, and agent. I was up as one of the top wanted list for a while; and now, I was magically off. The look on their faces told me they didn't believe I was off that list either. My face was straight as I tried to not be overwhelmed by the moment.

"I have to search you," she said. I stretched out my arms, and she swept my arms, my body and legs. "Okay, Colby, let's go," she said as she pointed to the gate that was being held open for me. She kept her hand on my upper arm. I looked over my shoulder, and Asher had disappeared in all the suits behind me. It made me uneasy. I'm sure they had questions for him too.

We went up an elevator and out into a sea of desks. She took me over to a hallway of doors to interrogation rooms. I held my breath. They can't hurt you like that here, I said to the part of me that was terrified at the thought of interrogation. They will fuck with your reality. We don't know how long this will last, but we can make it through. The real threat lay in the jail cell I was potentially headed for. I guess in all the running, I knew deep down that I would never get away from this. I sat down at the table, the metal table. Why do they always have a metal table? There was a metal chair, I needed it, metal chair moment.

"Can I get you anything?" the agent asked me.

"Something tells me we will be here awhile, so coffee?" She smiled and left me in there.

I stood back up, went to the wall and leaned my back up against it. I chewed on my lip, my anxiety climbed into my heartbeat, and it was hard to hold it down. I closed my eyes and said a prayer. I focused on my breathing. I had to calm down; no matter what happened it would be easy compared to Chin.

The door clicked open to the FBI interrogation room. I opened my eyes and continued to concentrate on my breath. I still leaned against the wall, trying to push down the anxiety of yet another interrogation. I almost couldn't believe I turned myself in voluntarily.

"Colby, I'm Special Agent Metz," he came in and left the door open. Then the agent who escorted me into the room came in behind him. "This is Special Agent Parker." She had two coffees. She set one down on the table.

I pulled out the chair and sat back down. "Thanks," I said to her.

"Well, are we going to talk about why I'm here?" I asked as they dug through the folders they had in front of them. I didn't need a run up; I needed to get this over.

Parker started, "What was your involvement in the attempted Boston bombing?" she asked.

"Other than trying to stop it, nothing," I said confidently.

Metz half smiled and turned to his notes, "What's your relationship with Jason Rasmussen?" Metz said, looking at me intently.

I have never been asked about Jason before; I wasn't ready to answer. "He was, umm..." If I wanted out of this, I had to answer questions. "He was involved in the same bombing as me."

"Well, that is a step in the right direction. He admits this as well," Metz said.

They had him in custody; Crystal was the only free one left. "Are we here to talk about the first bombing?" I asked and looked at both of them. "I think we have been around on that one."

"Jason says you were involved in this attempted bombing," Metz said.

"I have a dozen federal agents who account for my whereabouts during this attempted bombing," I said, unimpressed with their line of questioning.

"Specifically, Jason said you helped broker the deal to bring the goods into the states."

"That is untrue. Again, I've been surrounded by federal agents; there is no way I could have done this." They had nothing on me.

"Explain this photo right here." Parker slid a photo in front of me. It was me and Christian talking.

"That is me talking to a source that helped us crack this case," I said to them. Christian gave me the phone and tracking information for the shipment.

"So, you admit talking to Christian De Los Santos," Parker said.

"That was never a secret," I said. "My partner Special Agent Asher Findlay and Kevin McNally were with me when I went to meet him." I chose their full names to avoid confusion by just using Asher and Mac.

"No, check the date here," Parker said and pointed to corner with a date time. "This is about two weeks prior."

"I was on a mission in Nicaragua, then in a hospital, then a DIA prison in that entire time period. At no time, could I have met with Christian. The date on that photo must be altered," I said and pushed the photo back at them.

"DIA prison?" Metz said.

"Yea, they held me there for a while, beat the shit out of me. Until my team came and got me out of the prison."

"We heard others claim this too, the DIA claims that no such thing exists," Parker said.

I felt my chest tighten, and the anger flooded my veins. I looked up and then pierced my eyes into Parker and Metz.

"I don't know what to tell you; it's not like they gave me records for holding me in their prison. Did you talk to Chief Steve Steiner or Sergeant First Class Aaron Ericcson? They know all about it." I leaned forward.

"I don't know what Jason is doing, but I had nothing to do with this. If this is all you have, you are way off base. Talk to them. Ericcson helped find me, should be easy; you can ask him right now." Then it hit me, maybe Aaron wasn't here because he wasn't allowed to confirm anything about the prison.

"Jason also shows you had a secret boss for the first bombing; he now thinks you were working for Top Hat."

"The first time I heard of Top Hat was a few months ago. I don't even know how they are involved in this. This is insane. Jason is on drugs," I said and instantly regretted it.

"Who were you working for?" Metz said.

"The DEA. I was an informant," I would not admit to more than I had to in court before.

"We have travel records for you after the first bombing showing you traveled to meet with leaders of Top Hat."

"You're way off base. Wasn't I under surveillance until my arrest?" I could feel myself panic. They tried to tie me to both the bombings and the Iranians. Jason was in on it.

"We need more details," Parker said.

"Well, you have crossed too many lines now. Am I under arrest?" I asked and stood up.

"You aren't leaving," Metz stood up and motioned with his hand I should sit back down.

"I want a lawyer," I said and plopped into the chair. I trusted Aaron again, and I shouldn't have. That's why Aaron didn't come. I believe he loved me, but he still did his duty. He couldn't walk away from it. I would run into the same conflict.

Asher, what did he know. I just turned myself in for a crime I didn't do, and they had a witness who tied me to it and evidence. I felt so stupid. I shook my leg. I couldn't believe I fell for that entire act of his again. If I ever got the chance, I would pay Asher and Aaron back for tricking me. I doubt I would ever get out of this.

Metz and Parker left me in the room. I stood up, grabbed the chair by its back and slammed it into the wall and screamed "FUCK." Then I paced the room; I couldn't believe I fell for it. After what seemed an eternity, a different agent came and got me. "Come with me."

He took me to the elevator, and all I could think was, *here goes, it's Chin's turn*. I tried to bring acceptance into my mind. That this was just what was going to happen, and there was nothing I could do about it. I was stronger this time, and I was going to fight this time.

He took me to a row of cells and opened one door. I went in and chewed on my lips as he closed the door behind me. My stomach fluttered with the anxiety of knowing Chin was coming. I needed sleep; it was the only way I could fight.

40

"I AM SICK OF your agency's obsession with me," I said, standing and backing up against the wall. Chief Steiner entered the cell. I expected Chin; I guess there were others who could come too. First Aaron, then Chin, of course someone else had to get in their licks. It hit me right then, the DIA director had every reason to frame me and had all the information to do so. Plus, they knew when I couldn't get an alibi. Of course, Aaron was roped into this.

It was more than Jason framing for this. I had been in that cell for at least a day; I wasn't sure on the exact time, but I had a few meals.

"It's a real shame, you know," Chief Steiner said, standing at the entrance to my little cell with his hands on his hips.

"What is?" I asked as I let the frustration rise into anger. I got ready to fight; my hands were up at the ready.

"You. It's very rare someone can resist those levels of interrogation techniques. We could use someone like you to train our interrogators and our operatives," he sat down on the jail cell cot.

"What are you doing here? Decide Aaron and that other big motherfucker didn't do a good enough job? Had to get it in yourself?"

"Big motherfucker, oh, you must mean Fahrenbacher. No, no I will not do anything to you," he said and patted the thin mattress to signal me to sit down. I stayed up against the wall, my hands up, my feet ready to fight.

Aaron had mentioned Chin's name before Fahrenbacher—that is a good name for a big, scary son of a bitch. "Why would I believe you?"

"The people who framed you; they spent a lot of time cramming things you did into time frames when they thought you were missing, unaccounted for, when even the DEA couldn't cover for you." Chief Steiner rubbed his thumb over the palm of his left hand as he inspected it.

"What of it?"

"The director has stepped down. He will announce it here in the next few weeks. He's working to cut a deal with the special counsel to save the agency some face. He is giving up information on Ashenhurst too." He looked over and met my gaze. "Thanks to you," he said.

"That fucker dug his own grave; I had nothing to do with it." I was still agitated and ready to fight. I stared down at him wondering if Fahrenbacher was waiting outside. Or Aaron; he is the one who really fucked me in the head.

"You found out who blackmailed him and how."

"I found a picture, hardly meant anything."

"That picture is of him when he was in his early 20s in special forces stationed in Germany. He got caught up in a neo-Nazi motorcycle club."

"Then he is getting what he deserves; I could give a fuck. Why are you telling me this?"

"His last act is to disband the prison."

"So, he is closing a prison; is that supposed to make me happy? You probably have twenty other prisons and stand them up at the drop of a dime," I said.

"Anyway," Chief Steiner said, ignoring my comment, "he has released some key files. Files that will prove you could not do the things they said you did. Because you were in our prison..."

I cut in, "Being tortured."

He ignored me, "That is why you were missing and unaccount-ed for, when they say you did the things they say you did, like meet with key folks, send wire transfers, things like that," Steiner said. "That should override the claims from Jason Rasmussen."

I dropped my hands. There had to be a catch. "At what cost? What do you want from me?"

"You don't think you paid enough?"

If he is telling the truth, and I'm done believing anyone from their agency, I lost my career, anyway to support myself, my family, or my sanity. Maybe this is what Brickman meant by conviction. Really giving everything away for fortitude, not once but twice.

"How did you turn him?"

"When you said you would turn yourself in, Aaron knew he had to make sure you were safe. He flew back, and we went and talked to the director. After I showed him what we found, what you found, he seemed relieved. Then Aaron spent a lot of time with him telling him about you and what you did. He said it was a burden he was sick of carrying. The director did the right thing."

"It couldn't have been that simple."

"Well, that and the special counselor investigating all the old cabinet members was circling him. It was coming time. I think he saw it as an opportunity to cooperate with the special counsel, get leeway."

If he was telling the truth, I finally truly understood why we needed insiders in the DIA.

"So, what now? Am I going to prison for this shit?"

"You didn't do it, did you?"

"You think that matters to these people?"

He looked back at me and shrugged his shoulders. We stayed like that for a few moments, in our own heads but looking directly at each other. I misjudged Aaron; I kept misjudging him. He backed me every step of the way, and I just couldn't see it.

"Look, when they let you out, which they probably will, I'm serious, we could use you. We need real-life people we can trust to train our people."

"I fucking hate interrogators, and your fucking agency. You don't need my God damn help."

"I thought you might say that."

"Jackie, dinner is ready," I called out from the kitchen. I finished putting food on the plates and then headed toward the bedroom to see what she was doing.

When I walked in, I found her asleep on top of the comforter. She was completely out. I sat down on the bed and took a minute to take her in. I missed her. It was nice to have her in my house, in the bed I imagined her in a hundred times before this moment. I pushed her hair out of her face and leaned down and kissed her forehead.

She smiled and opened her eyes.

"I thought you came in here to shower before dinner."

She slowly blinked, "I did." She rolled onto her side and looked up at me. "I sat down for a second. I don't remember falling asleep."

"Are you in my clothes?" I asked of her in my T-shirt and a pair of my boxer briefs. She looked good in them. She looked good in everything.

"I don't know if you know this, but I try to keep everything I own down to what fits in that bag," she said, pointing with her head. "And those few sets of clothes need to be washed. Do you mind?"

I shook my head 'no.'

"Well, you're done with that now. Time to get onto life after being on the run."

She smiled and reached out and put my hand in her two. She blinked slowly.

"Are you feeling alright? You look pretty tired, and you didn't seem like that twenty minutes ago when we got home." Over the last two days we drove back from the doors of the FBI in Texas to my place in North Carolina. Jackie had been on the run for over six months when we finally found her. When we walked in the door, we were both starving, and Jackie wanted to shower while I put our dinner together. Our first dinner together in this house.

She smiled and kept tracing my hand with her fingers. "I'm more than alright. I feel good and calm and most of all safe. For the first time in months, longer. Safe enough to sleep. I don't think you get how long I have gone without really sleeping. I am always awake between the nightmares, the fear of being caught, and everything else. Then I'm near you, and it all just fades away into the background. It is the best feeling I have ever had."

"I will do everything I can to always make you feel that way."

"And what if you can't," she said with a sly smile.

"You're strong. I know you can take care of yourself."

"What If I don't want to? What if I need you?" she said, measuring her hand against mine. "At the end of the day I want to turn it off; will you be the one who takes care of it so I can rest? Rest like I can right now?"

"Well, I promise to do what I can, and then I will entrust you with the rest."

"Do you swear it?"

I smiled and looked around for something to swear on. On the nightstand was a book I took from her. I grabbed the book. "I swear by this here book, *Mental Toughness*, our book that I will do everything I can to protect you, us. When I can't anymore, I will pass the torch to you," I said to her. She looked calm, free of anxiety that so filled her when I found her and got her from that diner. Far from the look she had on her face when she said she would consider turning herself into the FBI. I wanted to keep her that way. "Don't worry though; it will take a lot and something terrible for me to pass that torch."

"I will remember this," she said. She had a soft smile on her face as she interlocked her fingers into mine.

"Did you want to eat dinner?" I asked her. I knew she was hungry, but it looked like sleep might win this fight.

"I always want your food, Aaron," she said as she leaned up on her elbow and brought her eyes off my hand to my face.

I couldn't help it; I leaned down and kissed her, pushing her into the pillows.

"What did you do with my clothes?" She asked as she came into the kitchen in her towel.

I turned to her and pulled her towel off, and she shot me a smile as I put my hands on her hips.

"Is this your plan, take my clothes away so I don't leave?" she bit her lip.

"That's a great idea," I traced my fingers down her back and pulled her body into me.

She kissed my cheek and picked up the towel I put on the floor. "Seriously?" she said.

"I made room for you in the dresser," I said as I swept my thumb across her cheek and went back to the stove. She left the kitchen.

She had spent the last three days mostly sleeping and sometimes eating. She kept saying how safe she felt and that her body needed sleep. I was happy she felt that way around me. I love her, and her loving me surprises me; her level of trust in me makes me love her more. Her feeling safe because of me was a responsibility I was happy to bear. A responsibility I could only carry out if I could keep her somewhat near me. I didn't need to protect her all the time; I just needed to be there when she got home. To be her safe place.

"Did you buy me new clothes?" she said, walking back into the kitchen in workout clothes that looked like something she used to wear when we worked out together.

"I had to do something while Sleeping Beauty just laid around," I said. I washed the clothes she left on the floor in the room and in her bag. They were worn out and gross. I didn't know what to get her other than what she seemed to wear most of the time outside of work.

"Thank you," she said as she rocked up onto her toes and wrapped her arms around my neck.

"You know you don't have to go to DC; you can stay here with me. We can start a life together," I said with my arms around her lower back as I looked into her eyes.

"Aaron," she said.

"I'm serious," I said. I just found her, and I wanted to convince her to stay before she left. Once she left, I don't think she would come back. "Let's get married, Colby James, start our lives together."

She turned red. "Ross, come on."

"I'm not kidding, you're the one for me." I wanted to marry her, and I was hoping she would say yes.

She kept her eyes on me, and I watched her version of us spin through her eyes. She bit her lip as her eyes danced between mine. "One day at a time," she said, then kissed me. I was overwhelming her. It wasn't a no; it was a not yet, not right now.

41

I WALKED OUT OF the Navy Memorial Museum feeling like I wasn't much closer than when I walked in there. My phone rang; Aaron insisted I had a phone. I stayed with Asher, who didn't have a home phone, and Aaron didn't like the idea of relying on Asher to talk to me. We settled on a flip phone, only for me to communicate with Aaron. I finally answered it.

"How's the search?" Aaron asked.

"I got a name, Thomas Hain; does it mean anything to you?" The clue Brickman left for me at the library linked to a series of naval ships, and a man named Thomas Hain was the only person on all of them. Although I don't think it was the Thomas Hain listed, if he was alive, he probably wasn't involved. He only led me to the name.

"No, not ringing a bell."

"Me neither," I said as I sat down on a bench. It was way easier coming here this time than last time. Last time was too close.

"Asher's looking for you. I gave him your number."

"That explains it, that weird number calling me all day. This is our phone. I can't have people getting used to getting ahold of me whenever they want."

"Call him back," Aaron said, annoyed with my shirking of cell phones and our debate over it.

Aaron hung up.

I called the missed call number back.

"Jackie?"

"This better be important for you to call my cell phone."

"CJ wants to meet up with you." That was a big step, a tricky step, but a big step.

CJ was already seated when I walked into the restaurant. I went up to him at the table, and he stood up as I got close. I wasn't sure what the pleasantry level would be when I walked up. I had fucked up pretty bad when I left them dealing with me running. He opened his arms, and I went in for the hug.

"Good to see you," he said.

"You too," I took the seat across from him. I was going to defer to him on all things. I didn't know what direction we would go in.

"You know you aren't supposed to be writing reports for your partner at all, let alone when you are wanted by the FBI," CJ said.

"I can firmly say I didn't write the report," I replied.

He shook his head, "You did everything just shy of it."

I didn't have a response; he knew the answer. Asher also paid the price for it already.

"Someone tried really hard to pin this stuff on you—would have been a shame if it worked. We didn't have you on the team anymore."

"Have?"

"If you want it," CJ said.

It was what I wanted but didn't think it was possible.

"I can honestly say I did not expect that."

"I thought you talked to Asher."

"We did. Asher is hopelessly optimistic. I left you guys with a hurricane mess to clean up. In the middle of all of it, Asher was convinced you would take me back then."

"You helped clean it up in your own way."

"Did you think I did it?" It was important to me to know if CJ's trust in me had wavered.

"No. I didn't think you were involved. The evidence on the other hand was mounting against you in the first couple months," CJ said.

"You questioned it though?" I asked.

"Of course I did, everyone did."

I weighed what he had said.

"You know that information you provided led to us finding a lot of drugs. We have made a big dent in dismantling that cartel. There are still ongoing investigations but might have helped us stop one of their major supply chains. More importantly, we found a container with more dirty bomb material that was still stuck in the port. We watched it with the FBI for a long time to see if anyone came for it, but all the companies and people involved in it disappeared overnight. We still got to find these people, the rest of this group, and if there is more material, we have to find it. We could really use your help to finish this up, close off this investigation."

I smiled. I wasn't sure if I could go back to the team.

"It helped change things. Even the lead you gave Asher on Top Hat, we could chase down some information on them."

"What makes you think Asher got that from me?"

"Fine. Have it your way. With Asher's lead on Top Hat, we could find some of their leadership here in the U.S. and link Ashenhurst's activities with corruption and more. They were using hawala, money networks, to fund the interpreters who ended up being the ones driving that van we were chasing in Boston."

"I'm glad Asher was able to figure that out," I said with a big smile.

"The Iranians the FBI arrested in Rhode Island even tried to claim your bombing, in a strange turn of events. That died quickly though. Other than loosely claiming it, they had zero to back it up."

I nodded. "I'm glad I missed all of that. Who did it?"

CJ looked at me curiously, "You helped us figure it out. It was members of a fringe Iranian Kurdish militia group..."

I cut him off, "Not the bombing, I know that. Who set me up? Who knew I was Colby and Jackie? Who framed me? How was Jason involved in all of this?" The questions poured out of me. The FBI didn't give me the answers.

"Jason committed suicide in jail," CJ said suddenly.

"What?" I asked. I was frustrated, confused and shockingly saddened by this. I loved Jason on some level. "I thought he was a witness against me. That he was cooperating on all the bombings. No one told me he was dead."

"He was... or was going to."

"Then suddenly commits suicide?" I both questioned it and agreed with it. *Maybe the guilt of lying against me. What a selfish thought. He's dead, and I'm worried about myself.* He could've been killed and made to look like a suicide.

"It took a couple days to extradite him from the Dominican Republic after he turned himself in. By the time they did, he was going into full detox."

I felt a tear escape my face. He was using again. Relapse is a part of recovery. Relapse could be deadly. Relapse had its own level of guilt.

"By the time he was stateside, he had to be hospitalized. After he was discharged into jail, he committed suicide."

I looked at the ground. What pain he must have been in relapsing. "Why would he, I mean?"

"He left a note."

I looked up at his face desperate to know its contents.

"I didn't want to kill her." CJ said with flat effect.

The words rolled in my mind.

"Do you know what it means?" CJ asked. Obviously he had tried to figure it out.

I felt our past come up in me... "I, uh..." I suddenly felt overwhelmed. He was dead.

CJ filled in the space, "We thought it meant he killed you. Or we feared it. There was a lot of speculation he did, anyway."

I knew what it meant. It meant a lot; he was still upset with me for having him kill Ashenhurst's girlfriend, especially after that woman in Iraq. "He, uh. It's something that happened in Iraq. He had bad PTSD over it." Also, I made it worse by having him do it again. Why had I not thought of this till now? I was so focused on the stupid mission that I didn't even realize what I did. The air left me, and a terrible ache washed over my body.

"Are you okay?"

"This is my fault." I made him do the one thing he couldn't live with himself. The thing that made him use in the first place. The thing he fought every day. I made him do it again. My stomach churned, and I grabbed onto it.

"No, it's not. It's suicide."

"I know him. I drove him to this. He probably wanted me to pay; that's why he started lying against me, to imprison me." He was on the run, and those two things, no wonder he was using again.

"You made powerful enemies when you dismantled a presidential cabinet. Any of them could have got to him, with the drugs. He probably wasn't in his right mind." Jason helped me with the first bombing and in the process, we got many people fired from their jobs in the president's cabinet. They could have found him and turned him against me. There were many avenues and reasons for people to use Jason against me.

I stood up and walked away. I needed to process this. I lost a good friend, someone who would've been a lover in different circumstances. I really was dangerous to be near. I felt vomit climb up in my throat. *Why is Chin right about me so often?*

I pulled myself together and came back to the table after a few minutes and sat down.

CJ broke the silence, "In any case, it wasn't Jason setting you up, not alone anyway,"

"The number of people aware of who I am, Jackie and Colby, that has to be pretty small."

"Do you know?" CJ asked.

"I have some leads. Thomas Hain."

"Sounds like you know," he said.

"I'm on a trail. His name came up; I don't know who he is or what he did. He is just on the trail."

"Sounds familiar, but I can't place it," CJ said. "What's the other lead?"

"An email address that leads to a server up in the Capitol Hill area. I need a work computer to get some off-the-shelf hacks to get in, though."

"Well, come back, and we can give you that."

I looked around the room. "If you don't know who burned me, then I'm not safe to work for you. That person can blow up any op we are on."

"Did you give this information to the FBI?"

I laughed, "No, definitely not."

"Jackie, you got to use the parties to figure this out," CJ said, maybe remembering the part of me that frustrated him.

"Let's just say I don't want to reveal my sources." Not like I could say I blew up a restaurant or blackmailed a U.S. Senator to get the information.

"Mac told me you and I would need to talk after Alabama and Florida." Mac had a real problem seeing in the inside of my Fortitude team's operations, from the things we used to our connections. I'm guessing CJ assumed I continued down that path without them.

42

I took my time going through the small house. It only had two bedrooms. It was a nice house for being in Northeast DC. This girl probably was a sorority girl, maybe even a queen bee in her world. She was smart. She had a master's degree hanging on the wall from the University of Virginia. She was a cheerleader there too, lots of pictures of that. Not a hair out of place for this girl.

I sat down in her little kitchen at her two-person table that fit in her breakfast nook. I could see the whole first floor from my cozy corner. She would be home eventually. I waited as the dark crept into the house. She was probably out at a happy hour, blissfully unaware of what waited for her at her home.

I heard the keys in the front door and waited. She came in, kicked off her heels. She dropped her purse, picked up her shoes and headed up her stairs. I heard her go into her bathroom, then over to her room. Then she galloped down the stairs in her pajamas. Her eyes weren't adjusted to the darkness like mine. She flipped on the light to the kitchen while looking down at her phone. She looked up and jumped, dropping her phone.

"Hi, Kami, you know who I am?" I asked rhetorically. We had never met, but she sure had spent a lot of time messing with my life.

She leaned to pick up her phone.

"Oh, I wouldn't do that," I said, "but you are more than welcome to scream." There was loud music playing outside. "I don't mind if you do."

Her eyes were wide as she stared at me.

"The problem with people like you is that you think this is a game. You don't know what to do when that game becomes real. You see in video games, you can die and come right back to life. You can kill someone and turn it off and move on with your day. It doesn't happen that way in real life." I stood up. "You can't frame someone for mass murder, then move on with your day. It's going to come back up. You are going to deal with those consequences. You can't turn off this video game. You turned it on, not me."

She started walking backward.

"You see, Kami, I know this is real, all too real. Do you? Do you know how to deal with what you started?"

She turned and ran for the front door. She opened it, and Asher was standing there. She slammed the door.

I picked up her phone and went through it. "Oh, he's a cute one," I said, showing her the picture I was looking at. "Is that who you just had drinks with?"

She was shaking and terrified as she pressed her body up against her front door. "What do you want?"

"Oh... you see, what I want, you can't give me."

"Why are you here?" she said. There was a knock on the door, and she jumped forward.

"You are going to call up this FBI agent," I said, handing her a card. "You are going to tell her you bought the cell phone information about the Boston bombing from Christian De Los Santos. You are going to show her the payment trail that was started by your computer, right here." I opened her laptop that she had left on the ottoman. I had opened the recovered files she thought she had deleted. "You are going to tell her who you gave them to."

"Why the fuck would I do that?" she said. She must still think this is all a game.

"So feisty," I said. I went back to her phone and pulled up a picture. "Because this is a picture you took with your phone when you were planting a bomb outside this restaurant."

She didn't take the photos; I did as part of an insurance policy. I keep a lot of things for insurance, stored away where people and not even hackers can find them. I planted these pictures on her, to give me leverage over her. I flipped to a different program. "Here is the program you ran to set off the bombs in quick succession." I had downloaded the things I had used for the bombs to her phone the night before while she was sleeping. I wanted to make sure Christian would want to go after her. This would force her to flee to the FBI. "The point being, if you don't call this agent and show her this, I will send this to our friend, Christian."

"I didn't do that. Why would I do that?"

I set her phone down by her computer. "Did you know that Christian is still going to physical therapy because of the injuries he sustained when a series of bombs went off in his restaurant and by his car? He is mad, looking for revenge. I know he is after me, but what happens when I tell him you are the one who helped me hurt him, and then provide him proof?"

"I bought information about you off of him, why would I turn around and bomb him?"

"Oh, so he met you face to face? Knows who you are?"

"Well, no, but I could..."

I walked toward her, and she pushed herself into the corner. "Now, Kami..." I said reaching out and putting my hand on her arm, "I own you. You do anything other than call that agent or tell her I was here, our friend, Christian will get all of that." I had to play by her rules. She wanted to frame me; I could hit back harder. She had never put her life on the line before. Also, I was way better at it than she was because I know what paying the price for those things looks like.

"If you do that, Christian will kill me and my family."

I gave a coy smile, "you never know."

"It wasn't me. I was following orders," she hissed at me.

"Who's orders?"

Her eyes welled up, but she held back tears, "I work at Top Hat, and my boss, he said to do it."

I stared at her longer and pulled a knife out from the back of my waist band.

She looked down at the knife then leaned off the wall. "I work for Ashenhurst; I do what he says."

"And just what did he say?" I held the knife to her throat and kept good eye contact with her.

"To find you, to stop you."

"Why? From what?"

"I don't know. He didn't tell me why, and I didn't ask." She shrugged her shoulders.

"What exactly did you do to stop me?"

"I tried to find all your old accomplices and offered them huge sums to give you up. The cartel pretended like they didn't know you, then offered you up out of nowhere. I didn't know you were a federal agent. I swear." She slid slightly along the wall and tried to get away. I pushed into her to keep her from moving.

"Now Kami, if you stopped when you found that out, you wouldn't be on the other side of this knife. I'm not a federal agent anymore, thanks to you."

"I didn't... I just... It was just some lies, that's all."

"Not as fun being on the other side, not knowing when the shoe will fall. If the knife will get you now, how long you will be in jail, if Christian will get you later, or who knows what else," I said to her. I wanted to ask her more, but I needed her to be fresh going into interrogation. I didn't want her to spill that I visited her, although given she just admitted to trying to frame me, I don't know that they would believe her.

She nodded her head slightly.

"You tell the FBI all they want to know, and I won't tell Christian. You don't show up there or don't cooperate, I will tell Christian. Remember Kami, I was never here." I opened the door. "Maybe the FBI will cut you a deal. There are bigger fish to fry than you." I walked out leaving her behind and the door open.

43

IT DIDN'T FEEL RIGHT to be back in the office, especially wearing a visitor's badge. CJ put me in a conference room with Asher. CJ had been working on my leads and was ready to bring me into them. I sat in a chair and traced my eyes along the microphone wires that ran across the table. The door opened, and Mac and Lee walked in. I brought my eyes to meet theirs. They definitely were not expecting me. They both stopped dead in their tracks. I moved my eyes slowly between them with a straight face. The air thickened in the room as they stared at me.

The door opened again, and Doc almost crashed into them. I could feel a scowl form on my face, and I quickly wiped it away.

"What the..." Doc started then stopped when he saw me.

I looked over at Asher and back at them. "It's great to see you guys, too," I said, trying to cut through the tension.

"Are you back on the team?" Doc asked.

"No," I said.

"Not yet," Asher jumped in behind me.

The guys spread out into chairs as CJ walked in. He brought the FBI Agents Metz and Parker. I wasn't exactly thrilled to see them.

"Thomas Hain," CJ started. "Jackie had a lead on who had burned her, and I knew I recognized the name. He is the guy who notified the FBI you are Colby," CJ said to me.

"Who is he?" I asked back.

"He is a DEA agent in Miami," CJ said.

"What did he do exactly?" I asked.

Parker jumped in, "He notified a local Miami FBI agent that you, Jackie Ericcson, were Colby James. He recognized you in the pre-mission brief call. It took the FBI hours to confirm your identity after he notified them. The op had started by the time they confirmed it and passed out."

I looked around the room so confused. "Why does a random agent in Miami know that I'm Colby?" I leaned forward in my chair. "One month prior to this incident the people in this room didn't know I was Colby. They had been working with me for a year and didn't know. Why does this guy know?" I asked everyone as I looked around the room exasperated.

I turned to Metz, "I'm sure there were FBI agents on that call who actually talked to me as Colby, and they said nothing nor tied those two things together. Why does Hain know and say something? Did you ask him that once he identified me?"

"Recognizing a known criminal is not something we typically question," Parker said.

"I was buried though. In my only picture in public, I was beaten badly. I was nowhere. My tracks are covered. If you didn't deal with me directly, how would you know?" I was getting frustrated. "Anyone else on the same page with me? If my supervisor doesn't know, how does he know?" The room felt deafeningly quiet.

CJ finally chimed in, "She has a point. We didn't know."

Asher piled on, "I wouldn't have believed anyone telling me. I only did since she told me with her own mouth. Has this Hain guy worked anywhere other than Miami?"

"We would have to check," Metz said. "We will check to see if he had any involvement or connection to Colby."

Mac chimed in, "You said it yourself, Colby..."

"What's that?" I was genuinely nervous about what would fall out of Mac's mouth.

"You said we can't check in with CJ from Miami because we don't know who Christian has in his pocket." Once again, I was genuinely surprised by Mac.

Parker asked, "Do you know of the cartel having someone in his pocket?"

"No," I said, "I just think you can't move drugs at that volume without somebody, some sort of spy in the cops somewhere. It's a hunch, a safety thought."

"Let's not jump to conclusions," CJ said, cutting me off. "Hain could have a legitimate reason to know you're Colby."

"Where did you get Hain's name from anyway?" Metz said.

I squinted my eyes and peered at them across the table. "Let me ask you this first, how did you know I was at the Navy Memorial? Where you literally had me in your hands and I barely got away?"

Everyone leaned in. Something told me the team didn't know about this incident.

"We got a tip, from a reliable source you were headed there," Parker said.

"Did you know why I headed there?" I asked. I thought maybe they know about the Library of Congress, but I guess not. I also had a strong hunch we both had the same source.

"My source gave me a cryptic clue that sent me there. I guess he called you after he sent me there."

We both knew we had the same source. They let the moment sit for a minute.

"We'll do some checking on Hain," Metz said. Metz and Parker looked at each other and both got up and left.

CJ pointed at Asher and nodded his head to the door, and they both left.

"Just like that, you're back in," Doc said.

"I'm not back in," I said, pointing to my visitor badge. He made it clear he had nothing to do with me.

"Why did you run if you did nothing?" Doc said.

"You all seem to forget the physical and mental shape I was in; I wasn't ready or able to subject myself to an interrogation again, by anyone," I said. It is easy for them to forget the torture when the bruises were gone, but the bruises were hardly the things I recall from my last stay. "You, of all people, Doc, should know what happened to me; you checked every injury. Did I not have enough broken ribs and bruises?"

"The FBI doesn't do that," Lee said.

I rolled my eyes, "Okay, I'm not explaining myself to you guys. You all turned on me on a dime, some fucking teammates you are." I pushed my chair out and stood up.

"Fuck that," Doc said. "We went through hell for you, Jackie. Even after finding out you're Colby."

"You guys really think on that day I was tricking you into setting off a dirty bomb? Is that what you think of me?" I paused. "After every..." I shook my head and looked off, biting my lip before coming back to them. I needed to remain focused. "Whoever blew my cover is a threat to this agency. That person also polluted the water with enough evidence to make the FBI question each one of you. They also launched a nationwide manhunt for me—a fellow agent who was not involved. In fact, I was part of the team, our team that had the leads and found the bomb and materials for more. The person who can do that to us, to our agency, I am here to get that person. That's it. CJ asked me to help, I'm here."

"You almost ruined Asher's career," Doc said.

"Asher and I are good, ask him. He regrets nothing he did for me."

"I don't know how you expect us to trust you," Doc said.

"Oh, I'm supposed to trust you? The man who instantly said, 'She did it. Give her to the FBI.'" My voice raised. I took a second to calm down. "Look, I get it, you don't want me around—that's fine."

After a few moments, Doc left the room, and Mac followed him. Mac stopped at the doorway, turned around and walked back in, "Hey, we should not have just turned on you like that. We fucked up."

I nodded, but I was too pissed at Doc to say much else.

He turned and left the room.

"Jackie, why is everything always so difficult with you?" Lee said, standing behind me.

"I wish I knew," I turned to him.

"This Hain guy did more than ruin your career; he ruined your life," Lee said, taking some level of pity on me.

"Well, shit happens; it's what you do next that matters," I said. I didn't care to delve into my life with Lee. "Could be worse. If he was successful, I would be in jail for this shit. I am thankful for what I have."

Lee stared at me; maybe he felt sorry on some level like Mac. I don't know if it mattered.

"I heard you are engaged, congratulations," I finally said, remembering the updates I got from Asher and trying to remember that these were my friends at one point.

"Yeah, we are," he said. "Dale's been worried about you. He blamed himself for a long time. Like if he showed up at the hospital sooner none of this would have happened." Dale, his fiancé, was supposed to pick me up from the hospital after my surgery. He was the one who notified everyone I went missing.

I shook my head in disbelief, "He couldn't have stopped what was in store for me."

"I know, he knows, but it's what he does—worries about the people he cares about."

"Tell him thanks. I'm good now, that's what matters."

44

Staring down the barrel of a 9mm at the motel while being in a position completely unable to defend myself. I didn't know if there is anything I could do other than freeze and wait for the end. I thought maybe I could get away after the shooting stopped. I climbed out of the bathtub and out the window, and now all I saw was a 9mm gun. With the sound of a shot, the gun suddenly fell, and the man who held it collapsed. It caused me to jump. I thought the sound was for me. Behind him was Doc. "Come on, Jack," he said to me as I continued my climb out of the window. I followed him to his position he had with Lee. We then headed back toward the parking lot across from the motel.

Parker talked in my ear again. I ripped it out of my ear. "God damn FBI almost got me killed," I said out loud to the team as I got to their circle.

"Isn't it the outcome that matters?" Asher said, using my words against me. I shot a look at him and turned my attention to Doc.

"Thanks, Doc, I thought I was toast."

Doc gave me a scowl. He may have saved my life, but he was not ready to acknowledge me as a human yet. "I guess I could at least not let them kill you after all you went through." I was wrong, maybe he might come around.

"I guess that confirms Hain is dirty," Lee said.

"Was that him in the sedan taking pictures?" The FBI had cut me off from most of the operation chatter because I wasn't one of them anymore. I only heard from Parker and her instructions. We set a trap for Hain. They set me up in a motel and had an informant tell Hain I was in town. Hain came and checked it out; next thing I knew, the motel was being shot up by the cartel.

CJ walked up leaving my questions unanswered. "Looks like the cartel is not happy with you," CJ said. I didn't exactly or not even mention my last interaction with Christian. I had enough trouble with the FBI. I kept a straight face. "Glad you made it out in one piece," he said to me. "More fire power showed up than anyone expected. We took a few out and arrested a few more. That room you were in took a significant hit."

"I'm only here thanks to Doc," I said. With all the crap he has said to me lately, I was pleasantly surprised he saved my life.

"So, we know Hain was in the cartel's pocket, but it doesn't explain everything else," Mac said. "Hain didn't have enough pull to pollute the water that much."

"Jackie has more leads we can chase when we go north," CJ said.

Asher took his gear off at the back of the suburban. I walked over to him. "That was fun," I said sarcastically.

"Hey, Jackie," he said, looking up at me and smiling. "I was a little concerned for you in there," he said, then stopped what he was doing. "I know you think you have solid relationship advice that clearly worked out for me. It's my turn. You should call him. Especially after something like that."

I didn't like it. I wanted to heed his warning. I pulled my phone out of my pocket and turned it on as I walked away from everyone.

"Hey, Colby," Aaron said as he answered. Colby was still his name, and I liked it. It made me smile. I didn't like reporting to anyone though.

45

"WHAT DID THEY SAY?" Aaron asked as I climbed into his truck. He waited for me outside.

"As if you don't know, you set this up," I said back to him.

He smiled a little, reached out and grabbed my chin with his thumb and finger. "You should come live with me."

He asked me this several times before. It was tempting. "I could still get back on my old team, maybe. Doc is coming around."

Aaron put the truck in drive and headed out of the parking lot. "Your talent is wasted there," Aaron said.

"Really?" I said as he smiled. "This from the guy who wants me to come and be his housewife?"

He laughed. "Like I said, your talents would be wasted around that team."

It made me laugh too.

"Seriously though, for you, these people you just met. That's you. That's what Colby James is made for."

I looked out the windshield. Sometimes the mystery of these places, their allure is greater than they are. People warned us against that. I was being drawn in. I also liked my team. I liked the DEA, maybe they had spots in North Carolina near Aaron. Aaron reached over and grabbed my hand. "Take your time, Colby. When the answer is right, you will know it." I interlaced my fingers with his. He came up to meet me after Miami and all that almost went wrong down there. I had more work to do to track down those who framed me before I made any life decisions.

"In the meantime, you can fulfill your real purpose in life, which is having my babies, just like two or three or four…" he said and laughed. I threw his hand back at him.

"Now, Jackie, I can't let you put fingers on the keyboard. Walk Asher through it," CJ said as we sat down at Asher's computer. Asher started by isolating the server for the email address we got from Christian. I pointed to the hack we should use to get into the system. The one I had safe on the server and didn't have access to while I wasn't a part of the team. Asher really was doing most of it without me. It also helped that I walked him through this before we went down to Miami when the FBI wanted me to be used as bait. We didn't want the FBI to muddy up the waters, and thought we could motivate her into cooperating.

He isolated on the laptop and its location at a house in Northeast DC. "Kami Hollingwood," Asher said. "We got her address." Asher did a few other searches. "Looks like she works for Top Hat. Here it is, former Ashenhurst staffer," Asher said as he scrolled through her LinkedIn profile. He found that information too fast; he wasn't doing a good job of pretending this was his first time looking for her information.

"Well, there's a direct link," CJ said. He implied she worked for Ashenhurst in the blackmailing and also was a part of Top Hat's involvement.

"Let's pay her a visit," I said.

"She doesn't appear to be as dangerous as Christian," CJ said. "We can bring the FBI in on this."

"That's bullshit, you said it would be us," Asher said. He played along well.

CJ walked away.

I was glad to have Asher with me. He was the best kind of partner.

"Make any decisions, yet?" Asher asked.

I shook my head no. I wanted Asher as a partner and CJ as a boss. I could take or leave the rest of the team. "Aaron wants me to move to North Carolina and have his babies. So, that's pretty tempting," I said with a smile looking at Asher.

Asher put his foot on my chair and pushed me away from him. "Pretty sure you aren't Jackie."

It made me laugh.

"You gotta come back, this place isn't the same without you. Plus, we still have to finish all that stuff with the dirty bomb and the corruption. There are so many more people for us to track down, and now we have real man power to get it done. You have been leading us in your own way, now come and do it for real."

"I know there is a lot to do, I want to. I have missed being here. Really, I missed you. You were the only one who had my back. I just don't know if the DEA is the right place for me anymore."

"We need you. I need you," he rolled his chair toward me and reached out for my face but stopped when someone walked by where we sat.

I blushed. I tried to pull my attention away from the moment and saw that the news was on behind Asher. I saw the headline "Corrupted Officials: Catastrophic Intelligence Failures," I grabbed the remote and turned up the volume.

"Not a surprise as this is coming to light on the heels of the bomb shells coming from the Special Prosecutor's arrest of former Boston Mayor Ashenhurst and several former directors of agencies all ousted a few years ago. It seems very logical they are turning on each other. We have really seen the Special Prosecutor tie together everything that went wrong leading up to this attempted bombing," said the male anchor.

"Let's hope we are nearing the end of these bombshells," the female anchor piped. "Coming out today, we are learning how Top Hat is aiming to recover from the arrest and indictment of several of its leaders. They are scrambling to maintain the hundreds of millions of dollars in contracts they have with the U.S. Government."

The headline changed, "Major defense contracting firm, Top Hat, rebranding to Favrilon."

A new voice over came with images of Top Hat's headquarters in Boston. "After some top officials at Favrilon, formerly Top Hat, were arrested a few months ago for involvement in a recent bombing attempt, the company seems to be undergoing a restructuring. To kick it off, Favrilon has announced a major partnership bringing Science, Technology, Engineering and Math, also known as STEM, into underprivileged communities," the female anchor said.

The male anchor joined in, "A Favrilon spokesperson indicated they want to provide opportunities to refugee communities and believe opening doors to STEM is a great path to brighter futures for immigrants to this country."

My mind flashed back to my talk with Brickman at the Peace Conference. He commented on top Defense firms, "They don't choose a side if they are any good. They survive no matter what is going on." Top Hat provided interpreters for both sides of the war.

As I thought about that, I wondered what that meant, Top Hat rebranding to survive the storm caused by this case breaking open. There had to be some reason they were targeting immigrant kids.

Brickman's words, "The best of our defense contractors are always involved in the..." he paused for a second and smirked, "...the bringing about of peace, or the need to bring about peace." They were up to something. I need to find out what, no way they just stopped meddling in all of this. Even if they could write off a portion of the company to save face. If I could choose my next mission, I would choose that one.

I turned down the TV when I saw CJ walk back into the room.

"It appears the FBI is in front of us," CJ said. "Kami is already in custody and cooperating."

"Well, there goes all that fun," I said and feigned surprise.

"She said Christian contacted her and initially acted as if he had done them a favor by helping them find the missing goods. Then she and Christian both realized you played him. She and Ashenhurst then agreed to purchase all the information Christian had on you. Ashenhurst wanted to find out what you were doing and why you were spying on them. Kami admitted that when they got information about your location, things moved faster than they all expected. They just wanted your fingerprints on the materials, maybe capture or kill you by walking you into a trap, but everything went sideways when they found out you were on a government operation. They didn't even conceptualize you would be an agent. They weren't ready to do the bombing, and when they got away, they stopped the bombing."

I looked over at Asher and back to CJ. She didn't tell me all of that.

CJ continued, "In the command center, it makes sense how things went sideways and also why there were some now known cops who went rogue. Those cops followed Ashenhurst's commands and shot at you all."

Asher and I shot looks at each other. I guess our trip to Kami's house worked out. I think it would be hard for her to convince them was in her house given the fact she was admitting to framing me.

"So uh, that's it?" I asked. It was anti-climactic like so many other moments that seemed they would have more weight. Fireworks would be more appropriate.

"Hain clammed up, hiding behind a lawyer and a union rep and isn't saying anything. They speculate Christian had something to do with it as he was very upset he was played by you."

I smiled at Asher and stood up in front of CJ.

"Sounds like we wrapped up a big part of this," I said.

CJ shook my hand, "Well, as always you helped us out. Are you ready to join us?" CJ said.

I stopped, "I wasn't expecting to be done today."

"We still have a lot of work to do," CJ said.

"I mean, the team?" I said with half a question, not sure they would take me back.

"The DEA could use you, if not the team."

"Can I have a few more days?" I asked. I wasn't ready to make a decision.

"Sure," CJ said and walked away.

I looked over at Asher and gave him a soft punch in the shoulder. He grabbed my hand and smiled at me. I went flush, and he let go.

I turned and headed out of the office. I grabbed my phone from the locker. I had two missed calls, one from Aaron and one from the people he had me talk to. I felt trapped; I was being pulled in too many directions. I suddenly missed the diner where I freely made my own decisions without the pressure of the surrounding people. I wanted to be with people who wanted to do the right thing, no matter the cost. I am not ready to be forced into anything. The phone rang. This phone was too much. It, in its own way, was forcing a choice. Aaron, DEA, something new, or do I choose my own path using my hacking skills and chasing my own missions? I bent the phone all the way back until it snapped. I dropped it in the trash can before getting in the elevator.

JOEY,

The choice I made next is why you are here. I'm so glad I made that choice if only for you. Your Dad was right there for me through it all. I just didn't see it. I know at the age you are at now when I'm writing this, it will be hard for you to see it too. One day though, when you are on the other side, you will.

I love you,

Mom

The epiphany to leave D.C. didn't hit Hollis until more than 15 years had passed. Those years included cutting ties with the shadier, drug-addicted, and delinquent—yet somehow loveable—branches of her family tree; letting go of true love twice; skipping her shot at a family; and, most notably, giving up any attempt to maintain good mental health.

It all started with a required polygraph to keep her security clearance—a test centered around making sure she hadn't provided aid to the enemy. The accusation, though implied, was downright insulting for someone who'd been dedicated to serving her country since the age of seven. The clearance got renewed, but the seed to leave was planted. A few more years of living through hell made it painfully clear: while the passion was still there, the tank was empty.

It was time to step back, join the ranks of the common folk, and support the country from way behind the lines. That's when the books started pouring out—straight from her soul and onto the page. Hollis found a new mission, one without the danger but full of purpose.

We call her H.K., and these are her tales.